W9-BGE-571

OCT 0 2 2008

FALSE PICTURE

FALSE PICTURE

An Abbot Agency Mystery

Veronica Heley

This first world edition published 2008
in Great Britain and the USA by
SEVERN HOUSE PUBLISHERS LTD of
9–15 High Street, Sutton, Surrey, England, SM1 1DF.

Copyright © 2008 by Veronica Heley.

All rights reserved.
The moral right of the author has been asserted.

British Library Cataloguing in Publication Data

Heley, Veronica
  False picture. - (Abbott Agency mystery series ; 2)
  1. Art thefts - Investigation 2. Detective and mystery
  stories
  I. Title
  823.9'2[F]

ISBN-13: 978-0-7278-6656-1   (cased)
ISBN-13: 978-1-84751-077-8   (trade paper)

Except where actual historical events and characters are being
described for the storyline of this novel, all situations in this
publication are fictitious and any resemblance to living persons
is purely coincidental.

All Severn House titles are printed on acid-free paper.

Typeset by Palimpsest Book Production Ltd.,
Grangemouth, Stirlingshire, Scotland.
Printed and bound in Great Britain by
MPG Books Ltd., Bodmin, Cornwall.

One

'We're a domestic agency, Velma. We don't *do* murder!' Velma wasn't listening. 'I'll tell you all about it when we meet. Lunch at Harvey Nichols, on me?'

Bea Abbot was desperate to get away from the paperwork on her desk, but hadn't considered getting out of it to investigate a murder. She'd answered the phone with her mind on a communication from the Inland Revenue.

'The Abbot Agency. How may I help you?' *The tax bill was horrific!*

'So you're not dead, then? I was beginning to think I'd have to report you as a missing person. Didn't you get my messages? I've tried and tried . . .'

Bea rummaged in the labyrinth of her mind and came up with the name of one of her oldest friends. 'I'm sorry, Velma. I've been at my wits' end to—'

'Don't talk to me about wits' end. I've been tearing my hair out . . .'

She hadn't, of course. Nothing would cause Velma to disturb her beautifully cut blonde mop. Bea ran her free hand up and through her own short, ash-blonde hair, realigning her fringe so that it lay at an angle.

Velma was in a state, but that was nothing new. Velma was always in a state about something. No, that wasn't fair. Or true. Bea knew she was being catty but couldn't help herself. *However much did the tax people want?*

'Then I thought you were the only person I could talk to about it. I'm desperate. Sandy's so scared. I mean . . . murder!'

Bea was impatient. Sandy was Velma's second husband whom Bea considered solid, in the nicest possible way. Velma, on the other hand, was somewhat given to exaggeration. 'We're a domestic agency, Velma. We don't "do" murder.'

Velma wasn't listening. 'No, I can't believe it, either, except that . . . oh, I'll tell you when we meet. Lunch at Harvey Nichols, on me?'

Was this an excuse for Bea to avoid dealing with the paperwork on her desk? 'I really can't spare the time.'

'All right, then. Patisserie Valerie at the bottom of Church Street, one o'clock. It won't take an hour.' She rang off before Bea could object.

Bea pulled a face at the receiver and put it down. She'd wanted a respite from paperwork, and she supposed this could be it. She picked up the tax bill. It appeared that the agency owed the Inland Revenue an enormous amount of tax for the last three years, which corresponded with the time that Bea's husband had been ill and left the management of the agency in her son's hands. Under that missive was more bad news, including a solicitor's letter from a disgruntled client.

Her dear husband was lying in his grave on the other side of the world, she felt every day of her sixty years, she owed the taxman more than she could pay, the agency rooms needed to be rewired and replumbed, and it looked like rain. She got her hands around the untidy pile of paper on her desk and tipped it into the wastepaper basket.

There! She felt better. Guilty, but better.

She knew she'd have to fish it all out in due course and deal with it, but for now it was off her desk, she was going to have lunch with one of her oldest friends, and she'd feel all the better for the break when she came back.

She checked to see if her cream T-shirt and dark chocolate trousers were reasonably crease free, renewed her lipstick, took her reading glasses off, put them into her handbag, and looked around for a jacket to wear. High summer it might be, but there was a nasty chill wind around.

She put her head around Oliver's door on the way out. 'I'm meeting someone for lunch. Back in an hour, right?'

Oliver didn't bother to take his eyes off his computer, but lifted a hand in acknowledgement. Bea wanted to tell him to get away from his computer and get a life, but restrained herself because he was practically carrying the agency at the moment. Oliver was a computer geek who'd only just left school and apparently needed only the slightest exposure to daylight.

Maggie was not in reception as she ought to have been, and as Bea climbed the stairs from the agency offices in the basement, she could hear nothing but the buzz of a pneumatic drill in the road outside. If her second assistant and house guest had been around, the house would have been full of Maggie's braying laughter set against a background of radio, television, phone, coffee grinder and food processor. Irritating girl. Maggie was obviously out.

Wait a minute; wasn't she having a driving lesson that morning? How many times had she taken the test? Bea shuddered. She felt sorry for the instructor.

She took the smartest of her umbrellas from the stand in the hall, and let herself out into the road.

He called himself Rafael. Behind his back, they called him Raffles, the master thief, because he notched up one art theft every few months. He'd never been suspected of the thefts – or of the murder. Make that murders, plural. Was it six or seven by now? He'd lost count.

On this last one, the old woman had opened the door, no problem. He was so small, so unremarkable that no one ever found him threatening – at first. One thrust with his knife and she'd fallen like a rag doll, legs all over the place, blood spurting. He'd jumped back, but not quickly enough to avoid getting some of her blood on him. Annoying, that, for it meant another dry-cleaning bill.

The grandfather clock had ticked on, and on. Nothing had stirred, not even a mouse. On with the latex gloves.

The flat was crammed with valuables but there was no point in being greedy; the collection of snuff boxes was what he'd come for. He slipped each one into a padded envelope and fitted them into his briefcase, lingering only over the plainest one, which really appealed to him.

She'd left the letter making the appointment with him on her desk, which meant he had no need to search for it. Good. He took the letter, checking that she'd not entered anything in the diary beside the phone. She hadn't. Empty diary, empty life. She was better off dead. It was the quiet hour, when no one was around to see a stranger leave the block. He dropped the briefcase into

*Zander's office to take home for him. He never risked carrying
the goods himself.*

The Patisserie Valerie was one of a chain which aimed for a
Continental atmosphere. No minimalism here, but excellent
cakes, coffee and snacks. It was the sort of place where you
could just about find room on the floor for your purchases from
Harrods and Harvey Nichols before making your appointment
at the salon round the corner to have your hair done for Ascot,
or Glyndebourne.

Not that Bea had ever been horse-racing, nor to Glyndebourne,
either. She'd always been too busy. Sometimes she thought she'd
missed out on things, having had to work so hard all her life.
Her darling Hamilton hadn't been keen on horse-racing or the
arts, really, with the exception of a routine visit to the Summer
Exhibition at the Royal Academy. He liked that because he
appreciated the eccentric, wherever it was to be found.

Bea pushed her way into the café, saw that Velma hadn't yet
arrived and snaffled a table for two in the window. The place was
filling up, the windows misting over. The cake display was fantastic,
as usual. Bea ordered soup and a quiche which she knew would
be well cooked and nicely presented. The food came and Bea
started on it, knowing that Velma would probably be late.

She was only ten minutes late, and for once not entangled
with shopping. In fact, she looked as if she'd lost weight recently.
Alarming. Velma had always appeared young for her age but
now it looked as if time were catching up on her.

'Sorry, sorry,' said Velma, diamond rings flashing as she threw
a cashmere and silk wrap over the back of her chair. 'Sandy was
on the phone, he's none too well, and I . . . but I must order something, I've not eaten properly for a couple of days. We had some
seafood a couple of nights ago, it was the calamari, I think, and
we were up half the night, didn't feel much like eating yesterday,
though that was probably the worry of it all. Anyway, I think I
could fancy a little something now.' She looked distractedly around
for the waitress.

Bea suspended operations on her quiche. 'Are you all right,
Velma? You look—'

'Frazzled, my dear. Totally and utterly. My dear Sandy is
usually such a rock, and to see him fall apart like this . . . though
I do agree that the seafood experience has probably not helped.'

'Calm down, dear, and tell me what's happened. You mentioned a murder, but I don't suppose you really—'

'What it is, we want you to investigate, or at least find out if Philip is involved, which we think he must be, though he couldn't have done it. You do agree, don't you?'

'You've lost me, Velma. Who's Philip?'

'Stepson, Sandy's boy.' Velma pushed her hair back off her face, looked up at the waitress with a smile, said, 'Something plain. Soup, a salad. Oh, I'll have what my friend's had, right?'

The waitress smiled, and nodded. Most people smiled and nodded when Velma wanted them to do something for her. She had a wistful air which captivated people into thinking her a beautiful woman, although in fact she was – as Hamilton had pointed out when he first met her – a nice woman who used her large blue eyes to good effect. Bea had known Velma since they'd been at school together, but even she was not impervious to her friend's charm.

'Black coffee for me,' added Bea to the waitress's back. 'Now, Velma; you know perfectly well that the agency doesn't "do" murder. Tell me what's happened in words of one syllable.'

'You were away when I got together with Sandy, weren't you? Well, the thing is that after my dear first husband died, rest his soul, I didn't quite know what to do with myself. After all, he'd been ill with this and that for so long and naturally I'd done what I could to help him look for cures and monitor his pill-taking so I'd grown used to not going out much. Then he had that totally unexpected heart attack and there was I, oh, terribly sad, of course, but a bit . . . well, I'm not sure quite how to put it.'

'Let out of school early? Not sure who to play with?'

Velma laughed. She had a pretty laugh, and a prettier blush which proved she wasn't wearing a lot of make-up. 'Something like that, yes. You were off with Hamilton on his dream trip around the world and then he died, of course, so sad, dear, and knowing you and him, it wasn't like me and my first, was it? I mean, you really did grieve, whereas I . . . well, of course I did grieve, but in some ways, though it sounds awful to admit it, and I could only do so because you are my oldest friend, but there was a certain sense of relief.'

Bea nodded. Velma's first had been a horrible man; a manipulative, selfish hypochondriac who'd kept her at his beck and call. 'So there you were, a wealthy widow looking for a new playmate, and . . .?'

'All of a sudden I was popular, being asked here, there and everywhere, and not everyone wanted me to back their financial propositions or get me into bed – though most of them did, I agree. Sandy helped me out when a particularly nasty specimen tried to drag me into his car. Sandy bopped him on the nose, and of course I asked him to see me home, knowing I'd have to make the running, because he's quite a shy old thing, you know. He's from a good family, not much money, works for a charity. I asked him to stick around and well . . . it wasn't long before . . . you know. So we got married. Sandy is a darling.' The waitress brought Velma's food, and got a dazzling smile of thanks in exchange.

'My coffee?' asked Bea. The waitress shrugged, and disappeared again.

Velma picked up her spoon and took a sip of soup but didn't seem hungry. 'I haven't any children, of course, my dear first wasn't able to, or I wasn't – it doesn't matter which now. I'm well past it, thank goodness. Sandy has a son by his first wife, a woman I've never met because she went off to live in Scotland somewhere with the intention of saving the planet, which is all very worthy though it's not clear how she meant to do it. Philip chose to live with his father and not his mother. Public school, not the tops because Sandy hadn't the money to do that and the boy is not exactly academic. A decent sports record, trials for the county, good enough to get him a job working in some television company, support procedures or something like that. You do see, don't you?'

'Not quite. Why do you think Philip has committed a murder?'

'Oh, he hasn't. Of course not.' But Velma's colour had faded and she looked more than her age, her pencilled eyebrows standing out against her fair skin. She pushed her half-finished soup aside and looked Bea full in the eye. 'It's just that he's got one of his godmother's pre-Raphaelite oil portraits – a Millais, would you believe? – which is worth hundreds of thousands which he says she gave him for his birthday which was yonks ago. Only, Sandy happened to see it in on the floor in her flat a fortnight ago, because it had fallen off the wall when the wire broke, and he offered to replace the wire and she said he wasn't to touch it because he'd only do it wrong. She was like that, you know, most ungrateful for anything he tried to do for her. She told him to put it in a cupboard in her bedroom, and that's what he did.'

'Oh,' said Bea.

Velma's face puckered as if she were going to cry. 'I know it looks bad, but I'm sure there's an explanation somewhere. Philip could have called in to see her because he is her godson after all. She didn't have many visitors. She hates – hated – people going into her flat, taking up her time. You know how old people get, a bit suspicious, not wanting to let anyone in and probably quite right, too, seeing what's happened. She is – was – a hoarder, you can hardly move in her flat, she never opens the curtains, you wouldn't believe what she's got in there – two Lawrences, a Romney, and a Fuseli for a start and some miniatures in her bedroom, not to mention her diamonds and a string of pearls which went right down to her waist, believe it or not. Sandy was always on at her to put the best stuff in the safe, but she said she couldn't because she'd forgotten the combination, and when he said he'd get someone round to see to it for her, she refused because it would have cost money.'

Bea nodded. Her coffee came. Black. She stirred sugar into it.

Velma's eyes went all round the shop, back to her food, looking anywhere but at Bea. Bea thought, What are you hiding, Velma? You *do* think he did it. Whatever *it* is. 'Her name . . .?'

'Lady Lucinda Farne. As in the island of Farne. Notorious in her day.'

Bea half closed her eyes, remembering a newspaper item about the woman's death a week ago? Longer? Now what did she remember about it? Yes; Lucky Lucinda, they used to call her. She'd been a famous model who'd gone on to become the long-term mistress of an international financier and married him when he was in his dotage. Her husband had left her a title, his money and a considerable collection of pictures and objets d'art from the late nineteenth and early twentieth centuries. The newspapers had put her age at eighty-five.

'How come she was Philip's godmother?'

'Sandy's first wife went to art school, the Slade. Lucinda had given up being a model by then and was very wealthy, so she was one of the patrons. Sometimes she took an interest in the next generation, letting them fetch and carry for her, that sort of thing. Though why she would be interested in Sandy's first wife is a mystery, since she's a selfish bitch – pardon my language but she is, always taking advantage of his good nature. She thinks of nothing but how she can "fulfil" herself, that sort of thing.

Almost the only thing she did for her little boy before she drifted
out of the marriage was to get Lucinda to act as his godmother,
thinking, I suppose, that she'd leave him some money when she
died.'

'So how come Sandy visits Lucinda?'

'When she – Sandy's first wife – left for distant parts, she
asked him to keep an eye on Lucinda, who was getting rather
peculiar even then. She wanted Sandy to keep reminding Lucinda
of Philip's existence because after all, who else would she leave
all her money to? My dear Sandy is so good. He was looking
after an old aunt anyway, so of course he said yes and so of
course he did and does. Visit. Every other week, usually. I went
with him a couple of times but you could see she really didn't
want to see anyone younger or more glam than herself.'

Bea sipped her coffee. The newspaper report had suggested
that Lady Farne had disturbed a burglar, been knocked down and
died.

'It couldn't have been Philip, could it?' said Velma, ready to
cry.

'How did you find out he'd got the picture?'

'A couple of nights ago we went round to collect Philip to
take him out to supper, which is where we ate the calamari that
made us so ill. Anyway, before we went out, Sandy had to use
the loo, one of the problems of age, and Philip's bedroom door
was open and there was the picture, leaning against the wall.
Sandy asked Philip where he'd got it, and Philip said his
godmother had given it to him months ago for his birthday in
February and of course dear Sandy knew that wasn't right but
he didn't know what to think. He doesn't think quickly dear, not
like you or me. So we all went out to supper and still he said
nothing till we got home that night and then he told me, and we
were both sick as dogs and . . . well, the next day he went off
to confront Philip and there was a terrible row, but Philip stuck
to his story and now Sandy doesn't know what to believe. Do I
fancy some black coffee? No, I don't think I do.'

'The picture was in Lady Farne's flat a fortnight ago? But
Philip insists he's had it for four months?'

Velma nodded, containing tears with an effort.

'Could she have given him a copy?'

'Lady Farne did not give house room to copies. Why should
she? She's a billionairess who could furnish a wing in a museum

with what she's got stuffed into that flat. She's become increasingly eccentric of late years, and miserly. She complained about the gas bill, so there's no heating in the flat. She had the phone cut off because she said the only people who used it were cold callers, and Sandy had to argue with British Telecom and pay something himself to get the service restored. She refused to wear one of those emergency thingies from the Social round her neck in case she fell, refused to have her light bulbs changed to energy saving because she'd have to spend some money out to get the benefit, you know. And as for insurance!' Velma lifted her hands in a gesture of helplessness.

'Sandy went on and on at her about keeping up the premiums, but goodness knows whether she actually did. Spending money on that sort of thing was unnecessary, she said. She was living on twopence a week and eating off gold plate. Metaphorically, of course. I don't *know* that she's actually got any gold plate, but you get the idea? Tried to get Sandy to pay for a cleaner for her place, and then said she wouldn't dream of letting anyone into her flat who might steal from her and . . . oh, I don't know! So, you'll help, won't you? I'll pay anything, within reason.'

'Me? What? How?' Bea thought of the tax demand on her desk; no, in her wastepaper basket. 'No, of course not, Velma.'

Velma leaned forward, dropping her voice. 'You think we should let it pass, let everyone believe that it was a burglary that went wrong?'

Bea stared at her fingernails. Did she really like this new shade of polish? That tax bill . . .

Velma said, 'You think it would be best to let sleeping dogs lie? Don't ask any more questions, don't do anything to draw suspicion on to Philip? Let Sandy get a stomach ulcer, because his indigestion is something chronic ever since it happened? Let Lady Farne's body be cremated and her estate wound up, and hope she hasn't left Philip anything in her will? Let Philip profit from murdering an old woman?'

Bea sighed, shook her head. 'What does Sandy say?'

'He dithers, poor darling. One minute he says we should tell the police about the picture being in Philip's flat, and the next he's defending Philip, saying it can't have been him because he doesn't carry a knife and wouldn't know how to use it.'

'But Sandy doesn't want his son's name being given to the police?'

'Would you, my dear? Would you?'

Bea grimaced. Her only son Max had recently been elected to the House of Commons, and was married to an ambitious young woman. Bea thought Max was squeaky clean, but suppose . . . some temptation? Some mischance? What would Bea do if Max happened to kill someone in a car accident, say? It was a dilemma. She hoped she'd do the right thing, but maybe she wouldn't.

Velma leaned forward so that no one else could hear. 'What we thought was that you could get someone into the flat to befriend Philip, worm their way into his confidence, get the truth out of him. Find an explanation for his having that picture. He's a loner, it should be easy. So, can you think of someone you can put in there?'

Bea had a sneaky, awe-inspiringly awful thought. Living with noisy Maggie was driving Bea insane. Could she possibly suggest that Maggie move into Philip's flat and befriend him? It would be the most enormous relief to have a quiet house again. Common sense told her Maggie would be useless as agent provocateur. 'No, I can't think of anyone. What do you mean, anyway . . . "put someone in there"?'

Velma got out a tiny notebook. 'The flat belongs to me, one of my first husband's better investments. Buying to rent in Kensington is as good as printing your own money, you know, all done through Marsh and Parsons, the estate agents just down the road. The flat's always been let to young professionals who can afford something a bit up-market. Four bedrooms – one is enormous and has twin beds in it – two bathrooms, large living room and kitchen. All mod cons.

'When I married Sandy and he moved in with me Philip came too, but I couldn't put up with him coming home all hours, mostly drunk and disorderly, breaking things, smoking a bit of this and that, the usual thing, dear, nothing really criminal, but disruptive.

'So I suggested he move into a vacant room in my flat which is co-ed now, men and women, thinking they'd be some kind of sobering influence on him. I'm not sure that that worked out, but one of the girls has left, so I thought you could put someone in there to find out what's really going on, someone who can befriend Philip, who's not the most . . . well, I'm not sure how to describe him exactly, but he doesn't seem to mix with the others in the flat. Surely you know someone who could do it? Preferably female, but it could be a male if the remaining girl moved into a single room and two of the boys bunked in together. I'll pay you well.'

Bea opened her mouth to suggest that Oliver might do it, and closed it again. Oliver was only eighteen, looked even younger and hadn't even learned the alphabet of socializing yet. No, Oliver was out of the question.

'Maggie might do it,' said Bea, feeling guilty but unable to stifle her longing for a bit of peace and quiet at home. 'One of my live-in assistants. She's early twenties, been divorced already. Not much in the way of computer skills but a brilliant cook and housekeeper.'

Velma wrinkled her nose. 'They're all professionals and we'd want a newcomer to fit in.'

'She could call herself a project manager; she's currently organizing new wiring, plumbing and decorating for the agency rooms in the basement at home, and she's not bad at that. Anything practical.'

Tears stood out in Velma's eyes, and she dabbed them away with a tissue. 'Oh, my dear, the relief! Bea, you are wonderful, I can't begin to thank you. I *knew* you'd come up with something. Just wait till I tell Sandy.'

'Don't tell him, not yet,' said Bea, wishing she'd never suggested Maggie could help. 'Look, if Maggie's going to go undercover the fewer people who know about it the better. You can tell Marsh and Parsons you've found a fifth person. I suppose they'll have to take up references—'

'This is an emergency, Bea. I'll tell the estate agents I've checked her out and she's OK, so they'll let her in. They'll need a deposit of a month's rent, and I'll see to that, too. How soon could you get her in?'

Bea wanted to say 'tomorrow' but had some degree of caution left. 'In a couple of days, I suppose. Are you sure this is what you want?'

'I'm not a fool, dear. I know that covering up a murder is just not on, but if we can only find some extenuating circumstances, perhaps we can get the case reduced to manslaughter. Perhaps it was an accident. That's what I'm hoping. But somehow or other we've got to get Philip to open up about it and that's where this Maggie person comes in. She's personable enough, isn't she? I think I met her briefly at that charity do the other month. Tall girl, looks like a model.'

Bea nodded. She'd been responsible for Maggie's make-over from Barbie doll to crop-haired model. The girl was quite present-able nowadays, and though still gauche, she was gaining enough self-confidence to socialize on a limited scale.

'Here!' Velma took a packet from her large handbag and shoved it at Bea. 'All you need, a cheque, a photo and as much information as I could get from Sandy about him. Ring me on my mobile, will you, when you've got going.' She fished out a mirror and lipstick, gave a little shriek at what she saw, and applied make-up. 'I'll go straight down to the estate agents, fix that end up. Oh, I hope, I do so hope you can prove it wasn't murder.'

'And if it was?'

Velma snapped her mirror shut. 'It has to be an accident. Right? I'm counting on you to prove it.'

Rafael was surprised her body had been found so quickly. The newspapers didn't say who had found her, but it hadn't been Philip or he'd have told them all about it. What with the drink and the pills, Philip was incapable of keeping his mouth shut, which was a teensy bit of a worry.

Philip was boasting that she'd given him a valuable picture on his last visit, When questioned, Liam had said that yes, Philip had got an old-fashioned picture in his room, but that it didn't look like anything much to him. Liam didn't have the background to know if it were valuable or not. If, as Philip claimed, it were a genuine Millais, then it would indeed be a passport to happi-ness. Though not for Philip, of course. Philip didn't deserve to profit from his theft . . . and it must have been theft, mustn't it? The old woman would hardly have given a loser like Philip anything worthwhile.

Tonight he'd get Philip to show him the painting and if it were anything half decent, he'd make him an offer for it. A couple of hundred, say.

The man in Amsterdam was avidly awaiting the gold boxes which Rafael had lifted the week before, plus the miniatures from an earlier incident. Rafael hadn't worked with him before, but he'd come highly recommended. Rafael was sure the Dutchman would be delighted to have a halfway decent Millais as well.

The only problem was how to get them there, for Rafael never

carried the goods himself. He had been using a reliable man as
carrier, but a car crash had put him in hospital.

Should he break his rule and take them himself? On balance,
no. The risk was too great. Besides, he had an open night to
organize for the gallery where he worked. What he needed was
a willing, innocent girl to act as a mule. Now, who did he know
who'd fit the bill?

Two

Friday afternoon

B ea walked back up Church Street, wondering whether she'd
suffered a senior moment by agreeing to help Velma, or had
acted with prudence and foresight. She was inclined, as she
turned in to her own road, to think she ought to ring Velma and
tell her the deal was off.

The Abbot Agency did not, emphatically *not*, do murder cases.
They were a domestic agency, pure and simple. Well, all right,
sometimes they had to disentangle misunderstandings between
client and employee; but they did not handle divorce work and
they were not a detective agency.

Granted, with the help of her two young assistants Bea had
recently exposed and dealt with a nasty charity scam, but that
was only because the agency had been partly responsible for
involving one of their clients in the first place. Check, check and
check again had been Hamilton's mantra, which Max had failed
to do.

Various other things had gone wrong during Max's time at
the agency. He wasn't perhaps best suited to the job, but when
Hamilton had become so ill, Max had taken over and had done
his best. Sort of. His heart really had been in politics and when
he finally got into parliament, he'd let the agency business run
down, assuming that Bea would not wish to keep it on after
Hamilton's death.

Max had left a lot of loose ends for Bea and her two new and untried assistants to tidy up on her return, and some of them – like the income tax affair – were serious. But that didn't mean they should stop doing what they were renowned for and start up a detective agency, did it?

Bea looked at her watch. Would Max be in the Commons now? No, wait a minute; the Commons had closed for its summer recess, and he'd be on his way north to his constituency for the holidays. She set her teeth. She simply must speak to him, straight away. That income tax problem . . . and one or two other loose ends.

'Whoo-hoo, I'm back.' Bea dumped her wet umbrella in the hall, bracing herself to meet an onslaught of noise. Maggie was in and seemed to have turned on every noisy machine in the house; television, radio – why did she need both television and radio on at the same time? – hoover and coffee grinder. Maggie was a natural born homemaker who aspired to be a high-flying businesswoman, or astronaut, or brain surgeon . . . any career, in fact, that she was least fitted for.

The girl appeared in the kitchen doorway, talking on her mobile phone. String-bean thin and bouncy with it, Maggie flashed a splendid set of teeth and waved at Bea. The hoovering continued. Maggie mimed 'Just a mo' at Bea and returned to the kitchen. The sound of the hoover did not cease. It was lying on its side in the living room, sucking in air not dust. Bea turned it off. And the television. This reduced the noise level some-what, but not completely.

Maggie brayed a laugh, and clanged saucepans about in the kitchen. She was probably gossiping to her new friend in the nail salon nearby; recently Maggie had taken to wearing false nails when she went out in the evenings.

Bea ground her teeth, fighting with herself. On the one hand Maggie was free, white and over twenty-one and therefore if she agreed to go undercover, it was no skin off Bea's nose. On the other hand, the girl was only just beginning to recover from the damage inflicted on a too tall, too sensitive girl by a destruct-ive ex-husband. Though reasonably bright, Maggie wasn't the sharpest knife in the drawer, and her attitude to life in general could be compared to that of an untrained but willing puppy.

Naïve was her middle name, and if unchecked, she'd dress from head to foot in DayGlo Lycra.

Would it be fair to ask her to go undercover? The coffee grinder stopped. For this relief much thanks. But the radio continued to churn out its tom-tom of doom and gloom.

Maggie shouted from the kitchen. 'Want some coffee? Oops, I've just remembered. Someone rang for you earlier, and I said I didn't know when you'd be back.'

'Who was it?' Bea dumped her bag on the table in the window – Hamilton's old card table, placed where she could sit and overlook the garden below.

'Dunno. I asked Oliver where you were, but he didn't seem to know. Oh, and the man came round to see about the rewiring and he wants to know if you need Wi-Fi or something. It costs extra, of course. Oh, bother, that's my phone again. Hello . . .?' Another burst of laughter.

Bea took the packet Velma had given her, and trod down the stairs to the agency in the basement. Definitely she must have these dingy rooms redecorated. Rewiring, yes; though she didn't understand about Wi-Fi. Oliver would know. She went through to the big back room which had once been Hamilton's office. Because the house was built on a slope, this room had access to the garden through French windows. She dumped Velma's package on the desk which was now hers, and bent to pick all that tiresome correspondence out of the wastepaper basket . . . which was empty.

Feeling stupid, Bea picked up the basket and shook it. It remained empty.

She began to panic. The letter from the tax people, the invoice from . . . that letter of complaint which must be answered, the communication from a solicitor about a case she'd never even heard of . . .

Gone.

Maggie came clattering down the stairs, and rushed through the hall to the agency reception office at the front of the house, still talking on her mobile.

Bea ran after her, short of breath. 'Maggie, did you empty the wastepaper basket?'

'What? Oh. Hold on a mo . . . Uh-huh. Dustbin day today.'

Bea told herself to take long, slow breaths. Recycling was the thing. All paperwork went into a green box in the well outside the basement steps leading up to the road. Of course the paper-work would be in there, safe and sound.

Maggie had turned on her computer, while still talking on her phone. Bea went through the tiny vestibule and out into the open air at the bottom of the steps. Maggie's perky little bay tree was doing well, and the steps were swept every day. The green recycling box was there, and the bag with paper for recycling was in it. Good.

Not so good was the fact that the most important letters were not in it. Including the ones from the taxman and the solicitor.

The rain had turned to a mild sort of drizzle.

Bea went back inside and stood over Maggie till the girl looked up from her phone call and realized something was up. She told her caller to hold on a moment and smiled up at Bea, all eager beaver.

'Maggie, have you been doing some shredding?'

'Uh-huh. Anything with our details on it. OK?'

During his time in the office Max had bought a new shredder, one that turned paper into confetti, and not strips. Bea closed her eyes for a moment. She told herself it wasn't Maggie's fault. The girl had merely been doing her job.

It was Bea's fault, and heaven alone knew how she was going to get out of this one. A grovelling letter to the taxman for a start. That is, if she could remember which tax office she was supposed to be dealing with, which she couldn't. Perhaps there was something in the back files . . . oh, and the solicitor's letter must be attended to, somehow.

'Maggie, how would you like to go undercover on a special job?'

They dragged Oliver away from his computer and sat in Bea's office with the lights on, for the rain hadn't let up.

Bea opened the packet Velma had given her, and extracted the cheque. She hid the shock which the total gave her, and put it in her top drawer without comment. Nevertheless the amount made her pulse beat fast. Why, it would cover almost all the bill from the tax people and wouldn't that be a good thing!

She emptied everything else out of the envelope on to the desk. 'We've been asked, as a special favour, to undertake an investigation into an incident in which an elderly lady died. It may have been an accident, or manslaughter, or murder. The death was reported last week. Here's the cutting from last Friday's local paper.'

Bea laid it on the desk and they both leaned forward to read the print, and look at the Forties-style photograph of a glamorous blonde.

'But we don't "do" that sort of thing,' said Maggie.

Oliver gave her a sharp look. 'It would make a change from finding people a new nanny or housekeeper.' Oliver liked a challenge.

Bea hid a smile. 'That's an old photograph. The subject was Lady Farne, widow of a man who left her very well off. When she died she was in her eighties, reclusive, miserly, sitting on a fortune in antiques in a large flat nearby. Oliver, would you like to see if you can dig up a more recent photograph and any other information about her? I expect there were obituaries in some of the better class papers.'

Oliver nodded. 'It says the death was due to a burglary that went wrong.' He flicked at the paper. 'There's a lot about her lurid life, but hardly anything about her death.'

'The police are probably working through their list of professional burglars who might have had a go.' Bea teased out another photograph from the pile. 'You don't need to know who our client is for the moment but she's done a good job assembling information for us. She suspects that a family member called Philip Weston knows more about the death than he should.'

Bea glanced sharply up at her two assistants. Oliver, swarthy, fidgety, still wet behind the ears, had a good memory and a clever mind. His eyes narrowed and sought Bea's. She could see him notching up the information that a Mrs Velma Weston was one of Bea's friends. He'd made the connection all right.

Maggie hadn't. She was grinning at the photo Bea was holding up for them to see. 'Grrr . . . just my type; tall, dark and handsome.'

Bea wondered if they were talking about the same photo, because to her Philip Weston looked very average, rather ordinary, perhaps a bit weak about the mouth. Discontented. 'You can't tell his height from a head and shoulders photo.'

'You can from this description, though,' said Oliver, who had pounced on a handwritten note in the pile. 'Five ten, dark, clean-shaven, dresses formally except at weekends when he shifts into casual gear. Works out at the local Virgin Active gym, no particular girlfriend, no car. Wonder if he's gay.'

Bea hadn't thought of that.

'He's not gay,' said Maggie, still focused on the photo.

Oliver flicked a glance at Bea, and looked away. Would Maggie know if he were?

'The thing is,' said Bea, 'that our client would like Maggie to take up a vacancy in the flat where Philip lives. Get him to talk about himself, his finances, that sort of thing. Particularly his finances. Apparently he doesn't get on very well with the other people in the flat, so a bit of sympathy from a nice girl like Maggie should do the trick, right?'

Maggie punched the air. 'Do I go in as myself, or under another name?'

'As yourself. You've been project-managing the make-over of the agency rooms here and that's your day job, but you need to crash out somewhere else at night. Stick to the truth about yourself. If asked, tell them about your ex-husband, how he did the dirty on you with the bimbo from the telly, that you haven't yet got the money from your half of the marital flat, that you went home when the marriage first broke down and then moved in as a lodger here, but need your own space and so on and so forth.'

'Couldn't I invent another name for myself? "Maggie" is so, well, ordinary.'

'Mrs Abbot's right,' said Oliver. 'If you tried to call yourself something else, you'd be bound to forget and they'd notice.'

'Boring, boring,' chanted Maggie.

'Maybe,' said Bea, through gritted teeth, 'but I agree with Oliver. Now Mrs Weston is going to fix it for you with the estate agents, pay your deposit and a month's rent in advance. She would like you to move in tomorrow' – and the good Lord knows, I'd like it too, thought Bea – 'but only if you think you can pack up and move there in time.'

'Where is it?'

Oliver had been shuffling through the remaining paperwork. 'It's one of those flats in that old block that faces on to Kensington High Street. You are to share a large bedroom and bathroom with another girl. It's not far. I could help you over there with your suitcase tomorrow morning, if you like.'

'All you have to do,' said Bea, having guilty thoughts about pushing the girl in at the deep end of what might prove to be a very murky pool, 'is act naturally. You're a working girl, been around a bit but not too much. Listen and learn everything you can about Philip. Go out for a drink with him, that sort of thing.

Turn up here every morning when it's time to open up the agency, and tell us what you've found out. That's all.'

Maggie was so excited that she had to get up and dance around. 'I'm going to be an undercover agent, I'm going to be a star in my own movie!'

Again Oliver and Bea flicked glances at one another, and disengaged.

'Don't overdo it,' said Oliver. 'Remember, this guy may have killed an old lady.'

'Oh, surely not, he looks such a sweetie,' said Maggie.

Bea sighed. Maggie never had been a good judge of character, had she? Bea was having second, third and fourth thoughts about this. 'Maggie, Oliver's right. You are not there to investigate anything. You're there to gather impressions and pass them on to us. Keep your mobile with you at all times, and keep it charged. Walk out of there the moment you feel uneasy. Understood?'

'I'm going to be an undercover star,' carolled Maggie, waltzing herself out of the room and up the stairs. As the thunder of her footsteps receded, Oliver sat back in his chair and sighed.

'I'll sign up at the gym he visits, see if I can get close to him there. Just in case he is gay.'

Bea blinked. What had brought this on? The idea of this under-sized geek working out in a gym had its funny side, but for the life of her she wouldn't hurt his feelings by showing amusement. Now she came to think of it, this was a better solution than she could have thought up by herself to get him out of the house.

'It'll be pricey, but yes; you do that and I'll pay the fees.'

Oliver shook his head. 'Let me. I'd rather.'

Bea stifled an impulse to tell him not to be silly. She reminded herself that he was growing up, a bit. Now and then. She must let him pay for himself if he wished to do so. 'Very well.' She shuffled the paperwork back into its envelope. Now she'd manoeuvred Maggie out of the house, she was inclined to think she'd done the wrong thing. 'I wonder if I ought to have asked Maggie to do this. I suspect she'll fall in love with Philip because she likes his looks and thinks we've got a "down" on him.'

'You can't stop her now.'

Bea knew she couldn't. She rose to her feet, stretching her back, grimacing. This damp weather reminded her to keep doing her exercises, or she'd get sciatica again. 'Oliver, do you know anything about pre-Raphaelite painters, Millais in particular?'

His head snapped round to her, and he gnawed at his lower lip. 'There's a good reason? I'll look him up on the internet.'

'You might try looking up Lady Farne at the same time, and perhaps even more important, see if you can track down any of the purchases her husband made, antiques, pictures, that sort of thing.'

'Pictures equals Millais?' He stood, his movements precise. He looked like an office boy on his first day in the job and could have walked into a position at NASA if brains were the only criterion.

Bea nodded. 'Pictures equals Millais. Specifically portraits in oils. I think perhaps I might take a trip to the library, see if I can track down a book with some reproductions in it, while you research the Farne collection.'

Dark eyebrows peaked. 'The burglar stole a Millais?'

Bea backtracked. 'I don't know. Maybe. We need more information about – oh, everything. Meanwhile, is there anything I ought to know about on the agency side? Complaints, letters missing, solicitors in a rage, that sort of thing?'

He reached in his pocket for his notebook, snapped back the band, frowned at the notes he'd made. 'Well, yes . . .'

She had second thoughts. If she told him the stupid thing she'd done with the tax return, he'd never look up to her again. 'Oh, never mind. Agency stuff will have to be put on one side for the time being. Maggie's been keeping the filing under control, hasn't she? Oh, and she did say she'd got some quotes for a make-over down here. Will you get her to give them to me before she goes?'

Oliver frowned at his notebook. 'There is just one thing I wanted to ask you about—'

Bea tried to sound off-hand. 'How are we fixed for cash, in case a big bill comes in?' The bill for income tax, for instance.

Maggie erupted into the room. 'Ta-da! Will this do?' She struck a pose to show off enormous dark glasses, a blonde chin-length wig, a beaded black top, rather too skimpy for her slender figure, and what looked like a short evening skirt in fuschia pink. She glittered with excitement.

Bea restrained an exclamation of horror and aimed for a kind, affectionate tone of voice. 'I think that might be a bit overwhelming, don't you, Oliver? Maggie, you're meant to be a professional woman. A good white T-shirt and jeans, perhaps?'

Maggie's face disintegrated. Was she going to cry? 'Is it the wig? My hair's so short now I often wear this in the evenings when I go out to the pub.' She'd cut off her own long hair a while back but the artist at Bea's hair salon had contrived her a neat cap of a pleasing auburn colour, which Maggie had pronounced 'Just not me!'.

'Yes, but . . .' Bea ignored Oliver, who was snorting into his notebook. 'Bear with me, dear. I know you can do "flamboyant" very well but I think in this case it might be better to try to appear ordinary, just till you've sussed out the other tenants of the flat.'

'Must I?' Maggie's beautiful eyes – really her only claim to beauty – starred with tears.

'I'll lend you something, shall I?' Bea had often found herself lending some of her classic garments in restrained colours to Maggie of late. 'It's about time I bought myself some new clothes, anyway. I usually . . .' She controlled herself with an effort, trying to smile. 'Hamilton always used to take me away for a week or so to Bruges at this time of the year. There's a good clothes shop there . . . and . . . well, enough of that!'

'You should go again, why not?' said Maggie. 'You deserve a holiday.'

'I wouldn't like to go by myself. Lose the disguise dear, while Oliver and I finish the routine jobs.'

Maggie flounced out. Oliver, grinning, licked his finger and turned over a page. 'About our finances. There are a couple of bad debts left over from Mr Max's time. Shall I organize solicitor's letters? But even more important—'

'Everything else can wait.'

Bea looked out of the window through the drizzle to the stately sycamore at the end of the garden, and through that to the graceful spire of the church beyond. She was worried about Max. A member of parliament had certain living expenses both in his constituency and here in London, where the rent of a flat was one of the biggest problems. Max's wife was no thrifty house-wife and mention of his finances recently made him look haggard. He had hoped that Bea would retire to the South Coast and leave her valuable Kensington house to him, but that was the last thing Bea wanted to do. Had Max got into a mess, moneywise, and used the money which was supposed to pay the tax bill?

Bea rubbed her neck. Then there was the lost solicitor's letter, which had been somewhat more than faintly alarming. What had their name been? Wasn't there some saint or other, probably Italian, that the faithful used to invoke to find lost property? She couldn't for the life of her remember his name, and it would have been useful at this moment. The nearest she could get to it was, *If there's someone up there, and I do believe there is – well, most of the time I do, and Hamilton certainly did – then could you please help me out of this mess? I know it's entirely my own fault that I've lost these papers, but . . . well, that's it, really. Please.*

Oliver was looking at her with a degree of impatience. Had he asked her a question, and she hadn't heard it? 'Sorry, Oliver. Wool-gathering. There were some letters in the post this morning that . . . no, we won't bother with them now. Let's have a look at those quotes Maggie got for us, and call it a day.'

The phone rang as she followed Oliver out of the door, so she went back to answer it.

Velma. 'It's all fixed up. Maggie can move in any time after six this evening. Tell her to ask for someone called Charlotte who's responsible for the lease. Must rush; Sandy's tummy pains are getting worse, and I'm taking him down to the hospital to get him seen to. Give me a ring when Maggie's moved in, won't you?'

The line went dead.

Bea cradled the phone, thinking that she now knew what it was like to stand in the middle of a rushing stream, lose your footing and get borne seawards. She wasn't, unfortunately, a particularly good swimmer.

Rafael left work with a slight headache. There was so much to think about at the moment, what with the invitations to the new exhibition at the gallery going out late, having to find a new carrier and Philip's refusal to sell him the picture.

On the other hand, it had occurred to him that Charlotte would make the perfect mule to carry the goods out of the country for him. Mind you, she was a squawker; heaven only knew how she got on at the library because when the flood-gates opened, she never stopped. Now she was agitating because another girl was going to move into the flat and the place was a tip. Fine. The rent would be shared between five and not four, which would please Liam and Zander, both of whom were perpetually short of money.

Better get Liam to calm her down. Liam didn't fancy Charlotte much, but he'd do as he was told for a bonus.

Rafael had an amusing thought. He had more stuff to move than Charlotte could feasibly take without asking questions. He'd have a look at the new girl; if she was anything like Charlotte, he could use her, too.

It was worrying, though, that Philip had disappeared with the picture after their little chat the other night. The picture had been genuine enough, though Rafael had told Philip it was just a good copy worth a couple of hundred at most.

The boy had wavered, tried to beat the price up. Perhaps it had been a mistake to threaten him? Rafael had only shown him his knife to help the deal along, and he'd had no real intention of using it, but Philip had been drinking too hard to realize that.

If it hadn't been for the little girl with the waist-length hair that Rafael had been chatting up, he'd have stuck by Philip till a sale had been concluded. It had been a mistake to leave him behind in the pub to go on drinking, but who'd have thought he'd have done a midnight flit?

However, all was not lost. Philip hadn't the brains to hide properly, nor the money. He'd be back, and when he returned it would be curtains and not pictures for him, right?

Three

Friday afternoon to evening

Bea tried to get hold of Max up in the Midlands, got through to his PA and left a message for him to phone her urgently. His PA didn't sound very encouraging; Max was out at some constituency function and would be going on to another meeting early that evening. In other words, don't hold your breath, Mrs Abbot.

How do you attract the notice of a busy man like Max, who

felt the burden of the Party resting on his shoulders, even though
he was a mere foot soldier and might never be anything more?
That tax demand . . .

Answer; you ring his wife. Bea didn't actively dislike the
over-thin Nicole, but she didn't cherish warm feelings towards
her, either. But needs must. Nicole wasn't at the house her parents
had bought for them. She would be out to lunch with her friends,
or perhaps at Max's side at a constituency event, smiling and
not meaning it. Bea dug out Nicole's mobile number, and rang.
Her phone was switched off. Bea left a message, trying to keep
calm, trying not to shout. There was no doubt about it, she was
thoroughly on edge.

Her own landline rang. Bea answered the phone in a clipped
voice.

'Abbot Agency, how may I help you?'

A laughing voice, a well-known voice, the voice of her ex-
husband, Piers, the well-known portrait painter and tomcat. 'I'm
coming round in—'

'No, you're not. Piers, I've got—'

'—ten minutes.' The phone went dead.

Maggie whirled into the room, snatching up papers, banging
filing cabinet drawers around. Max had experimented with having
a paper-free office, but hadn't backed up as much as he might
have done. Also, computers were fallible and Bea had decided
that although they would take every precaution to keep their business running via computers, they would keep some paper files.

'Must get it all straight before I go,' Maggie sang to herself.

Bea bit back a sharp retort. Maggie was still going to be here
from nine to five, wasn't she? Well, ten to five, more probably.
But her hours of work would not be affected. The girl burst into
song, 'I'm getting married in the morning . . .'

Bea tried not to wince. 'Maggie, where's the quotes you've
been getting for me?'

'Top right-hand drawer of your desk,' sang Maggie.

Bea reached for the drawer as the front doorbell pealed above.
That would be Piers, drat it. What a time-waster that man was.
Yet he could be helpful on occasion; Hamilton had liked him,
and kept in touch with him through the years.

'Shall I go?' asked Maggie, looking for an excuse to leave
her filing.

Bea shook her head, and went up the stairs to let Piers in. He thrust past her, carrying a large package wrapped in reused cardboard and tied up with string, which he took straight through into the living room. Of course, he'd borrowed the last photograph that Hamilton had had taken, and been doing a portrait of him.

Piers didn't bother with a formal greeting. 'Where will you hang it?'

He put the picture on the settee and looked around the room with a critical eye. 'It's come out quite well, even if I say so myself. I even found myself talking to him the other day. "Hamilton," I said, "is this portrait of you going to be a comfort to our beloved wife, or drive her insane?"' Sinewy hands made light work of the packaging, which flew off in all directions.

'What did Hamilton reply?' asked Bea, diverted in spite of herself.

Piers wagged a bony finger at her. 'He said I had to keep an eye on you, and so I will. Within reason.' He stripped off the last of the covers to reveal a portrait of Bea's much-loved husband, dark-haired, round-faced, not quite smiling. Kindly, intelligent eyes seemed to meet hers. Piers had caught Hamilton's air of serenity remarkably well. Bea sat down with a bump on the nearest chair.

'It's good, huh?' said Piers. 'I don't often get to paint a good man. Mostly they're fat cats with slimy souls.'

She nodded, unable to speak.

'You want to borrow a handkerchief?' Piers didn't normally keep handkerchiefs about his person, so the question was rhetorical.

Bea shook her head.

Piers prowled round the room, which was furnished with antiques of various periods inherited by Hamilton. The walls were hung with watercolours in gilt frames, some of them executed by his aunts. Piers took down one picture, shook his head, replaced it, and finally removed a large watercolour which had been hanging for ever over a small desk at the side of the fireplace. He hung Hamilton's portrait in its place and stood back, fingers rasping unshaven chin, to check the effect. 'There!'

Bea controlled her voice. 'It's very good, Piers. Very.'

'Hmm. Had a struggle to get the mouth right. I didn't intend him to smile, but he got the better of me. You'll be amused to hear I could have sold it to a client. A woman, naturally. I suppose I ought to have sent it for exhibition but no . . . I decided not. I didn't think he'd like it.'

'Thank you, Piers.' It was amazing how the eyes still met hers, even though she was no longer directly in front of the portrait.

Piers rubbed his hands down over his face. 'Well, that's that. We ought to break open some champagne to celebrate, but I know you're not much into the drinks line. Is there any coffee?' He yelled out of the door. 'Maggie, is there any coffee?'

Bea picked up the packaging he'd strewn around the place, and wondered what to do with the discarded watercolour. Hamilton had liked that picture, but she hadn't really looked at it for years, and wasn't sure now that she cared for it.

'I'll get rid of that for you, if you like,' said Piers. 'Genuine Victoriana, but not particularly good. Should fetch a good few hundred, maybe five on a good day.'

Here was someone who knew about pictures. 'How about a Millais, a portrait in oils?'

'What?' He swung himself into a chair and put his feet up on the coffee table. Patched jeans, ripped T-shirt, untidy black hair streaked with grey, a nose pushed to one side. Total charm. Total tomcat. It had been a disastrously unhappy marriage, but they'd made their peace after she'd married Hamilton and he'd adopted Max. Piers was someone she could rely on . . . unless she came between him and his painting.

'Who's putting a Millais on the market? They don't come up often. Is it a good one? He did a lot, and some are better than others. It depends on the sitter, partly. Male or female, famous or obscure. And there are some fakes around, naturally.'

'I haven't seen it, but I imagine it's a good one.'

Dark eyes sharpened. 'Bea, what are you up to now?'

'I'm not sure.' She folded up the packaging as best she could and stuffed it behind the wastepaper basket. Dustbin day today. Been and gone. And her correspondence with it. She looked up at Hamilton's portrait and he looked down at her, serene, not quite smiling. She seemed to hear him say, 'It'll all be one in a thousand years.' Yes, of course it would.

Maggie came in with the coffee, almost curtseying to Piers as she laid the tray down before him. Piers thanked her, gave her a professional once-over and dismissed her with a smile and a wave of his hand.

Bea said, 'I've been trying to get in contact with Max, but he's so busy, and of course I understand that, but . . .'

Piers grunted, slurped coffee, looked at the heavy watch on

his wrist. 'The boy's a fool. Don't know where he gets it from. Not from me or you and certainly not from Hamilton, who was worth more than all of us put together. Right. Must be off. Can't remember where for the moment, but it will come to me. Get me on the mobile if you need me. I'll be in London for another week, then off somewhere, can't remember where that's supposed to be either, but . . . oh, I know.' He grimaced. 'Painting another of the newly ennobled for an enormous fee. Flatter his ego, hide my true feelings, and never even think that he might have paid his way into the House of Lords. Well, I leave Hamilton in safe hands.' He stood in front of the painting, finishing his cup of coffee. 'Bye, old man. I'm going to miss you.'

He banged the front door to behind him, leaving Bea feeling limp. She had an impulse, which she knew to be mawkish, to kiss her husband's painted lips, but didn't, because she got overtaken by giggles. Hamilton seemed to be laughing, too.

'You old rogue,' she said, and then laughed out loud. Fancy talking to a picture! It was all very well for an artist like Piers, but for Bea . . .? Ridiculous!

She sat down at the card table in the window, from where she could look at the picture. Hamilton had been accustomed to play patience here, saying it helped him think. Ridiculous! But Bea pulled out a double pack of cards and laid them out. She was trying a new patience, eight across, decreasing by one card in each layer. Red ten on black jack. A lot of hearts.

She sighed, losing interest in the game. She really must get Maggie into some decent clothes and go to the library to research Millais – and oh, what about the taxman? She couldn't believe that she'd dumped important letters into the bin. She was supposed to be an adult, for heaven's sake, not a toddler throwing her toys out of her buggy. She had an agency to run, staff wages to pay. How could she have been so childish?

She went downstairs to look into the complaints file, which was not on her desk. Maggie wasn't in the agency, either. Even from the basement, Bea could hear Maggie, up in her room at the top of the house, doing a karaoke act along with the radio or her MP-thingy. '*I will survive . . .*'

I'm sure you will, thought Bea. I'm not sure I will, though. Now what do I do first? Answer: divert my thoughts by getting some books on Millais from the library.

* * *

Maggie decided to move into the flat that night. She had too much clobber to walk there, so ordered a taxi for herself and the three – no, four! – bags of belongings she wanted to take with her. Once she'd banged out of the house, Oliver and Bea turned in to the kitchen to tackle the chicken, chips and salad she'd left out for them.

The house seemed to settle down around their shoulders.

'Nice and quiet,' said Bea. Then, thinking that sounded like a criticism of Maggie, she added, 'I shall miss her.'

Oliver nodded, folding himself on to a stool and waiting for Bea to serve his food. He'd been the odd one out in his family, rescued by Maggie after a row in which he'd been thrown out on to the street. He was a nice lad, but used to being waited on by womenfolk. Not for the first time, Bea thought it would be a good thing if Maggie were not quite so protective of him. She did everything for him bar powdering his bottom after he'd had his bath.

Bea scolded herself. What was the matter with her? First she schemed to get rid of Maggie because she made so much noise, and now she was thinking about how she could get rid of Oliver, which made her the most ungrateful person she knew. Why, Maggie had been carrying the burden of looking after the house from the moment she arrived, and without Oliver the agency would have been finished months ago.

She dished up. 'Max didn't ring while I was out?'

Oliver shook his head. 'I got a lot of stuff about the Farnes off the internet, printed it off and left it on your desk. Lady Farne must have been quite a character. There's some stuff on Millais, too. He was another odd one. Did you know he didn't get his knighthood for years because he was playing around with another man's wife, though he did eventually marry her?'

She hadn't known that. Perhaps it was going to be more fun to research Millais than she'd thought it would be.

She'd returned from the library with an armful of books on art, which she didn't think was precisely her kind of bedtime reading. Not like the latest Maeve Binchy, for instance.

Oliver changed and went out after supper, saying he was going to see about signing on at the gym.

Bea wandered around the quiet, too quiet house. The rain had stopped, hurray. The scent of nicotiana and honeysuckle hung in the air. Bea deadheaded some roses, and swept up a few leaves which had fluttered down from the big tree at the bottom of the garden. She got the cushions out of the shed and sat down on the lounger under the tree with some of her art books. She turned pages. She yawned. All those pretty pickies of children and young girls and statesmen and . . . they were really just potboilers, weren't they? Only one or two of them stood out and one of them . . . she had to smile . . . was a portrait of his wife's first husband. Well, well. Who's the tomcat now?

Piers, currently painting a clientele whom he called the Great But Not So Good, was probably today's equivalent of Millais. She glanced at some of the sugary portraits of children which Millais had done. They were not fashionable today, of course, but they had a certain charm.

Which led her to remembering that Velma had the same sort of blue-eyed, innocent charm. Why, at school she'd got away with murder, not literally, of course, but . . .

Which led Bea to acknowledge a tiny crumple of uneasiness at the back of her mind. Had Velma laid on the charm a trifle too thickly? Of course not. Velma had known she was asking Bea a big favour and had acted accordingly. It was natural for her to do the blue-eyed innocent look. Still, there were one or two gaps in her story, now that Bea came to think about it. In the morning she would phone Velma and clarify one or two points.

She relaxed. The light faded gradually, so gradually that she hardly noticed it. Summer evening sounds carried far, a party in a garden some way away . . . a barbecue by the sound and smell. Someone was adjusting a television set, changing channels. Lights were switched on here and there. A woman was on a mobile, laughing, chatting, the words indistinguishable.

The phone ringing.

Her phone ringing.

She ran up the iron staircase to the sitting room, only to hear someone leave a message. Max? No. It was Nicole, explaining they were out but would get in touch soon, bye, bye. Bea tried to ring back, but Nicole's mobile was switched off again. Bother.

Bea tried Velma's mobile, but that was switched off, too. Velma wasn't answering her phone at home, either, so Bea left a message to say that Maggie had moved into the flat and would be reporting next day. Oliver wasn't back yet. Bea was faintly uneasy about him. And, she had to admit, about Maggie.

She tidied the house ready for bed, and took one of the art books up with her. After a couple of pages, she laid it down. She realized she was listening out for the youngsters, which was ridiculous, of course. Ten o'clock, and she tried to read a few verses from Hamilton's bible but couldn't concentrate. She read something about asking your neighbour for a loaf of bread when he'd turned in for the night, which didn't make much sense. She read it again. Ah, it meant that if your neighbour went on asking, you did eventually get out of bed, disturbing the whole household, in order to give him what he wanted. Hamilton would have said it was all about being constant in prayer.

Well, she didn't know much about prayer, but she was pretty sure that she wasn't capable of that much persistence . . . fancy sticking at it long enough to get your neighbour out of bed for a loaf of bread! Her mind wandered to what they'd have to eat at the weekend. Maggie usually saw to all that but if Maggie wasn't here, Bea had better do some shopping tomorrow. She turned off the light.

Eleven, and Oliver still hadn't returned. In all the time Oliver had been living with her, he'd never once been out this late. He had undoubtedly been run over and was lying in hospital, mangled beyond belief. If he wasn't back by midnight, she'd start ringing the hospitals.

She lay so that she could see the display on the digital clock on her bedside table. She thought it would be a good idea to pray for Oliver's safety, but she wasn't sure she knew any prayers of that kind. Would it be enough just to say, *Please look after him, please*?

And now she was about it, what about a bit of help for Velma and her Sandy . . . and she supposed for Philip as well, though it did sound as if Velma's suspicions were justified . . . and as for Maggie . . .

Bea smiled. *Yes, please do spare a moment to look after Maggie, because I honestly don't think I ought to have sent her to live in that flat. And yes, I am sorry I did it, it was selfish of me and I really wish I hadn't.*

The front door closed, soft footsteps went up past her bedroom door, and on again up to the top of the house where Oliver and Maggie had their rooms. Bea relaxed, turned over in bed, and went to sleep.

The new girl was cut from the same cloth as Charlotte but hid it better. All Brave New World on top, and insecure little beetle underneath. And how she chattered! All about her ex-husband – really one couldn't blame him for telling her to get lost – and her employer who'd given her a room in her house, and was recently bereaved and really ought to take a holiday, and was thinking about going to Bruges, and had anyone else been to Bruges and what was it like ... and on ... and on ...

That voice of hers could be heard all over the flat. She was almost as bad as Charlotte, who fluttered and squawked. Really, Charlotte was just like a hen when she got into a flap. But easy meat. Liam had hardly had to exert himself to have her eating out of his hand. The new girl had fallen for Zander. Hm, well, Zander had carried stolen goods around for Rafael twice already, even if he didn't know it. Rafael's lips twitched into a thin smile. Zander would play ball, if needed.

The big problem was Philip. He hadn't returned, he hadn't been back to the club, or the gym. It was irritating that Philip had chosen to disappear with the picture. What's more, if Philip got drunk – as he often did – and talked about the low price Rafael had offered him for the Millais, questions might be asked. Silence was golden, right? Dead silence.

As for getting the goods away, Charlotte had put the idea into his head, and the more he thought about it, the better it looked. The dear little squawker had seized on the idea of a few days' holiday in Bruges, and Bruges wasn't so far from Amsterdam, was it? As a tourist she could take the gold boxes out with her and his contact could easily connect up with her in Bruges. Charlotte would be the perfect mule.

There was a lot of pressure to get the miniatures out as well. He decided to get Zander to work on the Maggie bird, too.

Four

Saturday morning

It seemed strange and rather wonderful to wake up to a silent house. Bea stretched out in bed, enjoying those last few moments of peace and quiet. She usually woke to the sound of

Maggie turning on the television and radio downstairs. Dead on half past seven, Maggie would clump in with a cup of tea and draw the curtains back. It was amazing how some people could make so much noise, just by drawing the curtains back. This morning, there was nothing but silence.

No cup of tea, either. And nobody to make breakfast for them. Oliver wouldn't. Oliver couldn't.

It might be a good idea for Maggie to give Oliver some lessons in looking after himself, basic cookery for bachelors, that sort of thing.

Bea got herself dressed and went downstairs to find Oliver in the kitchen, looking lost even though his box of muesli was staring him in the face on the worktop. Bea passed him bowls, plates, mugs, and milk. She put on the kettle, made toast, asked if he wanted anything cooked and realized she was acting just as Maggie did.

Oliver got outside his plate of cereal in record time. 'I've applied to join the gym. It's good there, lots of help given to first-timers. They'll give me a regime to start on and I can also use the pool, have a juice or a snack afterwards. I paid on my credit card and they didn't need references. I said Philip Weston had told me about the place, that I'd met him in a pub. I'd hoped Philip would be there, but he wasn't. They said he hadn't been around for a while.'

'Do you mean that he hasn't been around since the burglary?'

'I don't know. I couldn't get a look at their records last night, but they do keep track of who comes and when, so it shouldn't be impossible for me to suss that out. Then an old schoolfriend was just coming out as I was leaving. I thought he might have known Philip, but lots of people use that gym and my friend couldn't be sure whether he knew him or not. I must take a copy of Philip's photo with me when I see him again.'

Oliver had had one good friend at school but had lost touch when he left home; correction, when he was kicked out by his father. Well, well. Little Oliver was growing up at last. Bea noticed he hadn't mentioned his friend's name. Would it do any good to ask, or merely irritate him? She understood that teenagers didn't like to be cross-questioned about their doings, and she could trust Oliver to be sensible, couldn't she? At least she now knew why he'd got home so late.

He helped himself to another bowl of muesli, and looked at the stove. 'Any chance of a couple of eggs?'

Bea put some eggs on to boil, adding vinegar to the water to prevent the eggs from bursting in the pan.

Oliver's appetite seemed to have improved with the exercise. 'I'd rather you didn't tell Maggie I've joined the gym. She's been ribbing me about being on the small side and she'll think I've done it to impress her, which isn't true. I can't help being on the small side. It's genetic.'

Bea hid a smile. Oliver was definitely growing up. 'Napoleon was the same, and Nelson.'

'I'm not really the fighting type.'

Bea served him his boiled eggs and toast as the front door burst inwards and Maggie appeared, waving the morning papers.

'Am I good, or am I good!' she said, whacking them down on the table. 'Mission accomplished, etcetera. And oh, he's totally, utterly gorgeous, and I seem to have made quite an impression on him, too, because he was all over me till I disentangled myself to get some kip. A bit quick, I thought, but I can't say I disliked it. Oh, my! I turn my back for five minutes and look at the mess you're in.'

She swept their cereal bowls into the dishwasher, removed the milk bottle, threw off her jacket, and went on talking. 'I just love this job. Going into a flat share is the best thing that could have happened to me. There's two other flats in the block rented by young people and they're in and out of one another's rooms, with a party in one flat or the other every weekend. There's one tonight upstairs that we're all going to and Charlotte – she's a sort of ugly duckling, but she seems to be responsible for the running of the flat – but if you, Mrs Abbot, were to take her in hand maybe you could stop her wearing those heavy dark glasses and hair all over her face as if trying to hide behind it, and her skirts are the wrong length, you know?'

Oliver said, 'Calm down, sit down, and tell us more about your latest conquest.'

She rolled her eyes. 'He's got a voice like whipped cream mixed with ginger and chocolate, and his skin's that colour too. He says his parents came from Grenada, but he's as British as you and me, and clever with it. He's going places, is Zander.'

'Hang about,' said Oliver. 'I thought you were there to get close to someone called Philip?'

Maggie put out her tongue at Oliver, but hooked the teapot towards her, and poured herself a mug. 'Philip? I didn't see him. It took me some time to work out who was who, because like I said, people from the flat upstairs seem to spend time in our flat, and vice versa. I nearly made a booboo with one man, thinking he might be Philip, but he wasn't; he was from upstairs.

'Anyway I did ask Charlotte – that's the ugly duckling – who the other men in the flat might be because I'm sharing a huge bedroom and a shower room with her, but there are three other bedrooms and one of them must be Philip's. She said one of the men seemed to be out and another went out early, I don't know where, but his name's Lee or something like that. Not Philip. Then I met Zander, that's the poppet I've been telling you about. He said Lee, or whatever his name is, had gone out for the evening and that Philip was a bit erratic, might be working late, they could never tell his movements, and that he might be in later, but he wasn't.'

Bea was beginning to feel anxious about the absent Philip. 'When did they see him last?'

'Dunno. I couldn't ask outright or it would have looked suspicious. I mean, I'm not supposed to know anything about him, and especially not that he's a murderer.'

'He may not be,' said Bea. 'We don't know that. We don't really know anything much about him.'

Maggie downed her mug of tea and said, 'Aah. I needed that, though I must admit I prefer coffee to kickstart me in the mornings. I didn't like to drink out of any of their mugs at the flat, because they're all stained and the dirt round the handles has to be seen to be believed. The place is a tip. I asked Charlotte why they didn't have a cleaner and she said that they had had one but there'd been arguments about paying her, and then they'd tried to get a roster going, everyone doing their share, but of course the men didn't lift a finger, and Charlotte's got enough to do at work without taking on a cleaning job as well, and why should she? I mean, it's not right, is it? So she asked me if I could find someone for them at the agency, because of course I was quite open about what I do as you said I was to be, and of course I said yes – and ta-da! Aren't I Miss Clever Clogs?'

Bea said, 'But we don't have any cleaners on our books who are capable of ferreting out the truth about Philip.'

'No, but *you* could,' said Maggie, dancing around the room.

'I said, I know just the person, someone a bit older but experienced and tactful. I said she's a widow, fallen on hard times, and she could start straight away. So here are your keys, Mrs Abbot, and if you like I'll take you over there and you can get started right away.'

Oliver choked on his tea. Maggie hit him on his back, and Bea . . . Bea didn't know whether to laugh or cry. 'But I haven't been out cleaning for years.'

'Keys,' said Maggie, dangling them in front of Bea, 'to the outer door, to the flat. There's a porter, has a cubby hole off the foyer, acts as janitor. Charlotte introduced me to him last night. She went down and told him I was going to bring in a cleaner, so it's all been cleared with Higher Authority. I'll help you get started and then I can get back here and get on with the usual, because it doesn't look like they've a reasonable hoover, or duster or a smidgeon of bleach anywhere. So, shall we get started, then?'

Bea couldn't go out to clean wearing one of her boutique outfits, so borrowed a gaudy T-shirt from Maggie, found some old black jogging trousers and a pair of reasonably decent trainers to wear. When she'd gone out on jobs for the agency in the old days she'd worn an outfit of black T-shirt and slacks, with a many-pocketed apron to carry her tools around with her. By great good fortune, she found it neatly folded in her closet, and slung it into a large plastic bag to take with her.

She took off her make-up and looked at herself in the mirror, feeling frowsty and boring, especially when she brushed her fringe straight down over her eyes, instead of at an angle.

Meanwhile, Maggie scurried around, putting together a basket of cleaning materials. 'If we can't get their hoover to work we might have to take ours, in which case we'll need a taxi to get everything there and back.'

Down Church Street they went, carrying the basket between them. Bea had a job to keep up with Maggie, who would have been hopping and skipping along if she hadn't had to wait for the older woman.

'I'm getting too old for this,' said Bea, as she sorted keys under Maggie's eye and let them into the hallway of the flats.

'You're doing all right for your age,' said Maggie, unconsciously making Bea feel even worse. 'Oh, this is Randolph, our wonderful doorman. Randolph, this is the cleaner that

Charlotte told you about, all right?' She led the way to the lift, saying to Bea, 'You need a holiday, that's all.'

'You haven't forgotten I've only just come back from a trip halfway round the world?'

'Yes, but you were nursing your poor dear husband all the time, and for ages before, weren't you? So, why not take off for a bit? Zander says he's been to Bruges and likes it. He thinks you should go on a package tour of some kind, so that you didn't have to go alone.'

Bea shuddered at the thought of a package holiday. She'd have to make an effort to be nice when she didn't feel like it, and probably have to share a bedroom with someone who snored. Not a good idea. However, Maggie had brought up a subject she hadn't thought about. What was she going to do about holidays in future? Find another widow to go around with?

The flat was on the third floor. As Bea opened the front door and sniffed the air, she knew what she'd find; closed windows, dirty socks, inadequately cleaned bathroom and kitchen. The fridge probably had mould growing behind it, the oven would be unused and the microwave brand new. The dishwasher might work, but the washing machine probably didn't. On the other hand, there would probably be a giant television in the sitting room, plus stereo equipment capable of filling the Albert Hall.

She sniffed the air. 'Ah, me. It takes me back to the days when I first worked for Hamilton, cleaning, cooking, doing everything bar plumbing jobs. I could even rewire plugs in those days. Is the sitting room at the end of the corridor?'

This particular block of flats had gone up in the early years of the twentieth century. Some of the original features, such as coving, picture rails, and fireplaces, had been retained, while an attempt had been made to combine ancient and modern by introducing good quality modern furniture and furnishings. The streamlined seating arrangements in blonde leather matched the cream carpet and the Venetian blinds at the windows. Two rather beautiful Swedish rugs provided accents of colour, but their patterns were smudged with coffee and other, less easily identifiable stains. As was everything else in sight.

Bea sighed. This particular lot of tenants had not been taking good care of things, had they? A blind at one window hung askew, broken, and nobody had bothered to empty the wastepaper basket, attend to rings on the furniture left by coffee mugs and wine glasses, or to clear away the debris left after several take-aways.

'How long did you say they've been without a cleaner?'

Maggie stripped off her jacket. 'Too long. I couldn't start clearing up last night, or they'd have me down to clean the place all the time. I'll begin on the kitchen and the boys' bathroom, shall I? Give you time to poke about, see what you can find. Our room's right at the other end of the corridor, you can't miss it. The ugly duckling says she could have moved into a single and made two of the boys share but no one else wanted to share, and anyway our room's enormous, almost like a little flat in itself, and she keeps that and our shower room next door clean enough. She won't let the boys anywhere near it, so you can forget our bit. Zander's room is next to the living room, and the other bod, the one who went out early, he's opposite. Which means that Philip must be . . .'

Bea tried doors. The boys' bathroom was going to need Mr Muscle himself to make an impression on the grime, the same went for a toilet next door . . . and the one after that was Philip's room.

Bea donned apron and rubber gloves before touching anything. There was a mixture of modern and Edwardian furniture in Philip's room, which was not large and whose window over-looked a wall and not the street. The bed looked new, as did the carpet and curtains, but both bore the marks of someone who drank – and smoked – in bed. 'Yuck!' said Maggie. 'What a fug!'

There was no sign of a Victorian oil painting, or of a package which might have contained one. The room smelled of dirty washing, the curtains were drawn against the light, the bedclothes were all over the place and a pair of pyjama bottoms was on the floor. The doors of a large built-in wardrobe hung open, the clothes inside were mostly on the floor instead of hanging on the rail, though a couple of empty dry-cleaners' plastic bags informed Bea that he – or someone else – had looked after his belongings better in the past.

A digital clock flashed on the bedside table, beside an empty wine bottle, a dirtied tumbler, some used tissues, an empty pack of cigarettes and a burned out lighter.

'Typical,' said Maggie, arms akimbo.

Bea waded through the stir fry on the floor to the window.

She drew back the curtains and opened the window so that they
could see and breathe properly, almost falling over something
on the carpet, which turned out to be a mobile phone. On the
table by the window was a takeaway foil dish which Philip had
been using for an ashtray, a freebie paper a couple of days old,
and a stained and almost empty coffee mug.

Bea picked the mobile phone up, dusted it down and tried to
switch it on, but the battery was dead. Bea slipped it into one
of the large envelopes she'd brought with her, tucking it into the
largest pocket in her apron.

Maggie objected. 'You can't do that. It's stealing.'

'There may be some messages on it. If he's disappeared, it
may just help us – or the police – to find him.'

Maggie's mouth made an 'o' and she made no further objection.
'I expect you'll want to search his clothes. You won't need me
for that. See you in a bit.'

Bea looked around. Still no sign of the missing picture. There
was no laptop, either, but there was a spell-checker, and a couple
of boys' toys, music orientated, a scatter of DVDs on the floor,
a small telly which looked second-hand and possibly didn't work,
a dead whisky bottle in the wastepaper basket and another under
the bed.

Might the picture be under the bed? Alas, no. There was enough
dust to make Bea sneeze plus a broken pen and some screwed-
up pieces of paper. She teased the scraps out. Receipts for wine
and whisky from a local convenience store. Oh, and the charger
for the phone, which he'd probably dropped and kicked under
the bed by accident. She surmised that without the charger the
phone was no use to him, so he'd abandoned it, as he seemed
to have abandoned many of his other belongings. She fished the
phone out of her pocket, plugged it in to charge and switched
it on.

A couple of drawers in the table by the window were filled with
coupons torn from newspapers but never redeemed, out of date
lottery tickets, some contraceptives and repeat prescriptions from
a local doctor. Philip had been on antibiotics recently, but his ongoing
repeat prescriptions were for antidepressants. Antidepressants,
antibiotics and whisky didn't go together, did they?

There were two unframed photos propped up against a pile
of *Men Only* type magazines on a scuffed chest of drawers. Girls
in the almost altogether. Or had they been cut from magazines?

No, they were real photos. Philip had obviously had the occasional girlfriend in the past, but not recently – according to Velma, who might or might not be biased. The dust was thick on the chest of drawers, except where a couple of framed photos seemed to have been standing until recently. Had Philip taken them away for some reason? Perhaps they had been of his father and mother? Or another girlfriend?

The bedside table drawer yielded aspirins, empty packs of prescription drugs, a couple of condoms. Dust. A small notebook filled with columns of numbers . . . what was that all about?

The bedclothes were rank. Bea stripped the bed and bundled the dirty bedclothes into one of the dry-cleaners' bags. 'Do we have any clean bedding?'

'He should have his own,' Maggie yelled back from down the corridor. 'Charlotte told me to bring my own and I did. Well, I borrowed from you, but I suppose that's all right.'

Bea opened a double-fronted, built-in cupboard, cascading smelly sports equipment on to the floor. On the top shelf of the cupboard were two sets of laundered bedlinen, still in their laundry bags. Bea smiled to herself, imagining Velma making sure he had everything clean when he moved in. Mind you, it didn't look as if he'd changed the sheets in weeks.

There was also a space where a man might conceivably have stored an empty suitcase or rucksack. Surely that was one item a flat-sharer would be bound to have? She thought of the items of luggage Maggie had brought with her the previous night; a large old suitcase which predated wheels, a sports bag and a couple of outsize carrier bags. So what luggage had Philip brought with him when he moved in? And where was it now? It did rather look as if he'd hastily packed a few things into – whatever – and lit out for parts unknown.

Bea started to make the bed with the clean linen, only to find that one set was incomplete. There was a duvet cover and two pillow cases, but no bottom sheet. What on earth had he done with it? She checked over the second set. That was complete.

Then she had an idea. She tipped up the mattress and discovered a flattened business envelope addressed to Mr P. Weston. It contained a flock of bank and credit card statements which made dire reading and a letter from a production company in Soho, dated a fortnight ago, terminating Mr Weston's employment after he'd ignored three previous written warnings about being drunk at work. There was also a polite letter on good notepaper from a club Bea had never heard of, reminding Mr Weston to pay his overdue account.

'Trouble.' Bea was thinking aloud. 'No job. No income. What was he living on?'

Maggie, also rubber-gloved, appeared in the doorway. 'I forgot to say, I think Philip's not paid his rent for a while. I was only half listening but the men were griping about it, saying it was just as well I'd come to join them to help with the rent.'

'Could you look to see how many shaving outfits are in the boys' bathroom?'

Maggie was loving this. 'You think he's done a runner?' She vanished, only to return within a minute. 'Two lots, in expensive toilet cases, one plain and one with a monogram of a letter "L" on it. Which means . . .?'

'Philip's is not there. This is getting complicated. I really ought to have brought a special camera with me to take copies of his paperwork, because I don't understand what's going on.'

'Like James Bond? His cameras are all disguised as something else, though, aren't they?'

Bea made a note of the club name on the letterhead and made up the bed, leaving the paperwork in place. She picked up the dirty clothing piece by piece, exploring pockets. Nothing but receipts and reminders of unpaid bills . . . there was also a letter from the gym pointing out that his membership had lapsed and suggesting that he renew. No wonder he hadn't been back there for a while.

She hung up the clothing that still looked reasonably clean, and stuffed the dirty bits and pieces into another dry-cleaner's bag. She tried to get the hoover going – it was an asthmaticky old thing – and failed. The carpet sweeper was clogged with hairs. She cleaned it out and did her best with it.

She considered wiping down all the dusty surfaces in the room but desisted in case the police had to be called in and looked for fingerprints. They wouldn't like her having changed the bed linen, either, but she'd left everything else in place, hadn't she? Well, except for the mobile phone.

If Philip turned up, then she'd have a go at the windows, which could do with a wash, and there were some unidentifiable stains on the carpet which needed specialist attention. However, the room looked and smelled a lot better than before.

She stood in the doorway, scanning the room. Had she over-looked anything? Possibly a trained policeman would have been able to draw a more accurate picture of Philip from looking over his things? Was she getting a false picture of him? She told herself it was wrong to jump to conclusions, but no, she didn't think she had. Philip was a bit of a layabout. He'd not told anyone he'd lost his job, he was in debt, drinking and taking tranquillizers. Plus it rather looked as if he'd lit out for parts unknown with a valuable picture, leaving no forwarding address.

She unplugged his mobile phone, hoping that even this short period might have charged it up. It had, a bit. She saw there were various messages on it, but wasn't sure how to access them, as the phone was a different type from hers. So she popped it and the charger into one of the large pockets in her apron, to be looked at later.

She passed on to the next room, the one occupied by Maggie's favourite, Zander. Was his name short for Alexander? Possibly. She wasn't going to search this room, but clean it quickly and pass on to the next. Correction; she would just check to see if the painting had been put in here for safe keeping.

Zander's room was slightly larger than Philip's, better furnished and much better maintained. Unlike Philip's room – which had given the impression of a transient dossing down for a few days – Zander's indicated a man who'd made himself very much at home. Zander was tidy, and looked after his expensive clothes. There was fluff under his bed, but no oil painting. Nor was it in the wardrobe or closet, or any of the drawers. However, there was a large suitcase and a sports bag there, which was as it should be.

His paperwork was neatly docketed in files in the drawers of a modern desk, not locked. Everything looked above board. Squeaky clean? He kept all his monthly wage slips, had a healthy balance at the bank, paid off his credit cards on the dot, his job brought him in a decent salary, he had direct debits on . . . .yes, yes. Very sensible, very well organized. She didn't know why she was looking at his paperwork. Habit, she supposed.

Another file contained his CV . . . yes, yes. It all looked good. Almost too good to be true. There was a locked briefcase under the desk which probably contained his passport, cheque book, that sort of thing.

There was no laptop, but Bea could see the mark in the dust

where it usually sat. Headphones for listening to music, a brand
new flat-screen telly and DVD player. A stereo sound system.
A camera, digital. Lots of books in a bookcase nearby; paperbacks
of modern authors on the trendy side. Condoms in the bedside
table drawer, no medication except some Piriton and a pack of
paracetomol.

Zander had thrust some lovingly phrased notes from females
into his bedside drawer, higgledy-piggledy, as if they didn't
warrant being filed away. Bea got the impression that Zander
probably operated most of his contacts by text message.

Two photos, not of girls, but of family groups; parents and
siblings, presumably. Bea wondered vaguely what country Zander's
family was from originally. Had Maggie said Grenada?

Bea looked under the mattress, but there was nothing there.
She made the bed, charged around with the carpet sweeper and
dusted with a damp cloth. The place looked a lot better.

And then . . . the front door opened, and someone called out,
'Hallo?'

Bea froze.

Into the dimness of the corridor came a girl who could only be
Charlotte, the ugly duckling. She had a fringe of dark hair which
hugged her cheeks, dark glasses, and was wearing a black suit
which was all the wrong shape for her. There was a hectic flush
on podgy cheeks, and she was talking in a squeaky voice.

'Are you there, Maggie? They're driving me mad at work and
if one more person asks me for change for the photocopier, I'll
kill them!' She caught sight of Bea, and stopped short. 'So you're
the new cleaner, are you? You understand you're only here on
a week's trial?'

Bea tried for a downtrodden employee's tone of voice. 'Yes,
of course. I think the hoover's broken.'

Would Maggie appear, wearing rubber gloves and stinking of
disinfectant? That would give the game away with a vengeance.

Maggie appeared, sans gloves, sniffing. 'Do hurry up, Mrs
Thing, or you won't have time to tackle the sitting room.' She
turned to Charlotte. 'I'm afraid she's the best I can do for the
moment. I may be able to get someone who works a bit faster
in a day or two, but . . . you know how it is with staff. You simply
can't get the best when you need it.'

Bea felt herself blush. How could Maggie! Though, to be fair,
the girl had taken the right line.

Charlotte ignored Bea to talk to Maggie. 'I thought I'd better pop back in my lunch hour to see how she was getting on. You won't let her keep the keys, will you?'

'Certainly not,' said Maggie. 'They always forget the keys if you let them keep them, and then where are you?'

'Exactly.' Charlotte put her head round the sitting-room door. 'Not done in here yet? Oh well. Perhaps you can manage to work a little faster next time. Three hours today and three on Monday, right?'

Bea opened her mouth to reply, but the girl had already turned back to Maggie. 'Are you free tonight? Liam's working late, so I wondered if you fancied a little something down the road first? Then we could go on to the party at ten. Have you got someone special you'd like to invite? Oh, I forgot. You're still getting over your ex, aren't you? Well, there'll be plenty of talent there tonight.'

'Suits me,' said Maggie. 'I have to get back to work in a minute. Half six here?'

At that moment Philip's mobile phone rang in Bea's pocket. Bea didn't know what to do. She couldn't possibly answer it in front of Charlotte.

'Oh, really!' said the ugly duckling. 'Personal calls during work time . . . and I expect she took a good half-hour off to have a coffee.'

Bea muttered, 'Sorry!' and sidled into the nearest room, which happened to be the sitting room. She pulled the phone out, and muted the sound. Another message had been left on it. She wondered how often it had been ringing in Philip's absence.

'What are we going to do about locking up when she's finished?' Charlotte followed Bea into the sitting room, but addressed her words to Maggie. Bea pretended she hadn't heard, and busied herself collecting discarded takeaway dishes. Charlotte continued, 'I don't like leaving her here on her own, but I really must get back.'

'Besides which,' said Maggie, 'she won't be able to lock the front door here if she hasn't got a key, though I suppose we could get Randolph to come up and see to it. No, tell you what, I'll come down with you now, and pop back up to the office, see what's happening there. Then I can come back in an hour, lock up and see her out.'

'You're a star, Maggie,' said Charlotte, her footsteps fading down the corridor. The front door opened and shut behind the pair of them.

Bea was alone in the flat, except for several bluebottles which were investigating the remains of last night's suppers. Bea wanted to ring Maggie's neck. For one thing, she wasn't going to be able to get the rest of the flat clean in an hour without help. On the other hand, she wanted to laugh because Maggie really had been rather superb, hadn't she?

Bea's own mobile rang. Velma, sounding controlled and tense. 'Bea, are you there? Have you got anything out of Philip? The thing is – I mean, it's a bit desperate – Sandy keeps asking me if he's all right, and I don't know what to say. He's in Charing Cross. The hospital, I mean.' There was a catch in her voice. 'We've been here all night, because the pains got worse and it's not indigestion, it's his heart. They did an ECG last night and that showed something really bad, and this morning he's been for an angiogram, and it looks as if one of the arteries is getting blocked and . . . Bea, I don't want to lose him, I really don't. Would you mind, if you haven't anything else on, would you come and sit with me?'

Still no news of Philip. Rafael decided he'd try Philip's father tomorrow, even though Philip had said there was no point his looking for help in that direction nowadays.

Charlotte was moaning that Philip had gone off without paying the rent. If she took it into her head that Philip really had gone missing she'd squawk for the police, and that was the last thing they wanted, wasn't it? He must get Liam to tell her that Philip had been in touch with him, saying he'd been off on a bender and was skint but trying to sort out his finances.

If only all this hadn't happened at the same time as things had blown up at work! The gallery was hosting a show for an artist who had a big following in the north. This would be his first show in London, and it had to go well. Rafael's boss was demanding his attention twenty-four seven.

Rafael did some deep breathing exercises to calm himself down.

Five

Hospitals are much the same everywhere. Why don't they upgrade their dim light bulbs? A brighter environment would make everyone feel better.

Velma was in a four-bed ward, sitting at Sandy's bedside and holding his hand. There were lines on her face which hadn't been there yesterday. Sandy was wired up to machines, and his eyes were closed. His big, athletic body looked at once lumpish and limp. When Velma saw Bea, she gave her husband's hand a pat and said she'd be back in five minutes. She led the way out into the corridor, but stood where she could keep an eye on her husband.

'How is he?'

Velma shrugged. 'They're moving him in a minute to a side room to keep a closer eye on him. Translation; they think he might pop his clogs any minute. Oh dear!' She stifled a guffaw. 'How stupid of me, making jokes when . . . but it's really serious, Bea. They want to operate, but they can't till Monday and then they're going to have to shove someone else out of the list to make room for him. Oh, Bea! He's always been so fit. Not like my first.'

Bea tried to reassure her friend. 'Sandy's strong. He won't let this kill him.'

Velma blinked. 'I blame Philip. Sandy got into such a state, worrying. The food poisoning didn't help, I suppose. If we could just clear Philip of . . . whatever.' She gulped. Her hand groped and caught hold of Bea's, and clung on. 'I'll be all right in a minute. I'm not going to go to pieces. Absolutely not. Only, I keep thinking that I ought to pray and I don't know how. Bea, will you pray for me?'

Bea thought that she hardly knew how to pray herself, but

she nodded. Hamilton used to pray all the time. She'd try to remember how he did it, and do the same.

Velma was keeping her eyes on Sandy. 'Have you any good news for me?'

The only news Bea had so far, was bad. How about this: Philip's in debt all round and seems to have done a runner with the picture. Yes, that would help, wouldn't it?

Bea said, with care, 'I'm trying to get an idea of what Philip is really like. What's your impression of him?'

Velma teased a handkerchief out of her pocket, and blew her nose. She shook back her hair. 'Forgive me, I'm somewhat distracted. Sandy over-compensated Philip for the loss of his mother, and now the boy thinks the world owes him a living. That sounds mean and petty and I don't mean to be. I'm sure he's a nice lad underneath.'

'He had a job?'

'A production company which sells to the television channels. Somewhere in Soho. Tuesday Next? Some name like that.'

Bea decided not to mention what she'd discovered about Philip's finances that morning. 'Is he still in contact with his mother?'

'I doubt it. Sandy says Philip went up there once for a holiday but came back early saying his mother had gone all weird, that there was no heating and she was living on lettuce leaves. He refused to go again.'

So it was unlikely that Philip had gone up there. 'Was Philip upset when you and Sandy got together?'

'He was over the moon. The first time we met, he gave me a hug and said, "My lovely, rich new mother!" He suggested I made him an allowance, but I couldn't see why he should need one if he was working, especially as he was always boasting about how important his job was. In my view, grown-up sons should be responsible for themselves. Sandy agreed with me.'

'Sandy didn't expect you to fund Philip's lifestyle, then?'

'I don't say he wouldn't have gone along with it if I'd wanted to throw money at the boy, but he certainly didn't suggest it. If anything, he's embarrassed by my being so well off. Incredible as it may seem, Sandy loves me for myself. It was he who proposed a pre-nuptial settlement, not me. He refused to let me put his name jointly with mine on our house, and he was keeping his job because it was a worthwhile thing to do. They think the world of him at work. People who spend their lives working for others are few and far between, aren't they?' She dabbed at the corners of her eyes, gave her head a little shake, and tried to smile. 'So, give me some good cheer, old friend. What has your little Maggie found out?'

Sighing inwardly, Bea produced an edited report. 'Philip wasn't there last night. Apparently he's somewhat cavalier in his comings and goings. There's a party on tonight at a flat upstairs and we're hoping he'll turn up for that.' Bea didn't think he would, but Velma needed to hang on to hope at the moment.

There was a stir of people around Sandy's bed and Velma's hand shot to her mouth. 'I have to go.'

'You don't intend to stay with him again tonight, do you? You'll make yourself ill. Look, ring me when they've got him settled and I'll come to fetch you, take you home with me. The hospital can contact you at my place if you're needed.'

'I can't leave him.'

'Then give me your keys and a list of what you need from home and I'll bring it to you later.'

Velma put her hand to her head. 'Yes, I could do that, but . . . I can't think straight. I'll ring you, shall I? I must go to him. Pray for us, won't you?' She almost ran to her husband's bedside.

Bea went out into the fresh air. The traffic sounded too loud. She hailed a taxi and took it back home. And tried to pray.

As she opened the front door, she could hear Maggie's voice, rising effortlessly above the television and the radio in the kitchen. Savoury scents permeated the house. Maggie had been cooking. Maggie loved cooking and hated office work, but had been indoctrinated by her ambitious mother to think that career women employed other people to do their housework, and that those who cleaned and cooked for others were second-class citizens.

'Oops!' cried Maggie, when she saw Bea. 'I'm meeting Cinderella, aka the ugly duckling, tonight for supper at Wagamama's before the party, but couldn't leave you and Oliver without anything to eat. Shall I yell for him to come and get at it?'

Bea realized she'd missed lunch and was extremely hungry. When Maggie went to shout down the stairs at Oliver, Bea switched off the television and the radio, and laid the table.

Maggie crashed back into the kitchen. 'Mr Max rang, a couple of times. He's tied up with visits in his constituency this after-noon and all day tomorrow. He said you'd been trying to get him and I said you were out on a job, though I didn't say you were out cleaning because he'd have had a fit, wouldn't he!'

Bea nodded. Yes, he would. And bother, because she really did need to speak to Max. The tax bill . . . the solicitor's letter. Ouch. 'Any other calls?'

'Oliver dealt with them. Oh, and your first, the gorgeous Piers, came round, looking all worried. Said he'd drop by again later. He took that watercolour that ended up on the floor. I suppose that's all right?'

Bea nodded again. A wedge of savoury sausage-meat pie landed on a plate in front of her, with mashed potatoes and beans. Her salivary glands went into overtime.

Oliver slid into the seat beside her, bearing a sheaf of messages on a clipboard. 'We're eating early? Good.'

Bea indicated the clipboard with her fork, her mouth full. 'Can those wait till we've eaten?'

Maggie helped herself to a small portion of everything, saying, 'I deserve a raise. Since you went off to the hospital, I thought I'd better finish the job at the flat for you. So I spent two hours ten minutes cleaning on your behalf.'

'You're brilliant, Maggie,' said Bea. 'Did you find any paper-work, anything in the third man's room? What's his name?'

'Liam. I thought it was Lee, but it's Liam. Irish, I suppose. I looked in all the usual hiding places men have—'

Oliver snorted. 'And what would they be?'

'You wouldn't know,' said Maggie, smugly.

'What did you find? A toy gun and a stash of cannabis?'

'Don't be childish. Nothing like that. Some porn under the bed.'

'Paperwork?' asked Bea. 'Passport?'

Maggie looked thoughtful. 'Come to think of it, no.'

Oliver guffawed. 'You mean you didn't find them.'

'Children, children!' Bea reflected that when they had first taken refuge with her, Maggie and Oliver had practically been joined at the hip, but they were getting more like quarrelsome brother and sister every day. She put down her knife and fork with a sigh of repletion. 'Maggie, you did well. I'll have another go at the flat on Monday morning, but in the meantime let me bring you both up to date.'

She did so, through a slice of cheesecake and a cup of decaf-feinated coffee.

'So, you see, the situation is serious. Sandy needs Philip to be innocent and yet his actions point in another direction. Philip stayed out last night, the picture's gone, and his shaving things aren't in the flat. What's more, there's no sign of a rucksack or suitcase in his room which probably means he's taken some of his belongings and lit out for parts unknown. He's in debt, according to the bank and credit card statements, has let his gym membership lapse and owes money at a club in the West End. He's on antidepressants – which are not in his room – and he's been drinking heavily. According to Velma he works for a company making television programmes called Tuesday Next, some name like that, but it seems he got the sack some time ago.'

Oliver's eyes narrowed. 'You think he was so desperate for money that he stole the picture? And now the police are taking an interest in Lady Farne's death, he's taken off into the blue with it?'

Bea threw up her hands. 'What other interpretation can we put on it?'

Maggie grimaced. 'If he's done a runner and is in debt, then what's he going to live on?'

Oliver knew the answer. 'He'll sell the picture.'

Bea said, 'Can you see a man they don't know walking into Sotheby's and saying, "Oh, by the way, I've just come by this painting, but no, I can't tell you how I got it, and will you sell it for me?"'

'They'd call the police as soon as his back was turned,' said Oliver. 'So—'

'He'd fence it!' Maggie gave a whoop of joy. 'I've always wanted to be a policewoman, and say, "You're nicked!"'

'Yes, dear,' said Bea. 'But in the meantime, is the spare bedroom fit to receive a guest? I thought I might bring Velma back here for the night if I can tear her away from Sandy's bedside.'

Oliver looked at his watch. 'Hate to break this up, but I'm due to meet a friend this evening, and Maggie, aren't you supposed to meet someone for supper?'

'And then on to the party!' Maggie jigged around the kitchen, throwing plates and pans into the dishwasher. 'I do hope Zander is going to be there. I really rather fancy him, you know.'

They knew. Bea thought a warning might be appropriate. 'I'd

go carefully with Zander, if I were you. We really don't know anything about him, and—'

'I know everything I need to know,' said Maggie, nose in the air.

Bea told herself to shut up and let the girl make her own mistakes.

Bea felt sluggish after that repast but refused to allow herself to flop into a chair and turn on the telly. As Maggie banged out of the house, Oliver disappeared upstairs. Bea settled herself at her desk to go through some of the paperwork that had accumulated in her absence . . . what about that tax return? And the solicitor's letter?

Well, there was nothing she could do about any of those things on a Saturday evening when everyone sane would have gone home to their families, or be spending time with their friends. Only Bea was left alone and lonely.

She stopped that thought in its tracks. Yes, she was lonely. Intensely, painfully lonely. Lonely for one special person. Occasionally she coasted through an hour without thinking about Hamilton too much, and then . . . bam! Something would come up and hit her and she'd be feeling as raw as ever. It was only a short couple of months since he'd died.

She thought of going upstairs to look at his portrait, but didn't. Instead she did what she'd often seen him do. She swivelled round in her chair to look out of the window, across the garden to the sycamore tree at the end, and above that to the spire of the church in the High Street. See a spire, and aspire, Hamilton would say, smiling, appreciating the horror of the pun.

See the spire, and aspire. Bea thought about it, looking up at the spire, wondering how long it took for the agony of grief to subside. She knew he'd often broken off in his work to look at the spire and pray. He said it calmed him, made it clear what he should do in difficult situations.

She took off her reading glasses to look at the spire better, and tried to pray herself. *Dearest Lord God, if you can hear me through all the noise outside . . . and the noise inside me, as well . . . would you show me the way through the tangle I'm in? Please? Look after Sandy, be with him and if it is your will that he doesn't survive, then grant him strength and comfort. And the same for Velma. I'm afraid they're both going to be badly hurt, whatever happens to Philip. As for Philip, only you know the truth about that matter . . . oh, it's such a miserable mess, and I'm not the right person to deal with it. I suppose what I mean is, show me what I can do to help them, because I haven't a clue.*

She put on her reading glasses and opened the Complaints Folder. Somewhere here there must be the case which had brought the solicitor's letter upon them. No, not this person. Nor that. The words 'vexatious client' came to mind on the third . . . a man complaining that his landlady had lost a pair of his socks. There really wasn't much there to worry about.

The house seemed very quiet, with Maggie out. Oliver appeared in the doorway, dressed in good but casual wear. 'I'm off to the gym, and afterwards I thought I might go to the pub with my friend. Don't worry; we'll only be drinking halves of beer.'

Bea nodded, astonished that all of a sudden this little grub of a schoolboy was turning into a butterfly. As he left, she clutched at her desk, realizing she was going to be left alone in the house. She wanted to call him back, to detain him . . . how stupid! At her age!

She unstuck her hands from the desk and set her files to one side, deciding to make notes of everything she knew about Philip. If he stayed missing, there was no way his disappearance could be kept from the police, and she'd better be prepared to tell them what she knew. While she was about it, she'd better see what she could find out from Philip's phone.

Unfortunately, she hadn't got a manual for this phone, which was the very latest of its kind, and quite impenetrable in its complicated workings to Bea. She pushed buttons and got nowhere. Besides which, it rather looked as if the battery were dead again. She sighed. She'd leave it to Oliver to sort out on the morrow. Meanwhile . . . she looked up the name of the club which had sent Philip a letter reminding him to pay his debts. She'd never heard of it, and it wasn't in the phone book, but she traced a phone number through the directory.

A suave voice with a slight accent answered the phone. 'Yes, madam?'

Bea didn't have a good cover story ready. 'I was given your name by a friend, who said I might need references to join. Is that right?'

'Certainly. What name do you have, please?'

'Weston. Mrs Weston.'

'If you will hold a moment, please.' He put the phone on hold. Bea wondered why on earth she'd given Velma's name. She'd been stupid. She hadn't thought through what she should say. She cradled the phone, only to have it ring again.

She stared at it, worrying that the club might have caller recognition and called her back, had perhaps been checking that this number was not the one registered for Mrs Weston. The ringing stopped. Then her own mobile rang.

It was Piers. Without preamble he said, 'The thing is, Bea, I went to a private view at a gallery last night. Everyone was talking about the Farne collection, telling stories about Lucky Lucinda and her dirty deeds in the past, and speculating as to who might have inherited the goodies; the odds-on favourites to inherit, by the way, are a home for fallen women and the cats' home. One of the guests had a funny story to tell which might interest you. He said that someone had recently tried to sell him a fake Millais.'

'I'm all attention,' said Bea.

'Thought you might be. I got a trickle down my spine when I remembered you mentioned the word Millais because you've never shown any interest in the pre-Raphaelites before. It's been on my mind all day. I called round earlier, but you were out. What have you got yourself into now?'

'It's a long story.'

'I've got time, if you have.'

Bea kicked off her shoes, and told him what had been happening, as succinctly as she could. ' . . . So the picture might have been a genuine Millais. We know Philip did have it but now he's gone missing and so has the picture. Meanwhile poor old Sandy is at death's door, and I don't know whether to call the police or not. If I do, it will only make matters worse for Sandy. If I don't . . . I don't know what to do for the best.'

A longish pause. 'Have you a photo of young Philip? Yes? Right. I'll pick you and the photo up in half an hour.' The phone went dead.

Rage must be kept under control, or who knew where it might lead? The antique dealer six weeks ago – well, he'd got away with that. The old woman hadn't caused him any problems, either. He'd lifted the boxes as easily as walking off with a kid's ice cream. It had never occurred to him that Philip might want to lift something for himself. Why hadn't he waited till the old woman died? The whole lot would have dropped into his hands then, wouldn't it?

Or, maybe it wouldn't.

Maybe Philip had been pressed to settle his debts now and hadn't been able to wait for his inheritance. Or perhaps the old woman had got wind of his particular weakness and changed her will?

Another, even more scary thought. Had the men with no necks caught up with Philip? But surely they wouldn't have killed him, knowing he had expectations? He'd boasted of them often enough; his godmother had promised him an inheritance, and he could expect something from his father's second marriage to a wealthy woman, too. One way or another, the club's money was safe.

Rafael was getting a headache. He went over all the places where Philip might have been, but wasn't.

The father's place in South Kensington was all locked up, milk on the doorstep. A neighbour said he thought the Westons were away but had forgotten to cancel the milk and papers.

Liam said Philip had talked a lot about women but nobody thought he'd really pulled all the girls he boasted about.

The idiot! His disappearance was spoiling a perfectly good set-up. Which reminded him he'd better brief Liam about taking Charlotte to Bruges. At least that plan could go ahead. And the new girl, Maggie? It was a temptation to use her as well. He certainly had enough stuff to get rid of.

Six

Saturday evening

Bea made haste slowly, to be ready in time for Piers. A quick wash. One of her caramel silk T-shirts would be best, over slightly darker, well-cut trousers. A swipe with the hairbrush, a dab or two of make-up, no time for eye make-up but surely that didn't matter with such an old friend as Piers. Reading glasses, a smaller handbag, a light jacket, shoes with a heel.

Piers rang the front doorbell as she made it to the hall, and at the same moment the phone rang. She let it ring, and went out to find her ex-husband waiting to hand her into a taxi.

'Piers, where are we going?'

'South Kensington. I've rung ahead and they know we're coming. This Velma; is it the same girl who used to spend hours on the phone to you when we were married, twenty or so years ago? A school friend?'

'I'm surprised you remembered.'

He huffed out a laugh. 'I remember all right. She slapped my face once. Nice girl, bit of a prude. Married a tightwad.'

'Did you make a pass at her? Oh, Piers.' She couldn't help laughing. Of course he'd made a pass at Velma. But Velma had never said.

He laughed, too. 'Her husband – that would be her first, right? – wanted me to paint him, a couple of years back. I said I might consider doing a double portrait of him and his wife together, but he wasn't interested. Perhaps my reputation with the ladies told against me.'

Bea had no kindly feelings towards Velma's first, having disliked him from the start. 'More likely he didn't want attention drawn away from himself.'

Piers tapped the glass and said, 'Anywhere here, cabbie.' He paid and they got out in front of a small shop front with an exclusive air and grilles over the window and door. It was well after seven o'clock and the shop looked closed, but Piers spoke into an entry phone, the grille over the door slid back and the door fell open.

Inside was a showroom full of minor but worthy eighteenth- and nineteenth-century paintings, with the promise of further delights in other dimly-lit rooms beyond. Bea looked for the cameras and security sensors which she was sure must be there, but they were too well concealed for her to spot.

A man in a good suit came forward to greet them. He was forty-ish pretending to be late thirties, as neat as a plastic model of a bridegroom on the top of a wedding cake. He had thinning curly blond hair, his teeth were blindingly white, his eyes crinkled at the corners and Bea distrusted him on sight.

Piers introduced them – 'Crispin; an old friend, Bea Abbot. She's interested in your visitor with the fake Millais' – before wandering off to view the pictures.

'What a palaver, my dears.' Was Crispin gay? He waved Bea to a divan and sat beside her. 'You are interested in the pre-Raphaelites?'

'A family picture has gone astray,' said Bea, picking her words with care. 'Could you bear to tell me about your visitor?'

Crispin was happy to oblige. 'He came in on the heels of a good client or I wouldn't have let him in the door. One does get a sense of when someone is not a customer, you know? I was anxious to look after our client, so got rid of him as soon as I could. I know it's the fashion to have a slight shadow – so macho, and can be attractive – but this was simple neglect, and there was a certain body odour, if I may put it that way . . .?'

Bea nodded, thinking this tied in with what she knew of Philip.

'He was carrying a medium-sized picture which he'd wrapped in a bed sheet, would you believe? He pulled the sheet off and the frame was, I grant you, very nice. The picture itself could hardly be seen for grime. "It's a genuine Millais," he says. "How much is it worth, and will you buy it?" I look at him with alarm bells zinging through my head and I try not to shudder, because if there is one thing I've learned in all my years in the trade, it's that a person of this kind does not own a genuine Millais.

'So I say, "I'm afraid we're rather busy this morning and anyway, we don't deal in copies, however good." He says it's not a copy but the real thing, and I almost laughed in his face. I mean . . . how stupid! Then he says he's desperate, and I'm looking at the frame and thinking it might set off one of our Victorian landscapes nicely, and I say we might be interested in that alone. My dear, he almost bursts into tears! He wraps the picture up again, telling me he's going to find someone who knows a good thing when he sees it, and I say bon voyage, but that if he wants to sell the frame any time, he can drop back with it.'

'When was this?'

Crispin shrugged. 'Last week sometime. Or maybe the end of the previous week? Time does pass, does it not?'

Bea produced Philip's photograph. 'Do you recognize this man?'

Crispin took the photo in one hand, and the lines of his face hardened. He looked at Bea, then looked back at the photo. 'Yes. That's him.'

A gnarled hand came over Crispin's shoulder and removed the photograph.

'My son,' said a wizened gnome, 'judges people by the cars they drive, and paintings by their frames.' Crispin's father was a foot shorter than his son, and a hundred years wiser. He held out his hand to Bea. 'Frank Goldstone, at your service.' He'd probably been born with a German name, but long since anglicized it. Bea liked him straight away.

He said, 'I retired from active business some years ago, but this story of a tramp trying to sell a fake Millais intrigued me. Even so, I was about to dismiss it from my mind when my old friend Piers rang to ask about the same thing.'

Crispin pushed out his lower lip. 'I told you, it was a copy in a good frame.'

Mr Goldstone ignored his son. 'Even when pre-Raphaelite pictures pass into private collections, everyone in the trade knows where they are. Regrettably, Crispin remembered more about the frame than about the picture, but he did recall that the subject was a young, fair-haired girl in a dark blue dress.'

Crispin shuddered. 'Her eyes went right through me.'

'Even her remarkable eyes failed to impress my son. However, his report interested me. I have time on my hands nowadays so I went back through my library of sales catalogues until I found a portrait by Millais matching Crispin's description. It was sold to a private collector through Sotheby's some fifteen years ago. You say that a family picture of yours has gone astray?'

Bea asked, 'Who was it sold to?'

The old man's face cracked into a grin. 'Softly, softly. You haven't mentioned the name of the people who have mislaid a portrait. It would, theoretically – and we are only talking theoretically, aren't we? – be interesting to compare details.'

Bea added two and two to make five. Mr Goldstone was prepared to tell them what he knew, but in return he would want ... what? The right to sell the picture through his gallery? 'Your son,' said Bea, 'recognized this photograph, and identified it as the man who brought the picture into your gallery.'

Mr Goldstone waved the photo away. 'I never laid eyes on the lad. I wouldn't know him from Adam.'

Crispin's colour had risen. 'It was a copy!'

'My son, we are having a theoretical discussion here, so why bring up your ill-considered opinion? Mrs Abbot here says that a family picture has gone missing, but the name of the family who bought this particular Millais is not Abbot.'

Piers materialized behind Mr Goldstone's shoulder. 'Try Farne, or we'll be here all evening.'

'Farne,' repeated Mr Goldstone, sliding a bony hand up and down his chin. 'Now where have I heard that name before?'

Piers laughed. 'Sorry, Frank. The doddery old gent act doesn't work on me, nor on Mrs Abbot. You've made all the right connections. I'd go bail you've got a reproduction of the picture out of one of your old catalogues, and have been on the phone ever since I rang, sounding out various colleagues to see if anyone else has been offered the picture. What have you been telling them, mm? That you're interested in a copy of a rather dull Victorian picture which is a fake, a copy of a work by Millais? You'll say it's in a good frame, but that if they are offered it, you'd wouldn't mind taking it off their hands for the sake of the frame, since you've got a mid-nineteenth-century oil that it would set off very nicely?'

'Hah!' said the old man, small eyes glittering. 'There's been no takers as yet.'

'But,' said Piers, 'you are hoping you've cast enough suspicion on the authenticity of the picture so that if it does turn up somewhere, your contacts will treat it with suspicion and pass the word on to you for the sake of the frame?'

'Or,' said Bea, 'they might just ring the police.'

The carpet was a rich, deep pile, but the word 'police' seemed to thud into it and echo off the walls.

Mr Goldstone's eyes practically disappeared behind tortoise-like lids. 'You are telling me the picture was stolen?'

'Not at all,' said Bea. 'I'm laying another false trail.'

Piers gave a short laugh and Mr Goldstone almost smiled. 'I can see you're no amateur at this game, Mrs Abbot. May I ask, what is your connection to the family who have . . . ah . . . *mislaid* a picture?'

Would it be wrong to divulge some information? She searched Mr Goldstone's deeply-seamed face and thought she could trust him, within carefully defined limits. Piers had brought her to see him, and Mr Goldstone certainly knew the art world in a way she could never do. 'In confidence?' she asked.

Mr Goldstone inclined his head, his eyes very bright.

'Crispin?' she said.

Crispin shrugged. 'Oh, very well. What a fuss about a fake.'

Bea chose her words with care. 'I have been asked to find Lady Farne's godson by a very old friend. Her husband – the boy's father – is seriously ill in hospital and asking for the lad, who appears to be in some financial difficulty. When last seen, he had in his possession a genuine Millais, a recent gift from his godmother, Lady Farne. Crispin has identified the lad who brought in the Millais from this photograph, and I confirm that this is a photograph of my friend's stepson. His name is Philip Weston.'

Crispin squawked, 'It's a genuine Millais?'

'Of course,' muttered his father. 'Crispin, I should turn you out to sweep the streets! To miss a Millais! My father would turn in his grave.' His eyes sharpened again. 'The provenance is secure? He has the right to sell?'

Bea met that one head on. 'We're not sure.'

'You mentioned the police?'

'We would prefer at the moment not to involve the police.'

'But the boy's gone missing?'

Bea nodded. Missing! Another unpleasant thought hit the carpet and echoed around the room.

'Pshah!' said the old man. He took hold of Crispin's arm and raised him from his seat without apparent effort and took his place next to Bea. 'A picture we could have sold, a man we should have detained. What other bad news do you have to give me?'

'He may or may not have been responsible for Lady Farne's death,' said Bea. 'And he may or may not have legal title to the picture. He's certainly lied about it. Also, he's in debt.'

'Who would he take it to, I ask myself?' said the old man, half closing his eyes. 'I tried everyone I know around here . . . zilch.'

'Sotheby's?' Crispin offered. 'Of course it would be some months before they could advertise and place it in the right sale.'

'Idiot boy! None of the big auction houses would take it without provenance and you say he hasn't got any. They'd look it up in their catalogues as soon as they saw it, and discover who used to own it. They'd know that Lady Farne has recently died, add two and two, and ring the police.' He stroked his chin. 'There's been no word from the police alerting us to look out for a stolen Millais, and if anyone's been offered it, they're keeping very quiet. I think we can assume that he didn't take it to any of the big art sale-rooms. So where is he hiding and perhaps even more important, what is he going to do for money?'

'As Crispin suggested,' said Piers, 'he'll sell the frame for whatever he can get.'

'Vandal!' scowled Mr Goldstone. 'To separate original frame from picture.' He shot a glance of dislike at his son. 'And this cretin here was responsible for putting that idea into his head!'

Piers wondered, 'Where would he take the frame? Portobello Road? No, he couldn't expect to get more than a few hundred there, if that. I think he might take it to one of the smaller antique shops in Kensington Church Street.' He stopped and looked at Bea, waiting for her to follow his lead. So what did he expect her to say?

Piers said, 'Would you be prepared to help us by making some enquiries in that direction?'

'Me? Oh, no!' A saintly shake of his head by way of reproof. 'I wouldn't dream of getting mixed up in anything shady. You should go to the police.'

Impasse. They couldn't go to the police. Or not yet, anyway.

Bea said, 'If you could help us to trace the lad, I'm sure the family would be grateful.'

It was the olive branch the old man had been waiting for. He smiled. 'Of course. Anything to oblige. If I did by any chance happen to hear something, I would be delighted to pass the news on to you. Meanwhile, I've made a copy for you of the relevant page in the catalogue which features the picture. Poor quality, I'm afraid, but it may help.'

The picture was that of a young girl with bold eyes and long fair hair in a dark dress. As Crispin had said, it needed cleaning. The frame was indeed elaborate.

Mr Goldstone ushered them to the door, jabbing numbers at a concealed panel to deactivate the alarm. 'The question is; who really has title to the picture? If we have to deal with whoever has inherited the Farne collection, I assume the family's gratitude would be, um, muted?'

Bea gave him a thoughtful look. She didn't know who would inherit the Farne collection, but she knew a man who did. In fact, she would very much like to pin him to an upright chair, shine a bright light in his eyes and give him the third degree at this very moment. Given that he was on the point of death, this did not seem likely to happen. But perhaps Velma knew more than she was saying? Now there was a thought.

Bea pressed one of her business cards on Mr Goldstone. 'Keep in touch?'

'Rest assured, dear lady. And here is one of my cards. Ring me at any time, day or night.'

As Piers and Bea went out on to the pavement, the door shut and was locked behind them. The grille slid across.

'Taxi!' Piers had the useful gift of being able to find a taxi at any time, anywhere. 'Do you fancy something to eat, Bea?' He turned his wrist over to look at his watch as he spoke.

'You're supposed to be somewhere else this evening?'

He gave an almost convincing impression of a man with time to spare. 'Oh, perhaps later on.'

'That's all right, Piers. You've done enough and I've eaten already. Drop me off at the hospital, and I'll see how Velma's getting on.'

Bea thought he'd probably got a date with a woman. Tomcats don't change their stripes. Whatever.

It took time to run Velma to earth at the hospital, but Bea did eventually do so. No visitors, except family. The glimpse Bea had of Sandy through the window into a small room showed him looking much the same, but a monitor above his bed was angled so that the nursing staff could check on him all the time.

Velma came out to speak to Bea, shifting from one foot to the other, her attention still on her husband. There were shadows under her eyes.

'Before you start,' said Velma, 'I'm not leaving him. Every now and then he opens his eyes and looks up at me, and I need to be there. He's frightened, poor lamb. Well, so am I, but I can act as if I'm not, right?'

Bea thought that Velma was a pretty good actress, but this was not the time to say so. 'I understand. You'll need some things from home?'

Velma handed over her keys, pointing out which were needed to get into her home, adding a list on a page torn from her diary. 'This is the code for the burglar alarm, and a list of the things I could do with. Oh, and if you've time, could you check on stuff in the fridge? I've a feeling there was some cream and milk in there that might be going off, and I expect the milkman's left some more in the porch. If it hasn't been nicked, could you take it in?' She glanced back at Sandy, who seemed to be trying to raise one hand.

'I must go.'

'Velma, before you . . .'

It was no good. Velma was already bending over her husband, soothing him. Bea shrugged. How could you question a client who was so ill?

She took another taxi, this time to The Boltons. Billionaires' row. The Boltons was rather special, the white or cream stuccoed residences curving round a graceful Victorian church situated on an island in the middle of the road.

Although there was a self-contained flat for live-in help over the converted coach house at the side, Velma had managed without servants since her first husband died. Instead, she made do with the services of a cleaner twice a week. And yes, there was milk and cream on the doorstep and a bundle of mail sticking out of the letterbox.

Before Bea could select the right keys to unlock the massive front door, she fished the piece of paper with the alarm code on it out of her handbag. She didn't want to dither inside with bells ringing out over the neighbourhood. Got it. First the mortise lock, and then the Yale. Buzz went the alarm. Bother, where was the alarm box?

Velma hadn't said, so it must be obvious. Obvious to Velma was not obvious to Bea. She told herself she must have observed Velma cutting off the alarm on one of Bea's visits to the house, but for the moment . . . ah, behind a small picture, yes? She set her teeth. Any minute now the alarm would go off and . . . got it, the third small picture frame opened to reveal the keypad inside. Bea keyed in the number and the buzzing ceased. She relaxed, and bent down to pick up the flurry of mail that had landed on the floor.

'Mrs Weston?'

A large man in a not very good suit stood in the doorway, with a woman behind him on the top step. Bea's mind suggested that they might be police, and her heartbeat accelerated. She dumped the pile of mail and said, 'No, I'm not Mrs Weston, I'm . . .'

They held up identification for her to see. 'DI Hignett. Mrs Weston, we'd like a word with your husband.'

'So would I,' said Bea, aiming for humour, 'but he happens to be six feet under in Australia.' Their expressions failed to lighten, so she hastened to explain. 'I'm not Mrs Weston. I'm a friend of hers, Mrs Abbot. Would you like to see some proof? Driving licence, library card, leisure pass, bank cards?' She reached for the handbag over her shoulder, but the man stopped her.

'Take it gently now. Suppose you pass your bag over to my colleague here, and she'll check out your ID.'

'What?' Bea started to laugh, but stopped herself. 'You imagine I've got a gun in here? You've been watching too much TV.' She handed over her bag, amused but also irritated. 'What's all this about?' As if she didn't know, or guess. This was about more than a missing picture, wasn't it? 'Look, I'm Bea Abbot, fetching a few things for my friend Mrs Weston. And when you're satisfied that I am who I say I am, then perhaps you'll explain why you're here and help me by picking up the milk and cream that's been left on the doorstep.'

The woman looked in Bea's handbag, and nodded to the man. 'She's who she says she is.' She handed back the bag, and bent to pick up the items from the doorstep.

'Can't be too careful,' said the man. 'You match the description, you see. Blonde hair, late fifties.'

'Thank you for the compliment,' said Bea, accepting the milk and cream from the WPC and setting them down on the hall table. 'Now, would you mind telling me what you want?'

They were over the doorstep. Oh dear.

'You say you're collecting stuff for Mrs Weston, so presumably you know where she's hiding? Perhaps you know where Mr Weston is, too?'

'They're not hiding, I can assure you. Charing Cross Hospital. Intensive care. No visitors except for family. If he lasts the weekend, they'll operate on Monday, but I gather it's touch and go.'

The man blinked, but the woman said, 'I'll check, shall I?' She went out on to the doorstep to make the call, while the inspector got out his notebook. 'How do you spell your name, Mrs . . .?'

'Abbot – A, b, b, o, t. Look, would you mind telling me what this is all about?' She had a very good idea what it was all about, but it would be best to act innocent.

'And we can find you . . . where?'

'Take one of my cards.' She produced one from her purse and handed it over.

He gave her a sharp look. 'The Abbot Agency. A private detective?'

Bea explained in a long-suffering tone of voice. 'A domestic agency, helping families solve domestic problems. Mrs Weston asked me to check her fridge, take in the milk, put some things in an overnight bag and take them to hospital for her, as she doesn't want to leave her husband's bedside. He really is very poorly. So, what is all this about?'

He nodded, dismissing her as of no importance. A cleaning lady, sent to tidy the house. His sidekick, on the other hand, had been sizing up Bea's outfit and was not inclined to dismiss her so easily. Sidekick reported to her superior. 'Yes, they have a Mr Weston in intensive care. I've taken a note of the ward but he's not receiving visitors.'

The DI was not giving in easily. 'Mrs Weston's trusted you with the keys? May we come in and look around?'

'What on earth for? Why do you want to speak to them, anyway? I'm not at all happy about this. You haven't explained anything. Look, I've got to put the milk and cream in the fridge and then find some things to take to Mrs Weston at the hospital, so if you don't mind—'

'Where's the harm in letting us look around?'

'Certainly not,' said Bea, putting a snap into her voice. 'You've given me no reason why I should let you in. I've told you where Mr and Mrs Weston are to be found, and unless you've a warrant to search this house – and I can't for the life of me think why you should wish to do so – then the door's behind you.'

'We'll be in touch,' said the inspector, snapping his notebook to, and producing a card. 'Here's my phone number. Tell Mrs Weston to get in touch with me, right?'

'I shall do nothing of the sort,' declared Bea, edging them back to the front door. 'The poor thing's got enough worry as it is, with her husband at death's door.'

'He's not faking it, then?' asked the inspector.

Bea just looked at him. She thought she was doing the outraged friend bit rather well. In fact, she did feel outraged, but not only

with him. She was furious that Velma had put her in this position, and furious that she had allowed herself to be manipulated
into taking on this case. She almost pushed the police out of the
front door, and closed it behind them, setting her back to it,
breathing hard.

So the police suspected Sandy of . . . what? They hadn't asked
for Philip. Possibly they knew nothing about Philip. No, they
wanted to talk to Sandy, and they wanted to 'look around' his
house. Did they suspect Sandy of knowing more about the death
of Lucky Lucinda than he ought? And what were they looking
for? The missing picture? This was getting to look very nasty
indeed.

Something made her look up. No, there was no one there. She
frowned. It had been a puff of air, as if from a door closing, but
all the doors in sight – upstairs and downstairs – were open.

Bea unstuck herself from the front door and pocketed the
policeman's card. She had no intention of leaning on Velma to
phone him at the moment, but the card might come in useful
later on. Now to deal with the fridge, and check the answerphone to see if there were any calls that Velma ought to know
about.

*How easy it was to con those who believed in love and marriage.
In his view, love and marriage did not go together like a horse
and carriage. In fact, the opposite. Luckily, the dreaded
squawker believed otherwise. She wanted a ring on her finger.
Fat chance. But Liam would play along for a percentage of the
proceeds. Liam would know how to disengage himself
afterwards.*

*Rafael didn't know why Charlotte wanted to go to Bruges,
but it suited him well enough that she did. Should he encourage
Zander to take the new girl over as well? If Charlotte took the
boxes, and Maggie took the miniatures, it would be a load off
his mind, not to mention cash in his hand.*

*If only he knew what had happened to Philip and his
picture! It was tantalizing to think of the Millais having been
in the flat for days before he heard about it. Philip's room
had been cleaned, which was a bore. There might have been
traces he could follow up. The only thing he could be sure
about was that Philip had been back recently, because his
mobile and charger had gone. So Philip was still around*

somewhere, and if he'd managed to put some credit on his phone, it should be possible to contact him, get him to crawl out of the woodwork.

But for now, there was a party to go to, a woman to seduce and a false trail to lay. He was the puppet master and they all danced to his tune.

Seven

Saturday evening

B ea wasn't able to see Velma when she arrived at the hospital, so she had to leave the overnight bag with one of the nurses. No visitors, no assurances that everything was going to be all right.

Bea shut off the alarm as she entered her own house and stood still, welcoming the silence. The house seemed to be breathing a sigh of relief that there was no loud music, no television blaring away, no clashing of pans in the kitchen. Bea hoped Maggie was enjoying her party.

Bea poured herself a glass of orange juice and went through into the living room. The game of patience that she'd abandoned the day before was still on the card table, but someone – Oliver? – had turned over a couple of cards, creating a space into which they'd put the king of clubs. She was annoyed. Then amused. What did it matter?

She drew the curtains at the front of the house, switched on a side lamp and opened the French windows at the back to savour the night air. Two moths circled her head, attracted by the light. There was a moon tonight, rising above the tree, illuminating the spire of the church.

On such a night as this . . .

Hamilton had died, quietly, peacefully. He'd known his time had come, and asked her not to grieve for him but to rejoice that his long acquaintance with pain was finally over and he could move on, closer to God. He'd not been a handsome man, but in death he'd achieved a dignity that had awed her. She'd held his hand while he'd slipped away from her. In death, he'd smiled.

She swiped the heel of her hand over her eyes, and descended the curling iron stairs to the peace and quiet of the garden. He'd often paced here at night, or sat under the tree with his hands, palm upwards, on his knees, praying. She couldn't pray as he did. He was capable of praying for half an hour at a time, sometimes longer.

For her part, she could send up arrow prayers and within a few seconds find herself thinking of something else. Should she have tried harder to get Velma to leave the hospital? Would she ever make sense of the jigsaw of facts and impressions that surrounded Sandy and Velma? And Philip – where had he gone, and was he in danger? Bea rather thought he might be.

She paused with her foot on the lowest rung of the stairs, letting the scent of the tobacco plants waft around her, listening in vain for the chiming of the church clock. In the old days it had chimed through the night, but no longer. Noise pollution, they said. Can't be doing with it, they said. Disturbs our sleep.

Bea had always found it a comfort, to hear it chime through the night. If you were deeply asleep you didn't hear it, and if you were awake and in pain or worrying about something it was a comfort, as if it were saying 'I'm here, always. Remember me.'

Bea looked up at the spire. *Remember me. Remember Velma and Sandy. If it is your will that Sandy should live, then I'd be so grateful. If it's your will that he should die, then please comfort Velma. I've been there, and I know what she'll be suffering. I watched Hamilton accept death, but he had a strong faith to sustain him and in the end I think he welcomed it. I'm not sure what Sandy believes in, if anything.*

As for Philip – you know him better than I do. Whatever good there is in him, let it guide his actions, wherever he may be. And if you really want me to get mixed up in this mess, then help me to see what ought to be done.

A breeze ruffled the leaves of the tree, and caressed her face. She shivered. It was getting late. She went up the stairs, closed and locked the grille and the windows, set the alarm and decided to retire for the night.

Oliver still hadn't come in, but he knew the code for the alarm. She could trust him to set it again once he was in. She hoped.

Sunday morning

Bea stretched out in bed, coming to consciousness with the church bells ringing. Oh dear, it must be quite late. Didn't they start at 8.45 a.m.? She'd meant to be up at seven but had overslept for once. The sun had entered the room through gaps in the curtains, which she never liked to shut completely at night.

She listened for sounds that would indicate other people moving around the house, and thought she heard the trickle of water from above, as Oliver had a shower. She sat up. Oliver might be able to solve one or two clues in the puzzle that the Westons had laid on her. She showered, dressed, put on her morning make-up and made her way downstairs to find him with his head inside the fridge, looking for . . . what? Eggs and bacon to appear ready-cooked? Or, possibly, the milk?

He was dressed in a good white shirt and jeans, casual but not cheap.

He said, 'If it's all right with you, Mrs Abbot, I thought I might go out with my friend today on the river, have lunch at a pub in Richmond.'

'Splendid,' she said, and hoped he hadn't picked up on the sour note in her voice. *She* wasn't going to be having a day off work. She was going to have to work, wasn't she? Anyway, she had no one to play with nowadays. She remembered Velma's take on widowhood, and grimaced. Lonely widows were all too easy a catch, weren't they? Although, to be fair, Sandy had been a good catch right up to the point that he'd fallen sick.

Bea cooked sausages and bacon for herself and Oliver, made coffee and toast. She said, 'Could you spare me an hour before you go off? There's one or two things only you can deal with, and time seems to be running out.'

'Correspondence?' he said, and she couldn't make out why he was smiling.

She thought of the missing tax return, and winced. 'No,' she said. 'Let me tell you what's been happening . . .'

She brought him up to date, laying Philip's mobile phone and the charger on the table for Oliver to examine. 'Can you retrieve his messages, and the phone numbers in the memory?'

Oliver loved a puzzle. He pressed buttons, frowning, trying this and that. 'The battery's dead, and there's no credit showing. Leave it on charge all day and I'll let you have the information this evening.'

She had to accept that.

She showed him the photocopy of the page from the sale catalogue. 'The reproduction isn't good, but you can see it's a young girl in a dark dress. It isn't in any of the art books I was looking at last night.'

Oliver put his finger on the small print where it gave the size of the picture. 'It's not very big. Somehow I thought a portrait by Millais would be much larger, perhaps half life-size.'

'I suppose he did all sorts.' She leaned over Oliver's shoulder to see where he'd been pointing to some figures on the page. 'You're right. A tallish man could carry it around under his arm. It seems Philip was carrying it around wrapped in a bed sheet. Suppose, for the sake of argument, that he was so desperate for money that he took the picture out of the frame. Would it roll up, do you think? Or would an old oil painting crack if you did that to it?'

'I don't suppose it would be recommended, but the frame is so deep that if he did take it out, it would be even easier to tote around.'

'Suppose you were Philip. You've lost your job and you owe money left, right and centre. You're on pills and have been drinking. You leave the flat some time in the night, with a rucksack or a suitcase and the picture. Why?'

'Is he being dunned? Threatened?'

Bea remembered the correspondence she'd seen in Philip's room. 'There was a letter in his room from a club whose name I didn't recognize, and he had a notebook with pages of numbers in it. The letter didn't seem threatening, but it did remind him of club rules about paying his debts.'

'The notebook might be his way of recording winning numbers at roulette or something. Lots of people think they can work out a system for beating the wheel. They can't, of course. But they try. Do you think he's the gambling type?'

'A gambling club . . . hmm. He'd lose, of course. Suppose it was that, and the club sent some heavies after him to make him pay his debts and he hadn't the wherewithal to do so—'

'Then he might easily want to disappear, taking with him his one saleable asset—'

'Which turns out not to be as saleable as he'd hoped. So where would he take refuge? I wondered if he'd go up to his mother's in Scotland, but he hasn't got a car or enough money for the train fare, and there's no credit left on his cards. Besides, going to Scotland won't help him cash in on the picture, which I assume is his priority. He's tried to sell it down here and been told it's a fake. He's been told he could sell the frame and I've got feelers out for anyone trying to sell that, but where is he, and what is he doing for food?'

Oliver sipped coffee, one eye on the clock. 'My friend said he'd pick me up in fifteen minutes. I didn't think you'd need me today.'

Bea made an effort to think of this from Oliver's point of view. 'Of course you must have time off. It's Sunday, after all.'

'Mm. About Philip. All I can think of is that when I was at my wits' end and thinking of doing away with myself, Maggie picked me up, dusted me down, and brought me here. She looked after me like a broody hen.'

'Ah.' Bea thought back to what she'd seen in Philip's room. 'He had a couple of photographs of girls there. You think he might have gone to one of them? But, how can I find out who and where? Velma's more or less incommunicado, and Sandy's too sick for visitors.'

'You can't,' said Oliver, chucking his dirty plates into the sink. 'You'll have to wait till tonight when we find out what numbers are on his mobile phone. I won't be late, promise. And then we can suss it out together, right? I'll put the phone on charge before I go.' He went out with it, and Bea took the dirty dishes out of the sink and put them in the dishwasher. She really must start house-training him.

She thought how pleasant it would be to have the house to herself, to have time off just to exist, and not to be busy about anything. Then she heard Maggie's voice in the hall, greeting Oliver as he was leaving. Several thuds later, Maggie appeared in the kitchen.

'Whatever are you doing here?' said Bea. 'It's Sunday.'

'You said to report every morning, and I need to borrow one of your suitcases on wheels. Is there any proper coffee? My head! I didn't get to bed till five.' Maggie turned on the radio as she passed it, and reached for some black coffee. 'Wow, that was some party and Zander certainly knows how to sweet talk a girl. I told him I'd met his sort before but, well, he is gorgeous!'

Bea turned the radio off, and told herself that patience nearly always paid off. 'Did Philip turn up?'

'Oh, him. No, he didn't.' Maggie frowned. 'They're ticked off with him actually, wondering how they can get him to pay up what he owes, and get rid of him. Charlotte said they've got to go carefully because their landlady put him in the flat, and they don't want to get on the wrong side of her. Liam says that in that case, the landlady ought to pay Philip's share of the rent. He's got a point, hasn't he?'

'Liam. That's the third man. What's he like?'

Maggie shrugged. 'Not my type, but he must be nicer than he looks because he's going to Bruges on business this week and he's asked Charlotte to go with him. He's promised her a boat ride on the canals, and a night-time tour of the town in a horse and buggy. She's over the moon, dreaming of a white wedding, though to tell the truth, I don't think he means to go that far. He's a bit . . . dunno . . . one minute he's all over her, and the next he cuts her off in mid-flow. But she thinks the sun shines, so it's up to her, isn't it?'

'Can she take time off work, just like that?'

'Says she's got leave owing and anyway she'll only be away two days. Says she might just claim she's got a tummy bug, not bad enough to get a doctor's certificate, but enough to get her time off. Anyway, that's why I wanted to borrow one of your big suitcases on wheels. Charlotte's only got a small one, and her big one is a soft top. She needs a solid case because Liam's taking over a Royal Worcester coffee set as a present for this friend he's doing business with and it won't fit into either of his bags. I said you'd got one that might do, which would save her buying another tomorrow, but she has to see it first. That's all right, isn't it?'

'I suppose it has to be,' said Bea, half amused and half annoyed. 'Take the one with the red stripe round it; it's easier to spot in a crowd.'

'Romantic Bruges.' Maggie was going all day-dreamy. 'A trip on the canal. A ride in a horse-drawn buggy. Wow. I wish Zander would take me, but he says he's not got any reason to go over there at the moment. I said wouldn't giving me a holiday be reason enough, but he just laughed. Well, I must be off. Zander's taking me to feed the ducks at Kew this afternoon, maybe have a picnic. I told him he was a cheapskate, but he talked me into it.'

'See if you can get him talking about Philip,' said Bea, sounding sharp and not regretting it. 'That's why you're there, after all.'

Maggie gave Bea a darkling look, but said, 'Right. I'll just fetch the case and be off then. See you tomorrow.'

She banged the case down the stairs and slammed the front door on her way out. Bea tried not to wince. That case had been round the world with her, she was attached to it and didn't want it scuffed. Then she laughed at herself for being so pernickety. What did it matter, anyway?

At some point she would have to get Maggie to understand that all this borrowing must stop, but not today. Today was Sunday. It was a day for relaxing, for being quiet, for not having to work.

The church bells had stopped. She looked at her watch. Too late for the nine thirty service. Should she make an effort to go later on that morning? Or relax in the garden? The sun was shining, the sky was blue, she could pick something light to read out of the bookcases in the living room and treat herself to a lazy day.

Or, she could go down to the hospital and chivvy Velma out for a walk. Velma wouldn't want to leave her husband's bedside, but it wasn't good for her to be cooped up with him day after day. When had she last eaten properly, for instance?

She ought to warn Velma about the police, too.

Actually, there was a list of questions she could ask Velma. Her friend must know a lot more about Philip and Lady Farne's death and Sandy's part in it, than she had said.

Grilling Velma would take a lot of energy and put a strain on their friendship, but was that a good enough reason for ducking out? Bea told herself that at her age she had earned a Sunday off.

But if she did nothing and the police jumped on Velma before she'd been briefed, before Bea could extract enough informa-tion to take the case further . . .? Hamilton had said once 'All that's necessary for evil to prevail, is for good men to do nothing.'

She could easily convince herself that she should do nothing. After all, she didn't really *know* how much Sandy had been involved with Lady Farne, did she? Her mind skittered away

from the effort that confrontation with Velma would involve. She
thought of Maggie yearning for a boat trip on a canal in Bruges;
little did the girl know how noisy such things could be, crammed
in with tourists galore, battered by a loud-speaker commentary
in different languages. And the horse and carriage trips finished
at dusk, didn't they?

But there were quiet walks by the less well-known canals, serene
squares with trees in them, swans on the canals and gorgeous
sunsets. Hamilton had spotted some rare bird or other last time
they'd been there . . . ah well. Perhaps some day she'd go again.

In the meantime, she'd better make a plan to get Velma out
of the hospital and into an interrogation unit.

Extracting Velma was easier than Bea had anticipated, for her
friend was so listless from lack of sleep, snatched meals and no
exercise, that she accompanied Bea out of the hospital without
too much in the way of argument.

'Only, I can't be away long,' she said, shading her eyes from
the bright sunlight in the street. 'I assume you haven't found
Philip yet? Of course not, or you'd have said straight away. Oh
dear, I'd forgotten how noisy Fulham Palace Road is.'

'It's a Sunday, remember. It's quiet by comparison.'

'Is it?' Velma was dazed.

Bea steered her across the road and into a quiet back street,
where she knew of a good vegetarian restaurant. Once seated,
Velma pushed the menu aside. 'You choose, something simple.
And quick.'

. Bea chose and ordered for them both. She considered
suggesting a glass of wine and discarded the idea. Velma probably hadn't eaten properly for days. Luckily the starter came
quickly, and though Velma took only small bites at first, she
soon picked up speed and cleared her plate as quickly as Bea
did. 'I needed that. I'm glad you made me come out with you.
You're a good friend, Bea.'

'Better than you think. I've been obstructing the police in their
enquiries on your behalf.'

Velma's beautiful eyes went blank. 'You've what?'

The waitress brought their main course. Velma looked at it as
if she'd never seen food before. 'I'm glad you didn't choose
seafood. That calamari really put the lid on it.' She asked the
waitress for some mineral water.

Bea lifted her fork. 'Eat. It will give you strength. It's time I gave you a full report, and then it's your turn to fill me in on the bits you've left out. Mm, this is good.'

Velma picked up her fork and took a tiny bite. 'I don't think I'm going to enjoy hearing this, am I?' But she attacked her plateful steadily if without relish.

'Maybe not. But you need to eat and you need to know. Now this is what we have discovered . . .' Bea told of her undercover foray to the flat and what she'd discovered in Philip's room.

Velma gaped. 'He got the sack? He's in debt? That club you mentioned . . . I've heard of it. Gambling for high stakes never did appeal to me. If he's in trouble with them . . . why didn't he say?'

'You'd said you wouldn't give him money, hadn't you?'

'Yes, but . . . I didn't realize . . . I had no idea!' She took a gulp of water. 'Sandy will be horrified.'

'Philip's drinking heavily and taking antidepressants, so he's probably not thinking clearly. He took the Millais out of the flat, wrapped in a bed sheet. You did set him up with some clean bed linen when you put him in the flat, didn't you? Yes, I thought so. Anyway, Philip arrived at a reputable gallery looking and smelling like a man who'd been sleeping on the streets . . .' She went on to describe what had happened there, and how the Goldstones had inadvertently put the word around that the picture was a fake, thus ending any hopes that Philip might have had of raising money from the picture. Bea fished the photocopy out of her handbag. 'Do you recognize the picture?'

Velma's hand trembled as she took the paper. 'I think so. It hung in the hall. Her walls were covered with pictures and the lighting was bad. Sandy would know, but . . .' Her face contracted, fighting tears. Finally she said, 'I could kill Philip, upsetting Sandy this way.'

Bea also pushed her plate aside. 'Sandy's the key to this puzzle, isn't he? Your turn to talk, Velma.'

'I'm exhausted. This is all too much. Why don't I just lie down and die?'

Bea grinned. 'You're a survivor, Velma. Remember how you used to flannel your way out of trouble at school? So let's hear it.'

Velma signalled to the waitress for coffee. 'I've got to keep awake somehow. We just have to get through today, you see. They'll operate tomorrow, although I'm having conscience-stricken pangs about pushing some other poor soul off the list, who might need the operation just as much as Sandy does.'

'No more diversions,' said Bea. 'Start with Lady Farne making a will. Sandy was one of the few people Lady Farne trusted. I'm guessing that she made him one of the executors.'

Velma nodded. 'We-e-ll, yes. It's true. He'd been on at her for ages about making a will, and finally she did so. She told him he was one of the executors and the other was a solicitor recommended by her bank. She said she'd left the bulk of her estate to charity, but that Philip would come in for a good bit if he behaved himself.'

'Philip knew?'

'He talked about it quite openly, but I don't think he'd have the guts – pardon me, but I really don't think he has – to kill her.'

'So how do you think he came by the picture?'

'It all makes sense now you've told me about his debts. He was desperate for money, so he visited his godmother and asked for help. She gave him the picture instead of money.'

'And he tries unsuccessfully to sell it. Next question. Was it Sandy who found the body and reported the murder to the police?'

The coffee came, and Velma drank it black, without milk or sugar. 'Yes. He was dreadfully upset because he'd known her such a long time and although she was pretty odd towards the end, he was fond of her. When he got home afterwards he cried, and I didn't think any the less of him for that.'

'Did the police say when she died?'

'Late on the Monday or perhaps early on the Tuesday morning before he found her. They asked him to look around, see if anything were missing, and of course as soon as he went into the sitting room he saw that her collection of gold boxes had gone. It was in a display cabinet, all rather dusty and not even locked up, can you imagine? It didn't look as if anything else had been disturbed and of course he didn't think to look in the cupboard to see if the picture were still there. He was very shaken.'

'Presumably he then contacted her solicitor—'

'Who was away on holiday. His secretary made an appointment for Sandy to see him on his return.'

Bea said, 'Go back a bit. What did Philip say about his godmother's death?'

'Sandy tried to ring Philip to tell him, but his mobile phone was switched off so we left a message on the landline at the flat. When he got back to us, he said how shocked he was to hear about it, and that's when we arranged to go out for a meal together.' Velma looked at her watch, and signalled to the waitress for the bill. 'My treat, this.'

'Velma, pay attention! When you met up, did he try to touch you for money again?'

'Well, yes, but I'd no idea he'd lost his job or anything. I told him not to be silly, end of story. He said he wasn't hungry and had Dover sole, instead of the calamari. I wish we'd had that, too. We were both as sick as dogs, and then Sandy told me about seeing the picture and not knowing what to do about it. I told him he ought to have it out with Philip so he did and came back in a terrible state. He started to have chest pains that afternoon, but we thought it was the food poisoning that was to blame. He hung around the house, getting under the cleaner's feet, dithering.

'I told him he ought to go to the police about Philip but he didn't want to, of course.' She bit her lip. 'We almost quarrelled about it. It was the first time we've ever had a difference of opinion. I put it down to the calamari and thought he'd be better next day, but he wasn't. I wanted him to go to the doctor, and he said he would if he didn't pick up soon and that I ought to keep my appointment at the dentist and he was out of cash, too, so would I get some for him. I was the teensiest bit cross with him, so I did go to the dentist, and then I thought I might as well have my nails done and do a bit of shopping. I wasn't punishing him or anything, but it seemed a good idea to give him a bit of space. Only when I got back I found he'd been to see the solicitor and that really put the kybosh on everything, because Lady Farne had made a second will, superseding the first, and leaving the Millais to Philip but not a penny more.'

'So it *is* his property, and it *is* a genuine Millais?'

'Oh, yes. But everything else now goes to Sandy.'

Bea's mouth dropped open. 'What?'

Velma nodded. 'Exactly. Then I realized that he's been looking after her all these years and, well . . . he was fond of her, you know. And she must have been so disillusioned about Philip. So it made sense. Not that my poor boy wanted all that money. But you see what it looks like, don't you? It gives him an

excellent motive for knocking her off. He didn't, but he can't
prove it because he often spends his afternoons round and about,
calling on people. He found her. He inherits. He's number one
suspect. I was going out of my mind with worry until I thought
you might be able to help.'

She started to hyperventilate, and Bea grabbed her wrist.
'Breathe deeply. In and out. In and out. That's it. Velma, you're
strong. You can cope, for Sandy's sake.'

'Yes, of course.' Velma downed half a glass of water in a
couple of gulps. 'I'm being stupid.'

'That's the last thing you are, Velma. You've always been a
quick thinker. As soon as you learned Sandy was a suspect, you
contacted me and threw Philip to the lions, rather than tell me
about the danger that Sandy was in.'

Velma gave a little wriggle. 'It wasn't quite like that . . .'

'Yes, it was. You told me you thought Philip had done it, while
denying that you did. A perfect Velma ploy. Did you want me
to give him away to the police, or were you going to do it
yourself?'

Velma wriggled again. 'It was a holding action. I didn't know
what to do. Sandy was so ill, not fit to be questioned, and I
didn't really *know* anything.'

Bea leaned back in her chair. 'Now I see why the police are
so keen to talk to you both.'

Velma grimaced. 'I can stall them till after the operation, but
I suppose I'll have to speak to them sometime. Advise me, Bea.
Do I tell them what I suspect, or pretend I'm an empty-headed
blonde?'

Bea rubbed her forehead. 'If we could only find Philip . . .
has he any girlfriends?'

Velma looked at her watch. Mentally, she was on her way
back to the hospital. 'Huh? He never introduced us to anyone.
I really don't know.' She gave the waitress her platinum card,
and passed her hand over her eyes. 'I could sleep for a week,
but I must get back. He keeps saying "Sorry" and I say I'm
sorry, too, but it doesn't seem to help. I tell myself that this time
tomorrow we should know whether he's going to live or die.
Only another twenty-four hours.'

'We'll probably be able to get some clues from Philip's mobile
phone this evening or tomorrow.'

Velma wasn't listening any more. She retrieved her card from the waitress and stood up, ready to go. 'Money's no object, Bea. Find Philip, and then we'll work out how to get the police off Sandy's back.'

He'd had to take the phone call in the pub, when he could hardly hear himself think.

Bad news. Van was pressing for the stuff. Not only the boxes but also the miniatures. Well, Liam would play ball and get Charlotte to carry the boxes. That was all arranged.

Could he arrange for the Maggie girl to take the miniatures over at the same time? She'd go if Zander went, too. Zander might not want to play, but then, he'd no idea he'd been carting stolen goods around for Rafael, had he? When confronted with that information, Zander would have no choice but to do as Rafael said. The girl had as much sex appeal as a giraffe, but there was no accounting for tastes.

He must set up a meeting with Liam and Zander for later that evening. No excuses accepted. Now where should he meet them? Certainly not at the flat. Ah . . . he'd been meaning to visit a prospective target out in the sticks, someone who was reputed to have a nice collection of medals. Easy to transport, medals. He'd written asking to visit some time ago – the usual thing, a query on insurance – and hadn't intended to firm up a date till he'd got the other stuff out of the way. However, he could kill two birds with one stone this way; a 'talk' with the medal collector followed by a meeting with the others at the nearest Tube station afterwards.

He scribbled notes to himself.

> *One: Liam must tell Charlotte that Philip had contacted him, and would be back next weekend.*
> *Two: Rent a car for the journey, pay by cash.*
> *Three: Liam must order the tickets for the Eurotunnel on line.*
> *Four: Liam to arrange hotel accommodation. Two doubles? Whatever he fancied.*

The boxes of goods were already packed, ready to be slipped into the girls' luggage. He'd give them a generous amount of spending money for the trip. Why not? It would be worth it. He was the grand master of this game, wasn't he!

Eight

Sunday afternoon

What do you do on a sunny Sunday afternoon? Take a stroll in the park. Go off in the car to meet with some friends. Visit relatives.

Bea hadn't any close relatives except for her son Max – who seemed to be incommunicado – didn't want to take the car out, and was feeling peevish.

Maggie and Oliver had deserted her, she'd lost some important papers, and was going to get into trouble with the police for withholding evidence.

She missed Hamilton.

She decided to walk back home from the hospital. It wasn't too far, she needed the exercise, and maybe the rhythm of walking would provide her subconscious with the time to work on the questions that were rolling around in her head.

Her shoes were comfortable enough, weren't they?

She set off up the road, and stopped. No, her shoes were not comfortable enough. She limped to a bench and got out her mobile phone to try Max. Once more into the breach, dear friends. Once more she got his voicemail. Oh where, oh where has my little boy gone? Gone, gone, far away. In the company of his anorexic, ambitious, fake-blonde wife. Out chatting up the constituency grandees, no doubt.

She delved into her handbag and came up with the card which the gnome-like antique dealer had given her the night before. He'd said she could ring at any time, day or night, and she had one important question to ask.

'Mr Goldstone, it's Bea Abbot here. You said there'd been no hue and cry after the Millais – and no, I haven't got a line on that yet, except to learn that it's genuine and that Philip had been left it in Lady Farne's will – but has anyone been trying to sell a collection of small gold boxes?'

The phone quacked excitedly. 'Ah, yes. Mrs Abbot, I was hoping you'd ring. You know that the police update us regularly about stolen art treasures? Nowadays I seldom concern myself with such things but your visit inspired me to look through the recent lists and there they are; twenty gold snuffboxes, stolen from the Farne collection. The coincidence hit me immediately. Did the boy take them as well as the picture? To think we had him on our premises, under our very hand!'

Bea picked her words with care. 'The man who found the body noticed that the collection of boxes had disappeared, and reported it to the police. But he didn't realize that a picture was missing until much later, because the last he'd seen of it, it had been stashed away in a bedroom cupboard. Days later, he discovered it had gone missing, but for family reasons . . .'

'Ah, family reasons. That I understand. This boy Philip is a member of his family, no?'

There was no point in trying to hide the truth from this man. 'Yes. That is, he might be. Let me outline a theory. Lady Farne's flat was stuffed full of antiques; pictures, objets d'art, snuff-boxes, some really good jewellery and so on. She lets someone into the flat and he walks out with the snuffboxes. He ignores everything else – even the easily portable stuff like her jewellery – but takes a picture out of a bedroom cupboard. Does that make sense to you?'

Silence. 'Mmhm. Mmhm. She had a safe, perhaps? He had no time to crack it?'

'There was a safe which she didn't use because she'd forgotten the combination, so the jewellery was on show, not in any secure place. The boxes and the picture were taken, but nothing else. What does that sound like to you?'

'The man who took the boxes is not the man who took the picture. The man who took the boxes is a professional thief.'

'Yes,' said Bea. 'That's what I was thinking, too. Not one but two people removed things from the flat. We've all been so carried away with the idea that Philip stole the picture that we haven't really looked at the bigger picture. Tell me; if you were a professional burglar, how would you have gone about stealing the boxes?'

He grunted out a laugh. 'You think I have an understanding of the criminal classes? Well, perhaps I do. This man you are thinking of, he comes prepared. He has a buyer for the boxes already. He is no amateur. He understands that he has to deliver the goods in perfect condition. These are priceless gold boxes, many of them inlaid with jewels. Some of them date back to the eighteenth century, from the court of Louis XIV.

'This man knows that gold can be scratched, that jewels can be knocked out of their settings. He would have brought something with him to wrap them individually, so as not to reduce their value. The collection would probably have been on a plane out of Heathrow that night. They would be sold, perhaps, to a private collector somewhere on the Continent. We may never seem them again.'

Bea said, 'This man you are describing is not Philip. Granted, Philip's in financial difficulty, but he's not the sharpest knife in the drawer and if he'd wanted to steal from Lady Farne, he'd have taken the jewellery as being the easiest to dispose of. Instead he goes into a bedroom cupboard and removes a second-rate Victorian portrait. I think we can take it that Philip did not steal the boxes.'

'It's not second-rate, but I see what you mean. It's not one of Millais' well-known pictures, though of course it has a certain value. The jewellery would have been easy to sell, as would the boxes – to the right customer. So yes, it was a foolish thing to take the Millais, which is not easy to sell. And to wrap it in a bed sheet! The height of folly! I would like a word with that young man.'

'So would I. Next question. Would you have heard if any of the boxes had been offered around over here, say to someone less scrupulous than yourself?'

'Possibly, but it's more likely they went abroad.'

'And the frame? Has that surfaced anywhere?'

'Sadly, no. I have set a whisper going around that the picture is definitely a fake, which should deter any of my colleagues from offering for it. They know I'm interested in the frame, and the likelihood is that they'll contact me if the picture is offered to any of them. We do these little favours for one another in expectation that they will be returned in due course. I believe I've enough credit to expect a return.'

Bea reflected that if the police were told about the picture, it would make life even more difficult for Philip. Which way would he jump? Towards the police or away from them? He couldn't expect help from his father . . . or could he? Before Bea had left Velma's house, she'd listened to the messages on the answerphone and there'd been a number of hang-ups among the usual calls from friends and neighbours checking on the times of a community association meeting, making a date for a coffee morning, that sort of thing. Were the hang-ups from Philip, trying to get through but afraid to leave a message?

Mr Goldstone was still speaking, and Bea had lost the thread of what he was saying. 'Sorry,' she said. 'Trying to think what's best to do.'

'Relax, dear lady. The police will be looking for those boxes, even though it is probably too late to catch the thief moving them out of the country. As for Philip, my guess is that he will surface sooner or later, probably having flogged off the frame and the picture separately for a few pounds. I would like to be optimistic about seeing the picture again, but I fear that on this occasion I cannot offer you much beyond my condolences.'

'As in . . . his death?'

'No, no.' The little man was disturbed by this. 'At least, it is my sincerest wish that does not happen, although I have a bad feeling about this.'

'So do I,' said Bea. 'We'll keep in touch, right?'

She switched off her phone, reflecting that she'd been using it a lot lately and it might need charging up that evening; but no, it was still registering almost full. Good. She looked about for a taxi to take her home. Walking in these shoes was not an option.

Sunday evening

Bea poached a couple of eggs for supper and ate them in the kitchen with the newspaper propped up in front of her. She channel-flipped through television programmes for a while, but nothing held her interest. She couldn't do anything about the things which were on her mind. Max didn't ring. Nor did Maggie. Philip's mobile phone lay on her desk, charging itself up, but the messages on it were inaccessible. She refused to tackle routine business letters on a Sunday.

Sundays were for resting from one's labours, giving one space to think. Doing a little praying on the side, if you weren't feeling too bolshy to do so – which was Bea's case at the moment. She could only manage some arrow prayers. *Please. If you could . . .? Such a mess. Look after Sandy and Velma?*

She had a long, refreshing bath and got into bed with a book that she'd read before. Like a sick child, she was rereading old favourites rather than trying to work herself into something new.

She woke with a start, to hear the house alarm set off its racket and then stop. Oliver must have come in and misjudged his timing. Only, suppose it wasn't Oliver, but someone who'd learned the code by torturing either Oliver or Maggie, who were now being held prisoners in a dungeon somewhere . . .?

Scolding herself for her stupidity, Bea nevertheless listened hard for a sound that would indicate either of her young friends had returned. It wasn't Maggie, because the house remained silent; no radio or television was turned on. Footsteps climbed the stairs outside her bedroom, going up to the top floor.

Bea shot upright in bed, dislodging her reading glasses. Was that the sound of a sob? But . . .! Oliver, crying?

His bedroom door opened and closed. He hadn't thought to tap on her door to announce his return. Well, surely there was no need for him to do that, was there? He wasn't her son, he'd turned eighteen and she wasn't his mother. She rescued her glasses and looked at the clock. Half past eleven. Not that late, really. Except that it was only recently that Oliver had taken to going out at night to the gym and to meet his friends. She'd been pleased that he'd started to socialize.

She took off her glasses and lay back on the pillows. Why should Oliver cry?

Well, if she came to think about it, there were many reasons why Oliver Ingram should be distressed. He'd always been the odd one out in his family and Bea suspected that he'd either been adopted or was the result of a sideslip on the part of his mother. Two blue-eyed parents do not produce a brown-eyed lad. Oliver's elder brother followed the family trend: well-built, sporting and of medium intelligence. Oliver had 'A'-grade A levels and was destined for Cambridge, right up to the point where he'd discovered porn on his father's laptop and his world had imploded.

Mr Ingram had thrown Oliver out, and the boy had huddled by the water in the park till Maggie had rescued him and brought him back with her. Oliver had kept the agency afloat while Max had gone off to play with his mates at the House of Commons. Oliver had rescued his belongings from his father's house and settled down to work for Bea when she took over the agency.

But, Oliver was eighteen years old and from looking forward to university and a brilliant career, he'd been dumped in a basement office, sorting out jobs for nannies. Meeting up with old school friends couldn't have helped, either, if they were full of plans for university and brilliant futures. The contrast must be painful.

Bea had suggested once that she help Oliver to get to university, but he'd declined, possibly out of pride? Possibly still raw from his father's rejection?

Added to which, he'd muffed disabling the house alarm and let out a sob on his way up the stairs. Conclusion: Oliver was in a bad way.

Of course Bea didn't have to do anything about it. It was none of her business. She'd offered him a room and a job and he'd taken it, period. She could turn off the light and go to sleep with a clear conscience.

Sighing, she got out of bed, found bedroom slippers and a towelling robe to go over her nightdress, and trailed up the stairs to the top floor.

As she approached, Oliver switched off the light in his room. He couldn't have sent a clearer signal. Oliver did not want to talk to her.

She tapped on the door. No reply. She tapped harder. 'Oliver, I know you're not asleep yet. Let me in.' No reply. She glanced down at her nightdress and robe, and qualified that. 'No, don't let me in, or I'll be had up for sexual harassment or something. Not that I . . . anyway, what I mean is, will you please come out of your room so that we can talk?'

The room remained in darkness. 'Nothing to talk about.' The words were muffled. Was he still crying?

'Humour me. I need to talk to you, even if you don't need to talk to me.'

'Can't. Need to go to the bathroom.'

Bea stepped back. 'All right. Ten minutes. Downstairs in the kitchen. I could do with a hot milky drink, couldn't you?' Without waiting for a reply, she set off back down the stairs to the kitchen, turning on lights as she went. The first thing she did in the kitchen was to turn on the radio, searching for some late-night music and turning down the volume. Maggie would have approved; except that Maggie would have had the volume turned right up and danced to it. Ah well. Bea wondered how the girl was getting on.

She fancied some buttered toast. Or would she like Marmite on it? No, plain. But with good butter. Hot chocolate? Mm, maybe.

She pulled down the blinds at the kitchen windows to shut out the blank blackness outside. Oliver shuffled in, still in his jeans and sweatshirt. Yes, he had been crying. No, she was not going to notice. 'Coffee, tea, hot chocolate, honey and lemon? Toast; plain, buttered and with jam? Biscuits?'

He shook his head. Hunched his shoulders. 'What do you want to talk about?'

'Life. Choices. Regrets. Why did I marry Piers at nineteen, when I could have gone to college and got a degree? My parents warned me, but . . .' She shrugged. 'Who listens to older folk? Perhaps a more interesting questions is; why did he marry me? Did he really imagine he'd stop chasing every woman in sight if he married a serious, chaste schoolgirl? Don't answer that. Instead, tell me what's going on with you.' She put some sliced bread into the toaster and depressed the handle.

'Nothing. The usual. I met up with my best friend from school. Naturally, it's made me realize what my life might have been like if only I hadn't upset my father.'

Bea thought that explanation had come out a little too easily. Yes, the boy was concerned about not going to university but no, it wasn't the whole story. 'I told you I'd help you get to university if that's what you want.' She rescued the bread as it flew up out of the toaster, and sought for the butter in the fridge.

A long, defeated sigh. 'It's complicated. I don't want anything to eat or drink. I had something earlier.'

'At the pub?' Bea put a mug of cold milk into the microwave. If it wasn't the loss of his university career that was bothering him, then what was? Mind you, she'd be devastated if he did go. How could she run the agency without him? She buttered slices of toast, cut it into 'soldiers' and pushed the plate towards him.

'My friend asked me back to his place after we'd been out for the day. It was his father who took such an interest in me before, taught me so many tricks on the computer. He'd been asking after me. I couldn't refuse to go, could I?'

'Of course not.' She removed one mug of hot milk, and put in another. Hot chocolate? Yes. 'I expect he was urging you to go to university too, wasn't he?'

Silence.

Bea stirred chocolate into one mug of hot milk, and left it at his elbow. She'd asked the wrong question, obviously. She took the first bite of her own toast, relishing it. Now what did she know about this adult friend of his? Mm-hmm. Oliver had said something a while back about not going to see him again, because his father had spread a rumour that it had been Oliver who'd been accessing porn.

She said, 'He asked you for the real reason you'd left home at such a critical time in your life?'

Oliver nodded. The phone rang somewhere in the house, but Bea let it ring. Whoever it was could leave a message. Were those Maggie's dulcet tones she could hear? Yes. Maggie sounded chirpy. Good for her.

Bea said, 'You told him the truth?'

The words burst out of him. 'I'd decided I'd never tell, because he'd have to investigate, being a school governor, and my father's only got that house because he's headmaster and if he gets thrown out, what will my mother do . . .' He swiped a hand across his eyes. 'I told him the lot. Everything. About my finding the porn on my father's laptop, and confronting him, and him saying . . . you know. That. And he believed me. I wish he hadn't. I wish I'd cut my tongue out before . . .'

'You feel you betrayed your father?'

'Yes.'

'Even though he traduced your character and threw you out?'

'I've ruined him!'

'He ruined himself. It was his decision to access porn.'

'He's a good headmaster, he's done a lot for that school.'

'If someone else had blown the whistle on your father, wouldn't you have thought it the right thing to do?'

A mutter that didn't make it into words.

'You still care about him?'

'I hate him!' The lad clutched his head. 'I've hated him for years, for his snide remarks to Mum and the way he used to put me down.'

'He's an inadequate personality,' said Bea. 'Afraid of a much brighter son.'

'I think he loved me when I was small, and I loved him. But when I got older, when it was clear I was never going to excel at sport like my elder brother . . . that's when it all started to go wrong. I realized I was cleverer than him, and that helped me not care so much what he said to me, and even to be sorry for him. I took the high moral ground, thinking myself so much better than him, but it turns out now that I'm just as filthy, just as . . . I don't deserve to . . .' He shook his head, unable to continue.

'I'm with you,' said Bea. 'Just. So you feel you did the wrong thing in telling on him? I'm not sure that you did, but then I'm looking at this from the outside. I think that a headmaster who accesses that kind of porn deserves investigation.'

'Oh, he'll get that all right. They'll be down on him with inspectors and police and everything. He might even go to prison.'

'We all make choices which affect our future as we grow older,' said Bea. 'Sometimes the choices we make alter our perception of ourselves. Until last night you hadn't realized you wanted revenge. Usually it's too late to do anything about a destructive action, but sometimes you can rectify or soften what you've done. Suppose you were to warn him, now, tonight? Tell him to get rid of his laptop. Dump it. Burn the hard drive, or whatever you have to do to remove the evidence. He'd still be investigated, still be frightened, maybe lose some credibility. But he might keep his job, and if he keeps his nose clean, he might see his time out in the usual way.'

Oliver looked at her, and through her.

She said, 'And you will rethink about going to university, won't you?'

The phone rang again. Bea started, but Oliver didn't seem to have heard it. Someone was leaving another message. Max? Yes, Max. Bea didn't move to pick it up. It was more important not to interrupt Oliver's chain of thought. What he did now might well affect the whole course of his life. She began to pray. *Dear Lord, be with Oliver. I don't know if what he did was right or not. Perhaps it was. But he's damaged himself almost as much as he's damaged his father. Put the right words into his head. Into my head. Be with us both.*

By the time she'd finished, Max had stopped speaking. Oliver brought his gaze back into focus, and reached for his mobile phone.

Bea said, 'You'll want this conversation to be private.'

She slipped out of the room with her mug of hot chocolate, which was no longer very hot, but would do. She drifted into the big living -room, without putting on the lights. She stood beneath Hamilton's portrait, and toasted him. 'Here's to you, my best friend and true love. I wonder what you'd have done in my place. Told Oliver he was right to tell on his father? I'm not sure he was. He doesn't think he was. Besides which, haven't I heard you say that every man deserves one warning? Although I must say, Mr Ingram doesn't seem the kind of man I'd normally go out of my way to help. But Oliver is, isn't he?'

The answerphone light was flashing, but she left it alone, her ears on the stretch to hear what Oliver would do next. He put his head round the door. 'Thanks. I'll be off to bed now. See you in the morning.'

Bea told herself that she didn't need the details, even though she would have liked to hear them. She depressed play on the answerphone. The first call was from Maggie, high on excitement.

'Mrs Abbot, are you there? I tried a couple of times earlier but you weren't picking up. Anyway, this is just to say not to expect me in tomorrow morning because I'm off with Zander, Charlotte and Liam to Bruges for a couple of days. Liam's rented a car and booked us on an early train through the tunnel. Luckily Charlotte has a driving licence. Can you believe it? I can hardly believe it myself!

'Zander didn't say anything about it when we were out today, but Liam's talked him round. I'm just walking on air, and so is Charlotte. I dropped by earlier to collect my passport and a couple of jazzy tops to make the boys' eyes pop out. I borrowed your small overnight bag, because Liam says Zander wants me to put in something else that he needs when we get over there. Hope you don't mind. I just didn't have room in my suitcase for everything we're taking. We'll be there in time for a late lunch tomorrow, back on Wednesday night, so I'll see you Thursday morning, if I don't oversleep.

'Oh, and by the way, you can stop worrying about Philip. He contacted Charlotte to say he was having a couple of days out of town – Brighton, I think it was – with a friend, and would be back next weekend. So we can go off with a clear conscience. Byeee.'

Bea shook her head, but smiled. She had a feeling that this romance with Zander wasn't going to go very far – it was too hot, too soon – but Maggie was old enough to make her own mistakes and if she did get a couple of days of pampering in Bruges, well and good. It was good news that Philip would be back at the weekend. She must ring Velma and tell her.

The second message was from Max, who sounded pretty peeved that she wasn't there after all the fuss she'd been making, leaving him messages all over the place. 'For you must realize I'm a busy person nowadays, trying to satisfy all and sundry before we fly out for our summer break. In fact, we're on our way to the airport now. The Maldives, three weeks of sunshine. I'll keep in touch, of course, but don't worry so much. You do get yourself in such a twitch, worrying about things quite unnecessarily. Nicole sends her love, naturally.' The phone went dead.

Bea would have given Max a piece of her mind if he'd been standing there in front of her. Would the taxman wait till he got back? Unlikely. Grrr.

Bea tried to phone Velma to say Philip would be back next weekend, but of course the phone was switched off, so she left a message.

She took her half-empty mug out to the kitchen. Oliver had left all the lights on in there, the radio still playing, and a plateful of half-eaten toast on the table. Of course. Bea switched off the radio, swept dirty plates into the dishwasher, refreshed her own drink and went upstairs to bed.

Rafael believed you made your own luck in life, but just occasionally everything seemed to conspire against him. The medal collector wouldn't let him into his house and then, after he'd been kept waiting half an hour for the others to arrive, Zander had said he wouldn't play. Apparently God had been telling him not to get mixed up in anything dicey. The Zander we all knew and loved had been brainwashed.

Rafael had tried to sit on his anger, but had made it quite clear that he couldn't afford to let Zander disobey him. For crying out loud, didn't he realize how deep he was in already? He wasn't being asked to do anything dangerous, was he? He didn't have to carry the stuff abroad himself. The girls hadn't a brain cell between them and would do it for him, no problem. Customs might check for explosives and drugs, but the car would be clean, the girls as innocent as newborn babies, so where was the risk?

But Zander had refused to listen, had even turned his back on Rafael! How dare he! Luckily they'd met in the quiet car park of a Tube station, dimly lit and deserted between infrequent trains. Before he had time to think, Rafael's wicked little knife had shot out and felled the brute. Brains against brawn. A few kicks to Zander's head made Rafael feel better. After a while killing really became the easiest option.

He told Liam to strip the body of all identification – they'd need Zander's mobile phone for a start – and roll it under some bushes for an early-morning commuter to find.

Thinking rapidly, Rafael decided how to explain Zander's disappearance. Liam must text Charlotte, using Zander's phone, to say he couldn't make Bruges as he'd been sent overnight to another office to deal with an emergency. His belongings must be moved from the flat. Liam could do that.

Liam was jittery. Was he going to become a problem? Stupid oaf! If Rafael hadn't needed him to collect the goods from the girls and hand them over to Mr Van, he would have got rid of him, too.

Everything would work out all right. Well, almost everything. Rafael was still angry about missing that picture. If only Philip would answer his phone!

Nine

Monday morning

Bea woke with a start. Had she set the alarm? Had she over-slept? At that moment the alarm shrilled, and she killed the noise. Then came the realization that there'd be no cup of tea brought up for her today, and that the house was unnaturally quiet.

She wasn't missing Maggie, was she?

Oliver; how was he coping this morning?

The next thought – which got her sitting upright – was that she was due to spend a couple of hours cleaning Maggie's flat that morning. She did not, definitely not feel like doing it. Suppose she got one of the agency cleaners to do the job and squared it with Maggie later? After all, there was nothing more to be found at the flat. Well, there was Liam's room to go through but Maggie had done that and surely it wasn't necessary for Bea to do the work herself?

She swung her legs out of bed. Hamilton had always said they should check and check again before taking action. Maggie might well have missed something, being infatuated with Zander. Bea groaned. By now Maggie, Charlotte and their two swains would be well on the way to Bruges, perhaps already in the Tunnel or even emerging into sunlight in France. It was all very well for some.

Oliver might be sleeping late after all that trauma yesterday. Bea told herself she would support him in whatever way necessary to get him to university. On the other hand, she sincerely hoped he wouldn't leave her.

She remembered that Philip was returning next weekend. Good. Sandy was going to be operated on today. Not so good. Bea sent up an arrow prayer for him and prepared herself to face the day.

Oliver was tousle-haired and sleepy-eyed at breakfast. Also monosyllabic. Bea decided that she wouldn't refer to their late-night discussion unless he did. Which he didn't. She remembered the lost correspondence from the tax office and winced. Well, she had more urgent things to think about now, didn't she?

She reminded him that she was due to clean at Maggie's flat that morning and he roused himself to say he'd work on Philip's phone while she was out. She told him to put his dirty crockery into the dishwasher and he did so, while sending such a wounded look her way that she wished she hadn't mentioned it.

Then off she went down the hill to the flats, wearing her cleaner's gear. She had a quick exchange of opinions about the weather with Randolph, the doorman, and went up in the lift to Maggie's floor.

Once inside, she sniffed the air. Surface dust, surface dirt, another stain on the carpet. Luckily the Friday night party had been upstairs or it would have been much worse.

The boys' bathroom was a tip, of course . . . how did they manage to get it so dirty in a couple of days? She would give Liam's room the once over and skim through the rest . . . except that there was a Do Not Disturb sign on Liam's bedroom door, the sort of sign hotels used.

She couldn't work out what it meant. Surely Liam couldn't be here still? He and Zander should be in France by now. Bea raised her hand to knock on the door and heard an unmistakeable fart. Someone was occupying Liam's bedroom.

Frowning, she went on into the sitting room and started work there. The stains on upholstery and carpet needed expert attention, but she did a superficial job of dusting and tidying. The boys' bathroom was next. Philip had taken his shaving things with him when he left. If Liam and Zander had left that morning, then their kits ought to be missing, too. But they weren't. Both were still there. What was going on?

Feeling anxious, she checked Philip's room, which looked exactly as she'd left it, except that someone had closed the window that she'd left open. Charlotte? Probably. Bea didn't bother to do any cleaning there.

She took the vacuum cleaner to Zander's room, which was a mess. This rather surprised her, since she'd assessed him as being neat and tidy. She stood in the doorway, trying to make sense of what she saw. His clothes had been pulled out of the wardrobe and chest of drawers and stuffed higgledy-piggledy into his suitcase and sports bag. Neither would close properly, and there were still a lot of his belongings left over. A good leather jacket hung over the back of a chair, and he'd forgotten to pack his shoes, or his books.

She moved into the room to see better. An expensive laptop had arrived in her absence. A black dustbin bag was under his desk. She lifted a corner to reveal the papers that had been stored in the drawers. His briefcase had been knocked over. It was still locked.

What was going on? If Zander had gone to Bruges, why had he left everything in such a mess? Surely he'd only need a small overnight bag for a couple of days in Bruges? But this . . . confusion? It looked as if he were planning to move out of the flat and had been interrupted before he finished packing. But why?

A noise from down the corridor made her jump, and she hastily picked up the vacuum cleaner and moved out of Zander's room.

A strange man dressed only in tracksuit bottoms opened Liam's door and blundered out, groaning, heading for the bathroom. He caught sight of Bea and froze, mouth agape. Unshaven and unkempt, he looked like a killer weasel with a narrow head and tousled, thinning mouse brown hair. His gaze fell on the vacuum cleaner she was carrying, and he relaxed. Yawned. Rubbed his eyes, clutched his head.

Would this be Liam? Presumably. She wished she'd had the sense to get a description of him. She wondered if she should offer to get him some black coffee but decided that a cleaner wouldn't, so she didn't.

He cleared his throat, still clutching his head. 'Mrs Thing? Forgot about . . .'

A mobile phone bonged. He staggered back into his room, reaching for the mobile phone on his bedside table. Bea could see him through the half-open door. She didn't want to start up the vacuum cleaner, which would have drowned out his conversation, so she got out her duster and started on the skirting boards, which certainly needed attention.

'Charley?' His voice was so croaky, he could hardly get the words out. 'Sorry. Bad head. Yeah, had to work all night, will join you later . . . yeah, sad about Zander, but Maggie'll get over it . . . yeah, yeah, I know the time.' Through the half-open door, Bea saw Liam look at his watch and half rise to his feet, horrified. He cleared his throat again. 'Yeah, it's later than I . . . look, hold on a minute. I've got to . . .'

He dropped the phone and lunged across the corridor and into the bathroom. There were retching sounds, and then the sound of running water. Bea moved down the corridor into the kitchen, leaving the door open behind her.

Liam returned to his room, wiping his mouth. He sounded more lively when he picked up the phone again. 'Sorry about that. The old tummy playing up . . . yeah, yeah, I'll be all right in a bit. So you're through into France, and everything's gone to plan?' A long pause while Charlotte quacked at him.

Bea could still catch a glimpse of him in profile, but apparently he didn't see her presence as a problem, for he continued his conversation without bothering to lower his voice.

'You find driving on the other side of the road difficult? I'm sure you're managing OK. Have you stopped for coffee? Well, you'll soon be in Bruges and . . . you need the name of the hotel?

Now what was the name? I can't think straight this morning. Oh, hang on. I've got it. The Belfry, right behind the belfry, anyway. Two double rooms booked in my name. If we miss one another, we'll meet in the Markt at six, on the steps of the post office . . . Yes, I'm sorry about Zander, too. He was really cut up about it, but if he wants to climb the ladder at work, he's got to jump when they need him to sort out a problem. Look, I'm taking the next Eurostar train, see you in the Markt at six. My friend's due then, and we can all four of us go out on the town, right? . . . What was that? . . . You're breaking up . . . curses . . . my battery's running down. Look, don't ring me again. I'll text you, instead.'

He shut off the phone with eyes that had difficulty in focusing and groaned. Addressing the air in front of him, he said, 'I did make the booking, didn't I? Ouch! She'll kill me . . .!' He scrambled off the bed and made it to the kitchen to switch on the kettle. Bea moved to one side, to let him pass. This time when his eyes fell on Bea, he seemed to have second thoughts about her being there. 'You can do my bedroom now, and then make yourself scarce, right?'

'But . . .' said Bea, thinking she ought to object to having her hours cut short.

'Just do it, right?' He reached for the instant coffee.

Bea went into his room. It stank of stale gin. She opened a window and started to make the bed, listening out for Liam's return all the while. How long did she have to poke around? Not long. Her foot kicked an empty gin bottle under the bed. She got down on hands and knees to check, but there was nothing else under the bed. Not even a dirty glass. He must have drunk from the neck of the bottle. Ugh.

The room was tidy enough, and after Maggie's ministrations on Friday, reasonably clean. There was a portable telly, new-ish. CDs, DVDs, whatever. An iPod. Liam liked porn magazines, apparently. Maggie had spotted them, too. Bea wondered whether Charlotte knew about them, or didn't care. There were two suitcases at the bottom of the big built-in wardrobe. He'd left his mobile on his bedside table. She would have loved to have seen what numbers were in its memory, but didn't dare.

Bedtime reading was raunchy paperbacks and spy thrillers. Well, at least he did read something. A locked drawer in a solid oak chest of drawers probably contained paperwork. There was a flutter of opened mail and some unpaid bills on the table by the window. A different outlook from Philip's. Nicer. Everything was just as it should be.

Liam appeared in the doorway, looking fractionally better than before. 'Out, you,' he said. Bea didn't dare protest. She shrugged, put her cleaning things away, and left the flat.

She was out of the building and walking up the street when her mobile phone rang. Maggie, in something of a state.

'Is that you, Mrs Abbot? Things have gone a bit pear-shaped. Zander's been called away by his firm so he couldn't come with us and as for Liam, he woke us up at some unearthly hour to say he'd had to work all night and we were to go on without him and he'd join us later. Charlotte said he looked ghastly and she's worried that he might be going down with flu or some-thing. She's tried to ring him back, but he's shut the phone off because the battery's running down, so she can't contact him. You've got the keys to the flat, haven't you? Do you think you could drop back and see if he's all right?'

'He's quite all right,' said Bea. 'Hungover, but recovering. He woke up and found me cleaning the place ten minutes ago and told me to get out. I really can't go back.'

'N-no, I suppose not.' Maggie didn't sound too sure about that. 'The thing is, we know the hotel's called The Belfry, so we can sign in there when we arrive, but we're supposed to meet this friend of his at six and if Liam's going to be late, we won't recognize him, will we? Liam's friend, I mean. It wouldn't matter really except that it's a business thing and we've got Liam's pres-ents for the man. Oh, I do hope Liam manages to get the next train, but even so, he's not going to be here for hours, is he?'

A prickle ran up and down Bea's back. The girls were carrying presents for someone they didn't know?

Maggie suddenly sounded brighter. 'Oh, Charlotte's just had a text from Liam. He's catching the 12.57 train. So that's all right. Sorry to have whinged.' She cut the phone off.

Bea stared at her mobile, cut the call and rushed up the road and into the house looking for Oliver.

'Oliver, what do you think of this? The two girls have arrived in Belgium without Zander – who's got to work – and also without Liam, who says he's joining them later. They're carrying gifts for a business friend of Liam's. What does that sound like to you?'

Oliver's swarthy skin took on a yellow tinge. 'Drugs! Tell me it's not true! They've really been stupid enough to carry gifts through Customs for someone else? Someone who didn't even travel with them?'

Bea sat down on the nearest chair with a bump. 'I hadn't thought of drugs, but of course it's possible. I was thinking it might be the stolen Millais. They could have cut the picture from the frame, rolled it up and put it in one case, and the frame – dismantled – may be in the other.'

'What!' He gaped. 'But . . . they wouldn't carry stolen goods out of the country, would they? That would make them accessories to murder!'

Bea ran her hand through her fringe, sweeping it across her forehead. 'It might not be that, it might be drugs, but . . . which is worse?'

Oliver tried to rise to his feet, and sat down again, both hands holding on to his desk. 'We've got to stop them.'

'How? They must be nearly at Bruges by now.'

'I'll get the next train. Oh, I can't. No passport. I was on my father's passport for years and then we didn't go abroad for some time and I always meant to apply for . . . I'm rambling.' Oliver ground his teeth. 'How could Maggie have been so stupid!'

'She's in love.'

'Which won't prevent her from spending some years in jail if what we suspect is true. The first thing Customs ask is, "Did you pack your case yourself?" And what will silly Maggie say? "Yes, of course," she'll say. And they'll have her banged up in no time. The stupid, stupid . . .!'

'It may not be drugs. It may be the picture. On balance, I hope it's the picture. My first thought was to ring the policeman I met the other day, he's not too bright but adequate. Only, that would be pointing him in the direction of Maggie and maybe the girls are only carrying tins of shortbread and . . . what was it? Some kind of expensive coffee service? I'm burbling. We don't *know* that they're carrying drugs. We don't *know* anything. It could all be perfectly innocent.'

'You don't believe that, and neither do I.'

Her mind was made up. 'I've got a passport. I'd better go after them. See if you can get me a slot on the train to take the car over. Or would it be quicker to fly? Can you find out for me? What will I need? Some Euros. No, wait. There are some in the safe for emergencies. For everything else, I can use my cards. See what you can unearth for me while I throw a few things together.'

She told herself not to panic, but couldn't help thinking that the facts pointed to danger. First Philip and the picture had disappeared. Now the two girls had been conned into carrying who knew what through Customs, without either of their menfolk to look after them. Zander had drifted off and Liam . . . who knew what scenario Liam had in mind? Would he really catch the next Eurostar train as promised?

This is crazy, Bea said to herself. I'm sure the girls are all right, and there's a perfectly good explanation for the men's behaviour. I hope. *Dear Lord, let it be so. And if there is something wrong, show me how to deal with it.*

She threw some things into an overnight bag – she had to use Hamilton's, since Maggie had taken hers – and hurried down-stairs to hear the good news and the bad from Oliver. 'I can't get you a slot to take the car over on the train. Fully booked, middle of holidays. The ferry would take too long. No seats for the plane till later this evening, and anyway, it takes ages to get to and from the airport this end and in Belgium. So I've got you a first class ticket on Eurostar, leaving just before one, arriving in Brussels two hours later.'

'That's the one Liam's supposed to be taking. Maybe I'll run into him on the train . . . but no, I doubt if he'll travel first class. We may well arrive in Bruges at the same time. It's going to be an interesting confrontation, isn't it?'

'What's the name of the hotel they're booked into?'

'The Belfry. I can't remember a hotel called The Belfry, but that's what he said.'

'It's the height of the tourist season. You usually stay somewhere else . . .?'

'The Europ. It's a bit further out, quiet, overlooking a canal, a family-run place. I'm sure they'll find me a room if they can. Can you get online to them? Or ring them. One of the big rooms at the top, if possible. How are we off for money?'

Oliver handed over two envelopes. 'One for euros, and one for sterling. The cab's booked and will be here straight away. Anything else?'

'A spot of prayer might come in handy.' She didn't know why she'd said that. She didn't know if Oliver believed in God or not. Anyway, it was said, and he didn't look astonished, so maybe it would be all right.

She didn't spot Liam in the departure area at St Pancras, but there were so many passengers milling about that she might well have missed him. She bought a newspaper to hide behind just in case. As they pulled out of the station, she rang Maggie. Ought she to warn the girls that they might be carrying a couple of bombs in their luggage?

'It's me, Mrs Abbot. I'm following your advice and taking a few days off in Bruges, hoping to arrive about five your time. Where are you now?'

'There's a thing!' shrieked Maggie, loud enough to make Bea to cower in her seat. 'Are you really coming, too? Charlotte, my boss is on her way over. Won't that be fun? Hi, Mrs Abbot, where are you staying? We've been trying to find this hotel that Liam booked us into but we think he's given us the wrong name, because there isn't one called The Belfry, though there is one just behind the belfry, which is a huge tower in the centre, and there are several hotels all round it, but so far we've not found one that knows anything about us . . .'

What on earth was Liam playing at?

Maggie was close to tears, but trying to laugh with it. ' . . . So here we are, sitting in the most amazing square, really stunning, the sun is shining, we're being chatted up by some husky Germans and a silky Italian . . . yes, we were, Charlotte. I know you are only waiting for your loved one, but I quite fancied the . . . yes, all right. Keep to the point. Well, the thing is, Mrs Abbot, that we're in a bit of a fix. I'm dying to dump the luggage somewhere and go off to do some sightseeing but Charlotte insists we have to sit here like lemons till Liam turns up and we haven't a clue when that's going to be . . . yes, all right, Charlotte, I'm not moaning but it is true, you know.'

Bea tried to think. 'It sounds as if there's been some mix-up over the hotel reservations. Listen, I'm booked into a quiet place that we always used to stay at. Let me ring them and see if they can fit you up for tonight, just till Liam arrives to sort things out.' This would at least get the girls and their suspect luggage off the streets. 'I'll ring you back in a few minutes.' She killed the call before Maggie could protest that Liam would see them right.

Had she got her address book in her bag? Thankfully, yes.

She got through to the hotel and yes, they'd booked her usual room for her, one of the family rooms on the top floor over-looking the canal. And yes, the one beside it was vacant if she would like to book it for her friends. What were their names? Delighted. They'd be arriving soon? Good. And yes, they had remembered that she liked an extra pillow on her bed, and a bottle of mineral water in her room.

Their thoughtfulness made Bea feel better. Hamilton had always booked them the same room at the top of the ancient building, because he liked its spaciousness and the way the ceiling was crisscrossed by huge wooden beams. Would she feel strange there now that she was a solitary widow? She told herself, You must look forward as much as you can.

She rang Maggie back. 'All fixed up. If you're in the Markt there's always a taxi or two cruising around by the post office. Take one to the Europ Hotel – the taxi will know where it is. I've booked you into a double room on the top floor, en suite. This will leave you free to dump your luggage, freshen up and do some sightseeing before Liam arrives. You can always fetch the presents for Liam's friends after you've made contact with him, can't you?'

There was a stir on the train. Bea added, 'We're just going into the tunnel now and I won't be able to use my phone for a bit, so . . .'

The signal cut off. Bea told herself to keep calm and every-thing would be all right. She remembered Velma and Sandy for the first time in hours and wondered if he were still on the operating table, and how Velma was coping.

Food was being served. And wine. Bea decided to forgo the wine, and to make some notes in case she had to call on the police to get the girls out of this mess. She needed to get it clear in her own mind, too. Paper? A pen? Where was the little note-book that always travelled with her? Not there. Sometimes she popped a notebook into the outside pocket of her overnight bag . . . but she'd got Hamilton's instead of her own and . . . ah, a notebook. His notebook.

She felt her breath catch in her throat. She'd bought this red leather-covered book for him at Smythson's three Christmases ago, knowing how he appreciated quality in every-thing he used. He'd used it as a commonplace book, to make notes when he was away from his computer, lists of things to do, odd reflections that had occurred to him about people, about life. He'd always used a black ink pen, his handwriting square, very deliberate.

On the first page he'd written his name, address and gone on to add 'The World, The Universe', just as small children did. Next there came a list of people they ought to send postcards to when they went on holiday. He must have popped it into his overnight bag, forgetting that they'd decided at the last minute to take only two large suitcases with them on their round the world trip. He'd never use it again.

She turned her head to the window, to the blank black tunnel wall, her throat closing up. She didn't realize she was crying until one of the train attendants asked her if she were all right. She forced herself to smile and nod.

She unclasped her fingers from round the book, found the first clean page, and jotted down everything she could remember people had said about Philip and the missing picture. Hamilton wouldn't have wanted her to waste the book. Hamilton would have wanted her to be methodical, to take notes, to double-check. Hamilton had inscribed a short prayer on the inside of the front cover. 'Dear Lord, be with me in all I say and do today.'

An appropriate prayer for all occasions.

One hour from leaving St Pancras and they were in France and approaching Lille. Oh, the flat, flat fields of France and Flanders . . . so different from the rolling English countryside. Once they'd left Lille, she tried Maggie again. 'Have you found the hotel, Maggie?'

'We've just got into the room. Wow! What a stunning view! Yes, it is, Charlotte. Don't be silly. Mrs Abbot, it's very good of you to go to so much trouble, but when Liam arrives Charlotte will want to be with him, though as Zander's not coming, maybe I'll . . . but we'll have to wait and see what he says. We don't mean to sound ungrateful, but you do understand, don't you?'

'Of course. Leave a note at the desk as to where you'll be, and I'll try to catch up with you.'

Maggie's voice went faint. 'Hang about . . . Charlotte's phone's making noises . . .' A pause, and Maggie came back to Bea. 'Charlotte's just got a text through from . . . who did you say? From Zander? Why is he . . .? Oh!' A pause, and then Maggie came through to Bea again. 'Zander's just texted Charlotte to say that Liam's missed the one o'clock train but will definitely be on the one leaving about two. Which means he won't be here till about half past six. I wish he'd texted me! I'd have given him a piece of my mind!'

Bea said, 'Yes, but Charlotte shouldn't—'

Maggie wasn't listening. Her voice came ever more faintly. 'Look, Charlotte, look out of the window. Wow, we're right by the canal. Aren't these little bridges just dinky, and look . . . there are swans on the water . . . and ducks, too . . .'

Maggie cut the call as Bea's train drew smoothly into Brussels station. Bea collected her overnight bag and alighted, trusting that Maggie would prevail upon Charlotte to abandon her lovelorn wait for her swain. Now for the next train to Bruges.

Rafael was furious. It was bad enough that Liam had muffed the disposal of the body, but the loon had failed to clear the flat of Zander's belongings last night. His excuse? He'd been so tired he'd fallen asleep! Rafael would give Liam 'falling asleep' when this business was done and dusted. How could he have been so stupid! And letting the battery on his mobile phone get so low that he had to use Zander's! Of all the cretinous . . .!

Enough of that. Next problem: Liam had spent the morning clearing out Zander's belongings, which meant he wasn't going to catch a Eurostar train till two or maybe half past. Allow two hours to get to Brussels. The trains from Brussels to Bruges ran at half-hour intervals, taking fifty minutes for the journey. Mr Van was expecting to pick up the goods in the Markt at 6 p.m. on the dot, not one minute later, but whichever train he caught, Liam was not going to make it in time.

Meanwhile, the girls were on the loose without a minder. Would they hang around, waiting for Liam? Charlotte . . . yes, probably. The Maggie bird was another matter. She was a singleton on the prowl, who could be picked up by anyone who took a fancy to her and then . . . Rafael started to sweat. Suppose she told a complete stranger that she was carrying a present for a man she didn't know? It didn't bear thinking about.

Rafael told himself that he was good at solving problems. So what should he do about this one? Answer: get Van to pick the goods up himself, or use his driver to do so. He could make contact with the girls, chat them up and relieve them of the goods. Liam must phone the girls, find out where they'd be at six and tell them to expect Mr Van. Problem solved.

Ten

B ea took a taxi from the station to the hotel, where she was greeted with pleasure by Erik the Red and his wife. They were a formidable pair, charming, intelligent and speaking four or more European languages. Bea saw them look past her as she came through the front door, expecting Hamilton to follow her in. She braced herself to tell them that Hamilton had died, and they commiserated without going on about it. Bea had been afraid she might burst into tears when she spoke his name, but managed not to do so.

Erik the Red – so called because of the colour of his hair – said her young friends had checked in but gone out again. And no, they hadn't left a message for her.

Bea confided in him. 'They were supposed to have been accompanied by their boyfriends for a short holiday, but one has been delayed and the other couldn't make it. They are, perhaps, a little naïve in thinking that the remaining one will meet them as arranged.'

The hotel manager was worldly wise. 'You think he might not be entirely reliable? If it had not been for your recommendation, we would not have given them a room tonight, because the dark one insisted her boyfriend had booked them into a hotel somewhere else, but given them the wrong name by mistake. We don't want to keep a room for people who might decide not to stay at the last minute.'

His wife was one step ahead of him. 'You think the boyfriend might have a bad reason for bringing the girls here, but not coming himself?'

Bea tried not to gasp. Did they think the girls were being targeted by white slave traffickers? Gracious! Knowing the reason the girls had been encouraged to come to Bruges, Bea was inclined to dismiss the suggestion out of hand. Of course she knew it sometimes applied to girls from poor countries, tricked into thinking they had jobs in a city only to find their passports confiscated and they themselves forced to become prostitutes.

This didn't apply to Maggie and Charlotte, but Bea decided to use this suspicion to her own advantage. 'Yes, perhaps the girls are somewhat naïve. I will pay the bill for their room, whether they occupy it or not. If the boyfriend turns up and whisks them off to another hotel and they want to go with him, I can hardly stop them. But like you, I feel something is not quite right about their arrangements. I will try to find them and check on the boyfriend, just in case.'

'The tall girl said she would take the one-hour tour in the citybus and then go on to the Chocolate Experience. The other said she'd go back to the Markt, because her boyfriend had promised to meet her there.'

'Good,' said Bea. She picked up her key. 'As a matter of interest, would you contact the police if girls disappeared from your hotel?'

'Of a certainty.'

This was reassuring, even if it was highly unlikely that her two girls were being targeted as sex slaves. Bea dumped her bag in her room, noting in passing that the flowers in the window boxes this year were vibrant, purple petunias. The last time she had been here with Hamilton . . . no, best not think about that. Yet she lingered at the window, renewing her acquaintance with the panorama of canal and ancient buildings, the skyline topped with towers, spires and twisted turrets. She leaned out, as she always did when she arrived, to check that she could still glimpse the restored windmills to the west. The sky was a pellucid blue. Egg-shell blue. The light-blue sky of Flanders.

She went downstairs and out into the sunshine, heading for the Markt in the centre of town. Somehow or other she was going to have to get Charlotte to open her luggage and check on what she'd been carrying for Liam. Drugs or a stolen picture. Which? And then what?

The Markt square was filled with tourists of all nationalities, posing for pictures, waiting in a queue to take a ride in a horse-drawn carriage, or gathering in groups around a tour leader to hear something of the history of the ancient buildings with their stepped gables and the towering belfry.

Nowhere was there a dark-haired, bespectacled girl with a fringe to be seen.

Bea tried to think how Charlotte would act, alone in a public place. She would have a coffee, of course. And then, perhaps, a tea and a cake? There were no cafés on the side of the square which contained the town hall and post office, so she would choose a café which would give her a sight of their steps. Bea walked past each one, searching the faces of tourists sitting at tables which were divided from the hoi polloi by ironwork stands of flowering plants. No, Charlotte wasn't in any of those.

Perhaps Charlotte would need to visit the toilets in the courtyard behind the belfry. As usual in Belgium, the toilets were immaculate, overseen by a dragon lady who made a living by charging tourists for their visits. Charlotte wasn't in the loos.

Would she have visited one of the art galleries housed in the same building as the belfry? No, she wasn't in either of those.

Bea thought that by now Charlotte might be as annoyed with Liam as she was besotted by him. She might well be lured into one of the main shopping streets which led off from the Markt. And why not? She could pop back to the square now and then. She could even see the steps of the town hall from the first shops. And there, not far down, was the entrance to Inno, a department store which would surely attract any woman with money in her pocket.

Bea reminded herself that Charlotte had probably started to prowl around the shops some time ago. She'd have done Inno and moved on by now. Did Charlotte like shoes? If so, she might well have indulged in some retail therapy. Bea wandered down the street, familiarizing herself with the latest fashions, tempted to enter one of the coffee shops, pausing to admire the colourful window displays. Would Charlotte have been lured into buying lace or chocolate? Belgian chocolate was the tops. But no, Charlotte wasn't in any of those places.

For some years now Bea had been buying clothes in Rubica, a shop which stocked well-made fashions with a flair. Hamilton had always accompanied her on visits to this shop, because his sense of colour and of what clothes would flatter Bea was spot on. So, when she came to the corner of the square where the shop was to be found, Bea hardly hesitated before walking in.

Annemie and Jeannine greeted her with warmth and, as the hotel people had done, looked for her husband to follow her in.

Bea had to explain again, and was touched by their genuine if restrained reaction. How long ago was it? Ah, what a pity. Did she need to buy anything today? Would it help? Sometimes it did.

Well, yes; she'd seen a swirly tobacco-coloured skirt in the window which would be just the thing for autumn, and what about a smart jacket to go over it? Rubica's styles were just that bit different from those to be found in the high streets of Britain.

Jeannine knew her size, of course. She could tell exactly what size anyone was, the second they walked through the door. Garments were produced with a swish and a flourish. Bea went into a changing cubicle, slid into the skirt and a creamy silk top, pulled on the matching jacket and stepped out into the shop to check on her back view . . . only to come face to face with Charlotte.

The girl looked exactly like a hedgehog, peering from under a too long fringe through heavy, dark-rimmed glasses. 'What are you doing . . .? I don't understand. You're Mrs Thing, aren't you? But you can't be . . . are you really Maggie's boss as well?'

'Well, yes, I am,' said Bea, wondering whether this was a stroke of luck or of dire misfortune. How could she turn this encounter to her advantage? 'I'm also newly widowed. My dear Maggie very kindly thought it would be a distraction for me if I went out into the field again, so . . .'

Charlotte was not convinced. She looked at her watch, gnawing her lip. She was holding a sad-coloured blouse which was all wrong for her colouring, and wearing jeans which bunched around her bottom and heels.

Bea said, 'Look, may I treat you to a coffee somewhere? I'm hoping to catch up with Maggie later on, but . . .'

'I mustn't be too long. I'm meeting Liam – my boyfriend – at six.'

'So we have time for a quick one, right?'

Charlotte was not gracious. She shrugged, gave the blouse to the hovering Jeannine and said, 'I wish I were tall enough to wear the clothes you've got on. They don't seem to have anything to suit me in here.'

They did, of course, but Charlotte was clearly unable to distinguish between what would and what would not look right on her.

'Coffee?' said Bea, being bright. And to Jeannine, 'Would you put these aside for me? I'll come back tomorrow for them, right?'

Once out of the shop Charlotte would have dived into the nearest café catering for tourists, but Bea led her across the road into a quiet lane where there was a coffee shop patronized by residents and regular visitors who knew a good thing when they saw one. It was quiet, immaculate, and with its dark panelling encouraged a feeling of warmth and security. Ideal for putting Charlotte at ease.

Charlotte grumbled, 'I've drunk too much coffee already.'

'I'm only just off the train,' said Bea. 'I really need something. My treat.'

'I've got to be changed and back in the market by six.'

Bea tried not to notice how ungracious the girl was. 'Plenty of time.'

'Are you really Maggie's boss? I don't understand. This is all just so . . . Liam missing the train, and Maggie being difficult and going off by herself, and now you turning up. It's all just so . . . stupid.'

'Let me explain. I run a small domestic employment agency and Maggie is my PA, currently organizing a make-over on the offices in my house. My husband died a while back and I've been a bit depressed. You know how it is?'

Charlotte nodded. 'My mum gets depressed. Takes pills for it.'

'Yes, well, I didn't want to start taking pills—'

The waiter took their order.

Bea continued, 'So I tried to work harder than ever. Maggie said I ought to take a holiday, and I told her I always used to come here with my dear husband and buy some clothes and . . . well, she said I ought to come again, though I didn't think, really, that I ought to do so. I thought it might make me feel worse, if you see what I mean?'

'My mum's the same. Wouldn't come down to visit me in London this year because she always used to come with Dad. I had to go up there, instead.'

Bea was pleased to see they'd established some kind of rapport. 'Then dear Maggie wanted to spread her wings, find herself a place in a flat where she could meet lots of new people. She's been through a nasty divorce, you know. I didn't want her to move out really, but I could see it was for the best.'

Charlotte nodded. 'Stand on her own two feet. Meet people.'

The waiter brought coffee and strawberry tart for Bea, and

hot chocolate for Charlotte. Bea paid the bill and decided to take a risk. 'Maggie moved out, and of course I was happy for her, but just a little worried that she'd fallen for a young man about whom she knew nothing.'

'Zander. He's OK. If you like that sort of thing.'

Bea said, 'I just hope Maggie's not going to get hurt again.'

Charlotte shrugged. 'I told her he wasn't taking her seriously, when she was griping about his letting us down. She didn't like that, but it was for her own good. It's funny, though. I was surprised when he said he'd come with us to Bruges – he's a workaholic, you know – but I was even more surprised when he cried off. I didn't think he was the sort to break promises.'

She dived into her handbag to produce a mobile phone. 'Just checking. Liam's phone is out of juice, so he's contacting me through Zander.' She sighed. 'No more news. I keep hoping . . . but I know it's ridiculous. He can't possibly be here before six, and maybe not till just after.'

'You must be looking forward to it. Where is he taking you tonight, and will he want Maggie in tow? Do you think I should take her off somewhere else?'

'I suppose so. I certainly don't want her around when I'm with Liam. She doesn't think of anyone but herself. It's all "me, me, me!" She never gave a thought to how I'd feel, being left all by myself in a strange place.'

Bea sought for something else to say. 'What do you plan to wear tonight?'

'I brought something dressy with me, though it doesn't really matter what I wear, because Liam's not like that. He loves me for myself, and despises those girls who spend all their time and money in beauty treatments, and starving to make themselves thin.'

Bea smiled, but didn't comment. Was the girl really that naïve? 'You'll be wanting to get back to the hotel to change.'

Somehow she got the girl to her feet and out on to the pavement. Charlotte stared around her. 'The waiter in the square said this is the main shopping street. It's not very grand, is it? More like a country town.'

'But more than adequate.' Bea pointed across the road. 'Have you been in any of the churches, or the cathedral? There's a wonderful Michelangelo statue which you ought to see.'

Charlotte wasn't interested in the statue, or in churches –

however old and beautiful. 'We mustn't be late. Maggie said we'd meet back at the hotel to change before we go out to meet Liam. I'm really looking forward to a ride in one of those horse-drawn carriages.'

Bea thought, but did not say, that Charlotte was living in cloud cuckoo lane. But there, perhaps Liam would treat her to a good evening out. Hopefully.

Back at the hotel Bea learned that yes, Maggie had returned and gone up to their room already, and that there were no messages for any of them. Bea went up to the top floor with Charlotte and made sure Maggie let the girl into their shared room, before going into hers next door.

She had a quick shower and put on a new-ish trouser suit in her favourite silvery-grey, wishing that Maggie hadn't borrowed a dull pink jacket that would have been ideal to go over it. It was about time that young lady learned that what was Bea's did not necessarily also belong to Maggie.

She was brushing her hair when the internal phone rang.

Erik the Red, speaking faster than usual. 'Mrs Abbot, a strange thing. Has someone come to your door? No? A young man came a few minutes ago, with a bouquet of flowers. He asked if the two girls, Charlotte and Maggie, were booked in here. When I said that they were, he wanted to go up to their room. Naturally, I refused. He then asked to use our toilets, which are in the basement. He did not return to the hall and he is not now in the toilets. Perhaps he has tried to go up the stairs without permission?'

At that moment there was a knock on Bea's door. 'I think he's just arrived. If I need help . . .?'

'I shall be with you in one minute.'

The knock came at the door again, and a man asked, 'Are you there, Charlotte? Maggie?'

Bea cradled the phone and opened her door, but there was no one there. A fire door closed off the short corridor to the right, which led to the other penthouse room. Bea pushed the door open and saw a huge bouquet of flowers in the hands of a tall man, who was now tapping on the girls' door.

'Can I help you?' asked Bea, stepping through the fire door to confront the intruder. He was so large that he loomed over her. How soon would Erik be able to get here?

The door to the girls' room opened, and Charlotte's head appeared. She looked puzzled. 'Who . . .?'

'Herman, very much at your service,' said the young man, pressing the bouquet upon her.

Charlotte gaped. 'Oh, but . . . I mean, we weren't expecting you yet. Liam said we were to meet you at six in the market place.'

'I thought it would be charming for us to become acquainted before, so that we will all have a perfect evening. With two such beautiful ladies, this will be a time to remember, no? May I not enter?'

'Afraid not, no,' said Maggie, her head appearing above Charlotte's. 'We don't know you from Adam and . . .'

'Of course we know him,' said Charlotte, protesting. 'Liam said his friend Herman would be meeting us and here he is.'

Was Charlotte taking the opposite point of view because she was annoyed with Maggie for leaving her on her own that afternoon? Charlotte tried to open the door, but Maggie blocked her. The young man pushed at the same time.

Bea thought it more than time to intervene. 'Girls, girls! Unseemly behaviour, don't you think? The hotel will have to call the police if you invite a strange young man into your room.'

'The police?' Herman took a quick step back.

'The police?' echoed Maggie, frowning.

'How ridiculous,' said Charlotte. 'He's a friend of Liam's, so of course he's welcome to—'

'Not to visit you in your room,' said Bea in her best schoolmistressy tone. 'Now, Mr Whoever, if you'd like to wait downstairs in the hall, the girls will be downstairs soon . . . after they've checked that you are who you say you are. After all, they only have your word for it that you've ever met Charlotte's boyfriend. How long have you known him, by the way?'

'Not long,' mumbled the young man, reddening. The outlines of his face and figure were beginning to blur with good eating and drinking, and he was on the verge of becoming flabby. He was expensively but casually dressed, exuding enough aftershave to asphyxiate everyone in reach. He looked at the door to the stairs, shifting from one foot to the other.

Bea said, 'Where did you meet Liam?'

'In a bar; what you call a public house. Holidays. London. Last year.'

'So you know him well? What's Liam's surname, may I ask?'

'It's Forbes,' said Charlotte, also reddening. 'Mrs Abbot, you are totally out of order. It's no business of yours if my fiancé arranges for me to meet one of his friends, is it?'

Bea noted that Liam had just been promoted from 'boyfriend' to 'fiancé' and winced.

'Look!' Charlotte flourished the outsize bouquet of flowers. 'He's brought me some beautiful flowers.'

The fire door opened and Erik appeared, gesturing the intruder should leave. 'I'm afraid hotel rules . . . we cannot allow guests to entertain men in their rooms . . . sure you understand . . .'

Herman departed with good grace.

'Well!' Charlotte flung herself back into the bedroom. Bea followed, closing the door behind her. The key was in the lock, and she turned it.

Maggie plumped down on the big double bed. She was wearing Bea's pink jacket over a pink top, and a long grey skirt. She looked presentable, her hair still chestnut in colour, though growing out to its natural dark brown. 'He didn't know Liam's surname and I don't believe he's a real friend.'

'So what?' Charlotte blustered, hiding the worm of suspicion. Charlotte was wearing a white peasant-style blouse, embroidered in red and blue, over a black skirt. She looked bunched up and uncomfortable. 'Liam sent him to look after us.'

Maggie wasn't so sure. 'How did he know we were in this hotel and on this floor?' She answered her own question, becoming indignant. 'Charlotte, you've been on the phone to Zander, and arranged it through him? How could you tell someone to come up to our room without consulting me?'

'It wasn't like that.' Charlotte twitched her blouse off her plump shoulders, and then hitched it up again. 'Liam's using Zander's phone because his own is out of order. Liam said he had a friend called Herman who'd collect us from the hotel and take the presents off our hands so that we'd be free to go out on the town and enjoy ourselves. I don't see anything wrong in that.'

Maggie was still frowning. 'But Charlotte, this Herman obviously isn't a great friend of Liam's, or he'd have known—'

'That's enough!' Charlotte snapped. She attacked her mop of hair with a brush, making it fly around her head in a fuzzy halo, hiding her face. 'Herman's perfectly charming and I'm sorry you don't like him. I'm delighted he's going to squire me around. You can stay here all alone and sulk, if you don't want to be seen out with him.'

Bea made her voice soft to defuse the tension in the air. 'What's worrying Maggie is the realization that you two have been set up in a scam, and if you're not careful, you're going to spend the night and the next few years of your lives in jail.'

'Wha . . . at?' Charlotte dropped her hairbrush and parted her bush of hair to look at Bea from under it. 'What on earth . . .? You evil woman, how dare you!'

Maggie had gone pale. 'Mrs Abbot, what do you mean? We haven't . . . honest, we haven't—'

'Let's put it this way,' said Bea, as calmly as she could. What if she'd got it wrong, and the 'gifts' for Liam's friend were just a coffee set and a tin of shortbread? 'You two girls have carried items through Customs on behalf of a friend who failed to accompany you at the last minute. These items are to be handed over to a man you don't know, by arrangement with your absent travelling companion. What does that sound like to you?'

'Doing a favour for a friend. And why not?' Charlotte was belligerent.

'The first thing a Customs officer will ask you is, "Did you pack your bag yourself?" And you will say—'

'Yes, of course.' Charlotte nodded like a toy puppet.

'And then he'll unwrap the "gifts" you were taking through Customs for your boyfriend—'

'Fiancé!'

'And what will he find? Not a coffee set and a box of shortbread, I'll be bound.'

Charlotte flushed with anger. 'You're being ridiculous. Liam showed me the coffee set. It's quite beautiful, Royal Worcester, all gold and hand painted.'

'You put it straight away into your case?'

'Yes. After he'd put some extra packing around the cups. He was worried they might be broken in transit.'

'You saw him do that? He took the box out of your sight for a while and returned it to you, all sealed up?'

Charlotte was silent. She pulled a hank of hair across her mouth and bit on it.

Maggie heaved the suitcase she'd borrowed from Bea on to the bed. 'There's one way to settle this.'

Charlotte squawked. 'You can't, Maggie. That's my suitcase and—'

'It's not your suitcase. It's the one we borrowed from Mrs

Abbot. We haven't even got keys for it, remember?' Maggie threw back the lid. Charlotte had unpacked and hung up her own things, and all that was left in the case was a large cardboard box, gift-wrapped and beribboned. Maggie ripped off the ribbons, ignoring Charlotte's cry of alarm. Under the gift-wrapping was a stout box in tasteful dark blue with gold lettering on it.

Inside the box was a layer of tissue paper.

Maggie threw that aside, and there were a number of bubble-wrapped objects, each one carefully positioned on a bed of more bubble-wrap. Each one Sellotaped into position.

'There you are, you see!' Charlotte had located her glasses and put them on. She was furious. 'Now look what you've done. How am I going to explain to Liam that you've ruined his gift-wrapping?'

Bea's pulse was racing. There was no picture here, so it must be drugs that the girls were smuggling. 'The packets are all pretty much the same size and shape. Where are the saucers, the cream jug and sugar bowl that you'd normally expect to see?'

'Why, underneath, I expect,' said Charlotte, reluctantly coming to look.

Bea picked up the nearest object and tore open the bubble wrap to reveal a small gold snuffbox, finely tooled. She turned it over and saw – or thought she saw, could she trust her eyes? – the logo for Fabergé on the back.

She collapsed on to the nearest bed. Her throat was dry.

Maggie seized another little bundle and unwrapped that, too. Another gold box, this time with a delicately painted miniature on the lid.

Charlotte said, 'I don't believe it!' Was she going to cry?

'How many . . .?' asked Bea.

Maggie counted. 'Nineteen. I don't understand.'

'If I'm right,' said Bea, 'these were stolen in a burglary not long ago. A burglary in which a man was killed.'

Maggie put both hands over her mouth.

Charlotte's phone rang. Moving like a sleepwalker, she took it out of her handbag and flipped it open. 'Charlotte here. Is that you, Liam? What have you got us into? There's no coffee set in the box you gave me to—'

Maggie snatched the phone from Charlotte, and shut it off. 'Forget it! Whatever he's got to say now, it's only going to lead us into more trouble. Think, Charlotte! Think! He's set us up. We're looking at years in prison!'

Monday afternoon

Rafael was furious at being interrupted at work. Hadn't he told that cretin not to phone him unless it were a matter of life and death? Liam was panicking, babbling. Out of control.

    The girls had rumbled what they were carrying.

    Rafael thought fast. 'Whereabouts are you?'

    'Just coming into Brussels. I'm not taking the train on to Bruges, no way. The girls will blab to the police, and they'll be waiting for me on the station when I arrive.'

    'Stop right there. Calm down.' If ever there was a time for Rafael to think quickly and calmly, this was it. First things first. 'What did the girls actually say?'

    'That they've found out what's in the coffee set box.'

    'Not the other?'

    'The tin that Maggie's carrying? Charlotte didn't say. We got cut off.'

    Rafael tried to concentrate. 'Get off in Brussels, go and have a coffee in one of the cafés in the station. Wait for me to ring back. I'm going to phone my contact, find out what's going on.'

    He cut off the phone. His boss put his head round the door, eyebrows raised. Rafael was needed. He did his best to smile. 'An emergency. A friend in trouble. One quick call should sort it.' He turned his back on his boss and punched numbers.

Eleven

Monday late afternoon

Charlotte collapsed on to the bed in a crumpled mess, hair tangled, blouse askew. 'I can't believe Liam knew about this. He owed someone a favour to help close a deal.'

'Who was this friend? Someone at work?'

Charlotte wasn't listening. 'He simply couldn't have known what was in the box.'

'Oh yeah?' said Maggie. 'Either way, he took you for a ride.' She whirled her own case on to the other bed. 'So, what am I carrying? Philip's picture?'

'What picture? Do you mean our Philip? What on earth are you talking about?'

Maggie pulled out a gift-wrapped box, about half the size of the one which had once contained a coffee set. She tore off the wrappings, handing them to Bea as she did so. This time Charlotte didn't object, though her lower lip came out in mutinous fashion.

'It can't be the picture. It's not big enough,' said Bea, thinking about drugs again. Oh, what had Philip got himself into?

Inside the box were some more bubble-wrapped packages, each one larger than the gold boxes they had uncovered before, but slimmer. Maggie unwrapped the first. A gold-framed miniature on ivory stared up at them, a sweet-faced, pink-cheeked young girl in a white mop cap with a pink bow on it.

'What the . . .?'

Bea put on her reading glasses. She unwrapped another with fingers that trembled. Another miniature, this time of a young man in doublet and hose, leaning against a marble pillar. He was holding a carnation in one long-fingered hand. 'Looks Tudor to me.'

Maggie swore under her breath.

Bea's mouth was dry. 'Are these from a museum, do you think?'

Maggie dropped the miniature she'd been holding as if it had bitten her. 'What do we do? Phone the police?'

Bea started to shake her head, reconsidered, and went back to shaking it. 'Explanations would be difficult and you'd be owning up to smuggling. Let's think this through.' She went to the door, unlocked it. 'We're assuming the stuff's genuine, but maybe it isn't. I've seen boxes like this in an exhibition in Somerset House, and their value is out of this world. I can't believe these are genuine. Perhaps they're copies with no real worth.' She hoped against hope that she was right. Bea held up the key. 'I'm just going to get my handbag from next door, make one phone call. I'll lock you in till I get back, to make sure Herman doesn't get at you.'

Herman wasn't in the corridor. She didn't think he would have been. Erik the Red was far too cautious to allow that young man out of his sight again. Would it be a good idea to ask Erik to call the police? No. Definitely not. They'd be stuck this side of the Channel with a load of stolen goods, without any good explanation as to how they'd come by them. Of course, if Liam could be lured to Bruges so that the police could arrest his contact here . . . but first things first. She needed to find out if these really were stolen goods.

She found her mobile and the card Mr Goldstone had given her. Fortunately he was at home and willing to speak to her.

'Mr Goldstone, I'm in Bruges trying to remedy a nasty situation which my young protégées have got themselves into. They were asked to carry presents through Customs for a friend . . . yes, I know, it was incredibly silly of them. One of the presents was supposed to be a valuable coffee set, a present for the friend's business contact over here. It turns out that the package contains gold boxes.'

The cracked, elderly voice put the right question. 'How many?'

'Nineteen.'

'There should be twenty.'

'Nineteen, each one swathed in bubble-wrap. There is also a box of miniatures. Do you know anything about those?'

The ancient voice grew stronger, reflecting the authority of the man. 'My friend Leo was killed for a collection of miniatures a couple of months ago. My dear lady . . . my very dear lady . . . forgive me. I must sit down.'

'I feel like that, too. Mr Goldstone, I was hoping they were just copies.'

He snorted. 'Rubbish! Gold boxes. Miniatures. I'd need to have a sight of them to be sure, but under the circumstances I think I can say you have stumbled across the proceeds from two robberies.'

'Yes.' Her voice faded. Oh, for a sip of water. She moved over to the table and poured herself a glass, blessing Erik, who never forgot that she and Hamilton always liked a couple of bottles of drinking water in their room.

He said, 'Have you a phone with a camera? Could you send me photographs of what you've found?'

'I'll see what I can do and ring you back.'

She returned to the girls' room, unlocking the door and locking it again behind her. Sweet chimes rang across the city. A quarter to six. There was a tense atmosphere in the room. Charlotte had her back to the room, talking on her mobile phone. Maggie was packing her bag, looking furious.

Bea said, 'What's going on?'

Maggie shrugged. 'I couldn't stop her. I turn my back for five seconds and she's on the phone, telling Liam everything!'

Bea drew in her breath. 'Before we do anything else, we've got to find out if these things are worthless copies or not. Lay those two boxes out on the windowsill where the light's best, will you, Maggie?'

Charlotte had heard. She relayed the information to Liam, listened and then turned in triumph to say, 'Of course they're only copies. How stupid of us not to realize.' She was flushed, with tears in her eyes. 'Oh, Liam, what a relief! You can't imagine what I've been thinking, worrying . . . so what time will you be able to pick us up? Shall we wait to have supper till you get here?'

Bea and Maggie exchanged eye-rolls.

Bea took photographs of the two boxes Maggie had unwrapped, turned them over to expose the hallmarks, and took more pictures. She sent the photos to Mr Goldstone.

He rang back straight away. His voice sounded strained. 'Fabergé, yes. And the other . . . I can hardly believe what you've shown me. They are priceless, both of them. If the others are as good as those . . . I think I need a brandy!'

So did Bea. 'Can you get me a description of everything that was taken in that particular robbery?'

Mr Goldstone grunted. 'Of course. It won't take me long. In the meantime, would you send me pictures of the rest? Only nineteen, you say? I wonder what happened to the twentieth.'

'The thief kept it for himself? As insurance against not getting a good price? Or perhaps he sent it over earlier, to prove he really had the goods? I really don't know. The other haul is perhaps even more important. I'll ring off and send you pictures of two of the miniatures.' She took photos of the miniatures, front and back, and sent them through to Mr Goldstone, who rang her back straight away.

'Genuine,' he said. 'Many, many times my friend Leo showed me his collection. I'd recognize them anywhere. Will you send me pictures of everything you've found? Then, if they're all genuine – and they look genuine to me – we have to decide what to do next. I've been trying to think . . . I have contacts with the police in various places, but not in Bruges.'

Despite her stated belief in Liam's innocence, Charlotte was hanging on to their every word, her face reflecting a swoop from hope to misery.

'Mr Goldstone, let me phone you back about this,' said Bea. 'In the meantime, may I ask you not to contact the police? Not until we've considered how best to get out of this tangle?'

'You don't want the girls to suffer? I understand.' A pause, while all three women awaited his verdict. Finally he said, 'If you involve the Belgian police, they will impound the goods and we won't see them again for years. Also the two girls will be arrested for smuggling. If you can get the goods back to Britain somehow or other, we might be able to hand them over to the authorities without involving your protégées.'

'It's not that simple. If we inform the police over here, we may be able to trap the people who were supposed to relieve us of the goods.'

Mr Goldstone grunted, said, 'Isn't it even more important to find out who is masterminding the thefts here in London? He's a killer, remember.'

Bea glanced at Charlotte, whose lower lip had come out. Charlotte was not going to help. Bea said, 'Charlotte's friend Liam was doing a favour for someone else when he asked her to bring the goods over here for him, but we don't know who. Liam may or may not have known what was in the packages. I don't know what to do, either. There's no obvious right or wrong solution, is there?'

'Keep me informed,' said Mr Goldstone, and switched off his phone. Bea switched hers off, too.

Charlotte was in tears. 'I'm not going to lead Liam into a trap.' She pressed buttons on her mobile. 'Liam, Liam. Answer the phone . . .'

Maggie made as if to stop Charlotte, but Bea held her back. 'He already knows we've discovered what's in the boxes, so he's not going to show up here, is he?'

Charlotte got through. 'At last! Listen, Liam, you're not to come to Bruges, do you hear? The police will be waiting . . . oh, right. That's good.' She deflated, her colour returning to normal.

Listening to him, she turned away from the others to face the window, though she probably wasn't seeing anything of the beauty outside. 'Yes, yes. I understand, of course I understand . . . no, of course you mustn't risk the police arresting you . . . as you say, it was all a joke that's gone wrong. If you could tell me who put you up to this, I'm sure that will help . . . you can't. Why not? . . . oh, I'm sure he wouldn't really do that. I mean . . . that's sick! No, of course I believe you, but . . . when shall I see you again? . . . oh, but . . . no, of course, but . . . Liam, you do love me, don't you?'

After listening to his reply, she dropped the phone, tears spurting. Throwing herself back on to the bed, she went into full-scale hysterics, feet thrashing away, hands clenched, eyes tightly closed, bawling her head off.

Maggie put her hands on her hips, appalled and astonished. Bea went into the bathroom, poured a glass of water, and threw it into Charlotte's face. The girl hiccupped and gradually calmed down, her colour returning to normal.

Bea said, 'There's no point alerting the police this end. He's going straight back to London, isn't he?'

Charlotte hiccupped some more. 'He says he won't be able to see me again . . . oh . . .!' Her voice rose again.

Bea said, 'If you want some more water thrown over you . . .?'

Charlotte shook her head, trying to control herself. 'He said not to ring him back, that he was going to throw away his mobile, that he was fooled into this by a friend, but he won't say who it was because he's frightened what the man might do. Liam says . . . he says this man is capable of killing! But I can't believe that . . . not really. He's just joking, isn't he? Anyway, it's quite clear that none of this is Liam's fault.'

Maggie didn't accept that. 'Tcha! He knew we weren't carrying a coffee set and shortbread. He wrapped up the goods and gave them to us to carry, so how can he make out that he was fooled?'

'Come to think of it,' said Bea, 'how has he got hold of Zander's mobile phone?'

Charlotte held her bush of hair back from over her eyes. 'I don't know, do I? Oh, maybe he did say . . . yes, he said that his phone was running out of power, so Zander lent him his. Zander was getting a company one for his new job in the Midlands.'

Bea sat down to think about this. The explanation didn't seem to hold water. Liam hadn't known his phone was out of juice until that morning when Bea had been at the flat to clean and overhead him talk to Charlotte. Zander had already left by that time, hadn't he? Although there was the question of Zander's shaving kit. What was going on there?

Charlotte wailed, 'Everything's gone wrong. I was so looking forward to coming here and having a romantic evening with Liam, going on the boats and riding by moonlight in a horse-drawn carriage.'

Maggie was having none of it. 'And being serenaded by a gigolo? Yes, I was looking forward to it, too.'

'Zander wasn't in love with you, though. He was just passing the time. Liam really loved me.'

Both Maggie and Bea looked sceptical, but Charlotte was digging herself deep into the role of abandoned fiancée. She threw herself back on the bed, crying, 'My own true love!'

Bea was about to fetch another glass of water when the internal phone rang. Being nearest, she answered it. It was Erik. 'Is that Mrs Abbot? That young man is still here, waiting for the girls. He says he wants to take them out in his car to Damme for a meal. Shall I send him away?'

'Tell him I'll be down in a moment.' She cradled the phone, thinking that she didn't like the sound of the girls being taken out to dine some miles out of Bruges, where streetlights might not penetrate the shadows between the ancient buildings. Yet if she voiced her doubts, Charlotte for one might easily take the opposite point of view and insist on going.

'Girls, Herman's downstairs with a car to take you out to supper at Damme – that's a village some miles out of Bruges. Would it make you feel better to go?'

'I couldn't face it,' wailed Charlotte, enjoying the role of lovelorn lass. 'How could he possibly ask?'

'Is the food good?' asked Maggie. 'I'm hungry.'

Now it was Maggie who was feeling contrary enough to take the opposite viewpoint to Charlotte. Bea realized she'd have to handle the situation with care. 'Damme has many excellent restaurants. Have you enough money to pay the bill, in case he defaults – as Liam has done?'

'Herman wouldn't default,' said Maggie. 'Why should he? He's invited us out to make up for the boys' running out on us. At least . . .'

Bea seized on that moment of doubt. 'He's personable enough, and an evening out in Damme might be just fine, provided only that he isn't doing it to get at the "presents". I don't suppose there would be much harm in your going, provided you don't let him get you alone in a dark alley. Oh, and you'd better take enough money with you to cover the bill at the restaurant and a taxi back. Just in case.'

Maggie sank on to a chair, thinking about this. 'No, Mrs Abbot, you're right. It's not a good idea. Anyway,' here she looked at her fellow traveller in mingled pity and dislike, 'I don't think Charlotte's up to it.'

'Of course I am.' Charlotte sat upright, reaching for a tissue and blowing her nose. Her skin was blotchy and she looked a mess, but in her present mood she was as determined to oppose Maggie as Maggie was to oppose her. 'Just give me ten minutes to get myself organized.'

Bea held back a sigh. 'How about I go down and tell him you're still getting ready, but would prefer to dine somewhere within walking distance? If he insists the "presents" are handed over to him before he takes you out, then we'll know he's only inviting you out to get at the treasures. Is that all right by you?'

Both girls nodded assent, though with some reluctance on Charlotte's part. Bea considered that the girl would soon forget Liam if another suitor were to offer himself. That is, if Liam could ever have been considered a suitor, which Bea rather doubted.

Maggie was trying to be businesslike. Anything practical, and she was worth her weight in gold. 'While you're gone, I'll unwrap everything for you to photograph on your return.'

Bea went down to the foyer where Herman was sitting, long legs stretched out to trap the unwary. He looked annoyed to see Bea and not the girls. Erik the Red was behind his desk and dealing with someone enquiring for a room, but held up a folded piece of paper to Bea as she approached. 'A message for you, Mrs Abbot.'

Herman got to his feet, looking over her shoulder. 'Charlotte and Maggie?'

'Too upset to come down yet.' She thanked the hotel manager, unfolded the note, and read it.

Herman asked, 'Bad news?'

Bea crumpled up the note. 'Something from the London office.

I'm afraid Charlotte's in a bit of a state. Your friend Liam's let her down, won't be joining her this evening.'

Did this mean anything to Herman? His stolid face failed to register surprise. Did he already know that Liam was opting out of the situation? She couldn't be sure.

'All the more reason for me to take her out, make her forget her friend. A good dinner, a bottle of wine, no?'

'Perhaps, if we went somewhere local? I don't think she's up to anything else. We could all four of us go to some place in Vlaamingstraat nearby?'

'All four?' He looked towards the front door, frowning. Was there someone out there waiting for him to emerge with the parcels? The note in Bea's hand was in Erik's hand. A car registration number – Dutch, not Belgian – and the query 'Do I call the police?'

'Don't you think it's a good idea for us all to dine together?' said Bea, mentally checking that she had her credit cards with her, and enough money for a taxi back. It wasn't far to Vlaamingstraat, and they had to eat somewhere.

Herman smiled widely, his voice softening, adjusting to the situation. 'Why not, eh? A parcel of beautiful women for me to take out for the night. Is that right . . . parcel of women? I'm afraid my English is not very clever.'

'It is a very good word,' said Bea, thinking that this man could be charming when he chose, and how would Charlotte react to him in this mood?

'Then I will cancel my reservation in Damme, and in half an hour we will all go out to make a great occasion, no? Oh, I nearly forgot. Liam asked me to pick up something from the girls to deliver to his partner here in Bruges. Two parcels? Something to grease the wheels of industry?' He rubbed his thumb against his middle finger in a knowing gesture. 'I can take them with me now to save the girls the trouble, and then we will all be as free as . . . as air, is that how you put it? As free as air?'

So Herman was in on the scam. Perhaps she could get a little more information out of him? She made her eyes widen. 'What sort of parcels might they be?'

'A tin of shortbread, and a coffee set made by one of your great English potters. Wedgwood, perhaps? Worcester? A great treat for us here in Belgium.'

'The girls didn't mention any presents,' lied Bea. 'Are you sure you've got the message right?'

He smiled, a gold tooth glinting. 'I check, right?' He went to the front door and disappeared down the steps to the street just as three tourists entered, noisily complaining about the difficulty of parking their car in Bruges. While Erik was reassuring them, telling them where they might park, Bea went after Herman to see what he was up to.

Was he phoning someone . . . Liam? His boss? No, he was leaning forward to speak to a man in a large car which had been parked right in front of the hotel. It didn't have a sign on the roof advertising that it was a taxi. No, it was a private car, and the number matched that on the note Erik had given her.

An elderly couple decanted themselves from a genuine taxi and had to manoeuvre their way around the stranger's car to reach the hotel.

Bea tried to see who Herman was speaking to, in the car. Could it be Liam? No, Liam was on his way back to London, wasn't he? Was this the man Liam was supposed to hand the goods over to? A fence? A Dutchman, not a Belgian?

A gaggle of twenty-something girls arrived on foot, each with a rucksack, and pushed past Bea into the hotel. Erik was going to be tied up for some time.

Herman gestured to Bea to join him in the street. She did so, clutching her arms because a light drizzle was beginning to mist over the landscape. She was thinking too many contradictory thoughts to be wary of him. He caught hold of her wrist. 'Why you interfere in this, eh?'

Bea revised her first estimate of him; his grasp on her wrist proved he was far from flabby. 'Let go! You're hurting me.' She looked around for help. This was a quiet part of town, but there were usually tourists lingering on the bridge over the canal, and cyclists dashing hither and yon. For once, the place was deserted, but the hotel lobby was full of people. She could scream for help if Herman couldn't be shaken off by other means.

Herman tugged her towards the car. The tinted window on the driver's side was wound down, and she could see a middle-aged man with a heavy white face sitting in the passenger seat. The car stereo was playing a Mozart wind quintet. Was this the car in which Herman had intended to take the girls to Damme? Was the passenger his driver . . . or his boss?

Herman shook her arm. 'Answer me, old woman!'

'What? How dare you! Let go, immediately!'

He shook her arm again. 'Silly old women who poke their noses in, have their noses cut off. You hear me? The girls have our presents, and we want them. Go and get them, now!'

'I don't know anything about any presents.'

He tightened his grip even further on her arm, and she heard herself mew with pain. She was frightened, but she would not give in. She looked for help to the man in the car, but he was smiling, lighting a cigarette, approving Herman's tactics. He was Herman's man, then.

She opened her mouth to scream, and Herman punched her in her midriff, causing her to jack-knife, out of breath. She might have been a two-year-old child, for all the effort he needed to control her.

He said, 'Shall I kick your legs down, and lift you into the car? I'm no amateur, understand?' He twisted her wrist with the detached air of one conducting an experiment.

Pain screeched up her arm.

He said, 'Is my English clear enough for you? Understand that if you do not hand over the presents at once, we will drive to a quiet place and see how much pain you can take. So, now you go and get the presents, yes?'

Monday, late afternoon

Rafael tried three times to get Liam on the phone before the idiot finally answered. Liam was on a train already, judging by the background noise.

'Why didn't you answer when I rang before? You know I've got this big "do" on tonight.'

'I thought it was Charlotte trying to ring me but . . .' his voice faded.

'Are you on the train to Bruges? I told you to wait in Brussels till I'd decided what was to be done.'

'I couldn't think what else to . . .' His voice came and went. Bad reception. Or perhaps the battery on Zander's phone was running out as well? ' . . . but she's in a terrible state.'

Rafael was impatient. 'So what! She won't dare go to the police or she'll land herself in jail. Now listen carefully. You're going to arrive in Bruges too late to pick up the goods from the girls so I've arranged for someone else to do it. I want you back here in London tonight. The train stops at Ghent on the way to Bruges, right? Get off at Ghent and take the next train back to Brussels. If you manage the connections properly, you can be back in London and at the flat well before midnight.

'I won't be able to leave the gallery till the early hours, and tomorrow morning there'll be all the clearing up to do. I'll meet you at your flat at, say, twelve o'clock tomorrow morning. I've got another job for you, and this time you'd better not mess it up.'

'But what if Charlotte—'

'Herman will deal with the girls. Once they're safely back in London you can chat Charlotte up as much as you please, promise her another jaunt to the Continent in the autumn. After taking the stuff over there for us once, she won't be able to refuse when we ask her to do it again. And next time, she'll know better than to open the parcels in her luggage.'

Liam quacked like a duck. 'You intend to use her again?'

'Naturally.' Rafael shut off his phone, and returned to the foyer. The guests were arriving, and he needed to flatter one, mislead another, and seduce a third. All in a day's work.

Twelve

Monday, early evening

Bea's wrist was on fire, and she'd been pushed off-balance. She couldn't breathe properly. She'd no doubt at all that the two men intended to take her off in the car till she agreed to hand over the two packages. There weren't any helpful passers-by coming and going over the bridge. But she had one last weapon she could use.

Well, two weapons, actually. She brought weapon number one into play. *Dear Lord, help! Surely you don't expect an old-age pensioner to tangle with hard men like these? I need some assistance here.*

Weapon number two. She lifted her free hand to show him that she was holding a piece of paper. Her voice came out in gasps. 'The registration number of your car . . . it was noted because . . . you behaved strangely.'

'What?' Herman's grip on her relaxed, and he turned to look up at the hotel.

Bea's voice wobbled. 'If anything happens . . . he'll ring the police.'

Herman didn't know what to do. He bent down to speak to the man in the car. Would they still try to whisk her away, even though they now knew the car could be traced?

'Get her in!' said the man inside the car. Herman swung Bea towards the back of the car . . . just as a large coach drove over the bridge and came to a halt outside the hotel with a sigh of air brakes.

Bea yelled 'Thief!' as loudly as she could – which was not very loud – but the first tourist to descend from the bus turned his head to see what was happening.

'Help! He's stealing my watch!'

A burly German dropped down into the road, followed by another of similar bulk. They were not young and they carried too much weight for perfect health, but they relished a call to arms.

The man in the big car yelled something and thrust open the driver's door.

Herman sent Bea spinning across the pavement into the path of the tourists and slipped into the car, the door swinging shut even as he started the engine and accelerated, screeching round a corner and away from the canal. Bea was caught and held by the foremost tourist, while the other pounded after the car only to give up the chase as it disappeared out of sight.

The coach load of tourists were shocked and helpful, but they were also tired after a long journey and were only too happy to be assured by Bea that there was no damage done – no really, she was quite all right. Shaken, of course, but a quiet sit-down for a few minutes would put her right.

The tourists trouped into the foyer, their baggage following them. Erik sent an anxious look in Bea's direction as she tottered through the foyer to the lift. She gave him a thumbs-up sign, and pressed the button for the second floor.

Her wrist burned.

She leaned against the side of the lift, trembling, wanting to cry and not allowing herself to do so, telling herself that she was in shock, that she had never, ever, had such a thing happen to her before. Telling herself that she was too old for these shenanigans. Her knees wanted to sag. She told herself she was pleased that she hadn't given in. Hamilton would have been proud of her.

She got herself out of the lift, couldn't face the stairs to the top floor and let herself down gently on to the settee on the landing. She wept a little, allowing herself a few minutes to give way, annoyed with Hamilton for dying, because if he'd been with her none of this would have happened. Men do have their uses, don't they!

The last time someone had hurt her physically had been at school, when a bullying sixth-former called . . . what was her name? . . . Petronella something . . . had given Bea a Chinese burn over some fancied slight or other. That had hurt, too.

The lift whirred, and she realized that the first of the coach party would be disembarking on to the landing any minute now. She couldn't be found, weeping, on the settee.

She dragged herself up the stairs to the top floor, holding on to the banister, thinking, You can do it, girl! She reached the landing. There! She congratulated herself. You did it!

She tapped on the door to the girls' room. Maggie flung it open, arms akimbo, in a state about something. There was no sign of Charlotte but water was running in the bathroom.

'Believe it or not, she's washing her hair,' said Maggie, grinding out the words.

'What!'

'Apparently she feels the need to wash her hair in moments of crisis. I'd like to shake her till . . .'

Bea wanted to laugh. She wanted to sink down on the nearest piece of furniture and have a full-scale hysterical fit. She wanted someone to take over for her, decide what needed to be done. She wanted to be back home in her own quiet little house, contemplating a quiet evening with a smoked salmon sandwich and a not-too-worrying programme on the telly.

She gulped, controlling herself with an effort. She touched the corners of her eyes to flick away tears. Maggie wasn't looking at her. Maggie was pacing the room, muttering. If Maggie had been a cat, she'd be lashing her tail. It seemed that relations between Charlotte and Maggie had deteriorated even further. Oh. Dear.

Maggie pointed to the window sill, where she'd laid out nineteen gold boxes in three lines, and almost as many miniatures. 'Nineteen boxes. Twelve miniatures. You wanted to photograph them?'

Meekly, Bea got out her mobile phone and took pictures, sending them off to Mr Goldstone.

'What about fingerprints, Maggie? It would be better if yours didn't appear. Will you clean your prints off everything with a tissue, and wrap them up again?'

Maggie slapped her forehead and delved in her handbag for a pack of tissues. 'A fine investigator I'd make! What did Herman say?'

'He wants the goods and is prepared to turn nasty if he doesn't get them. He was waiting downstairs in a big car with an older man in the passenger seat. I suppose the other man might be the fence. An interested party, anyway.'

'What's wrong with your wrist?'

'Nothing.' Bea noticed she had a couple of voicemail messages on her phone, so turned away to listen to them. The first was from Oliver, back at the office. He'd had a phone call from Velma. Sandy had come through the operation well enough but would be in intensive care for a couple of days, and had Bea any news for her? Well, no. Bea hadn't. She was horrified at herself for having forgotten about Sandy and his operation.

The second message was from Piers, light-hearted as ever. He'd been invited to some junket or other that evening and thought it might amuse her to go with him, if she were free. She wished he were here with them. She scolded herself. What could Piers do, if he were here? Answer; lift their spirits. Take them out to supper. Make them laugh, even. She rang her office, but the phone was engaged, so she left a couple of messages. 'Oliver, would you please ring Piers and tell him I can't come out to play tonight but will get back to him as soon as I can. And as for Velma . . . on second thoughts, don't ring her. There's no good news and she doesn't need to be worried with what I've found out so far.'

Charlotte clicked open the door to the bathroom and emerged, her head surrounded by a bush of hair even more electric than before. She said, 'I've come to a decision. If Liam's in trouble, then my place is with him. I'm going back to London straight away, to stand by him.'

Bea was happy to endorse this. 'A good idea. Perhaps you can change your tickets to go back on the ferry tomorrow.'

'Maggie can do what she likes, but I'm going back tonight.'

'Better check that you can get the car on a ferry tonight, before you decide.'

'You needn't speak to me like that. I'm not an idiot, you know.'

'Of course not. Have you also decided what to do about the smuggled goods?'

'We must hand them over, get rid of them. Then we can go back through Customs without any trouble, and there'll be no proof that Liam was ever involved in anything.'

'Sounds good,' said Bea, 'though I can see a couple of snags.'

Charlotte was becoming aggressive. 'What's it got to do with you, anyway?'

Bea's arm hurt. 'I want to keep you two out of jail if I can.'

'We hand the stuff over to Herman, there's no problem. I can manage perfectly well without you, thank you. Or Maggie. If Maggie wants to go back with you on the train, that's perfectly all right by me and she can move out of the flat straight away. Once we're back in London I don't want to see her ever again.'

'Mutual, I'm sure,' said Maggie, shoving the last of the miniatures back into its tin box.

Bea tried not to look at her wrist, which was colouring up nicely. 'Calm down, both of you. We're all in this together, aren't we? I have a nasty feeling that we haven't seen the last of Herman. Charlotte, he's a bully boy with a nice line in hurting women. I'm glad you decided not to have supper with him.'

Charlotte was busy on her mobile. 'I haven't time for all that. I'll eat here in the hotel and by that time—'

'The hotel doesn't do evening meals,' said Bea. 'Only breakfast and drinks in the bar.'

'What sort of hotel is it that doesn't do food?'

'A Continental one,' said Bea, through her teeth. 'We'll have to go out for something to eat. I know a couple of places locally that do Flemish dishes.'

Charlotte said, 'I'm not hungry. Anyway, do you two mind leaving me alone? I've arrangements to make.'

Bea shrugged, collected Maggie with an eye-roll, and returned to her own room.

Maggie plumped herself down on the big bed. 'I've messed up again, haven't I? I shouldn't have let Zander fool me. I shouldn't have accepted the package for Liam, and I shouldn't have let Charlotte rile me.'

'Easy to do.' Bea sat down at the dressing table, found some hand cream in her bag and put it on her wrist, which had stiffened up. She could have done with some arnica but hadn't any with her, not having anticipated that she'd be tangling with a no-neck man.

Looking in the mirror, she saw that Maggie was weeping, without sound. Bea was tempted to pretend she hadn't seen anything. Fatigue hit her. It was impossible to get off her chair and cross the room to comfort Maggie.

Impossible or not, she did it, somehow. She put her arm around Maggie's shoulders, and pulled the girl to her. 'There, there.'

Maggie swiped the back of her hand across her eyes. 'I really liked Zander, you know.'

'I know.' Bea's mobile phone rang, and she released Maggie to search for it in her bag. It was Mr Goldstone, confirming that the goods were the real thing, and wanting to know what she was going to do about it.

'I'm trying to think,' said Bea. 'There's a thug over here trying to get the stuff off us. It would be easiest to let him have it and then we could get back to England without being tripped up at Customs for smuggling.'

'I would agree with you, dear lady, if it hadn't been for the fact that Leo and I were friends for fifty years. I want his death avenged.'

'I'm not much of an avenger, I fear,' said Bea. 'I'll let you know what I decide.' She clicked off the phone as Charlotte barged into the room.

Charlotte was in a temper, hair whirling around her head, eyes snapping. 'I can't get anything on the ferry till midday tomorrow. Oh, you may well laugh, but how am I to stop Liam doing something stupid if I can't get back to look after him?'

'I'm not laughing,' said Bea. 'Far from it. And neither is Maggie.'

'Oh, pooh to Maggie. Let her find her own way back.'

A mobile trilled, and Charlotte's face changed. 'It's Liam!

Oh, Liam! Where are you? . . . What do you mean, you want to warn me? . . . He intends to use us again? He can't do that, can he?' She turned away to the window, lowering her voice, but Bea and Maggie could still hear her side of the conversation.

'But Liam, I wouldn't . . . no, I understand that but . . . your friends don't frighten me!' Charlotte collapsed into a chair. 'Yes, but Liam, listen to me! I'm coming back on the ferry at noon tomorrow and then we can talk, right?' She listened some more, then turned the phone off. She was weeping, too.

'Liam rang to warn me. He says that I've no idea how vicious these people can be, that if we don't hand the stuff over, they could do all sorts of horrid things to us. He says they'll take photos of me handing over the parcels to Herman, and then they'll blackmail me into carrying stuff through Customs again and again. He thinks we ought to hand the stuff over, but be careful not to be photographed with them. He says . . .' She wept, sagging against the wall. 'He says I mustn't try to contact him again, that he's not going back to the flat, that I must forget all about him. He says he was taking a big risk warning me . . . oh, I could just about die!'

Bea pushed herself off the bed. 'That's because you haven't eaten anything much today. I feel the same way, but we'll all be able to cope better when we've got some food inside us.'

'Not hungry.' Charlotte turned mulish.

'I am,' said Maggie, sniffing. 'Mrs Abbot, did you say you know some place local?'

'Get your jackets on, girls, and we'll be off,' said Bea. 'Lock your door behind you and meet me downstairs in the foyer in five minutes. I'll order a taxi.' It wasn't far to the restaurant but she wasn't risking another encounter with no-neck Herman.

The Bistro den Huzaar was her restaurant of choice. They knew her there, of course, and looked behind her to welcome Hamilton as usual. Bea explained that he'd died, and they looked shocked. How many more times was she going to have to tell people he was dead?

The restaurant was a popular one but the maître d' found them a table reasonably near the front. Dark wood, modern paintings on the walls including one of the chef, a long bar, waiters and waitresses who all spoke five languages each.

Bea said to the girls, 'I'd advise drinking beer not wine.'

'I'd like a glass of wine,' said Charlotte.

Bea tried again. 'I recommend the Flemish dishes; the pork casserole with cherries or the rabbit with prunes are both excellent.'

Charlotte shuddered. 'I couldn't eat a dear little bunny rabbit to save my life.'

The waitress met Bea's eye with a flicker of sympathy, but was too professional to grimace.

Maggie said, 'What's this . . . smoked eel soup? I don't think I've ever tasted eel, never mind in soup.'

'It's very good indeed. Hamilton – my husband – always used to order it.' Bea's throat closed up on her, remembering how much he'd enjoyed their visits here.

Charlotte threw her menu down. 'I'm vegetarian, anyway.'

Maggie lost her temper. 'Charlotte, you aren't! When we had supper the other night—'

'That was then. I don't like fancy cooking.'

Bea struggled with her own temper, and pointed to an item on the menu which she thought would appeal to someone who didn't want to be taken out of their British comfort zone. 'Maggie, suppose we skip the first course and share a Flemish chicken casserole between us? And for Charlotte . . .?'

The waitress patiently suggested a couple of vegetarian items to Charlotte, who grudgingly said she supposed she could force some chicken down if she tried hard.

Bea wanted to shake the girl. She told herself that once this was over, she'd be glad never to see her again. Some pâté arrived with French toast. Charlotte took a tiny bite, grimacing, but graciously said it was quite nice, considering. Bea was tempted to tell Charlotte that it was made using some dear little bunny rabbit meat, but refrained.

Bea ordered beer for herself and Maggie, and a glass of wine for Charlotte. All the time she worried what on earth she was going to do about the stolen goods.

The girls ate in silence. So did Bea. She was worn out, couldn't be bothered to make polite conversation. Maggie revived with her first helping of the casserole, had a second go at the dish and finished all their deliciously thin, crusty chips. Charlotte started by picking at her food, but polished off her plateful in record time.

'No dessert for me,' said Charlotte, shuddering as the sweet menus were brought for them to see.

'Three special coffees, then,' said Bea.

'No coffee for me,' said Charlotte. Predictably.

'Two special coffees,' said Bea to the waitress. 'But perhaps, three spoons?'

A special coffee at this restaurant was expensive, but included a sorbet, an ice, some tiramasu, and a slice of chocolate dessert. Maggie said 'Wow!' when hers came, and Charlotte said she wished she'd known, as she'd have decided to have some, too.

'Have mine,' said Bea, pushing it across the table.

'Allow me to order another,' said a man's voice. It was Herman's boss. Seen out of the car, he was a large, plump man with pale eyes. He seated himself, unasked, in the spare chair at their table. He was grey all over, from smooth hair and waxen skin, down through an expensive suit – cashmere and silk at a guess – to hand-made shoes. Bea guessed that he had a wallet full of credit cards, all platinum or gold. The waitress flicked a glance at Bea, who hesitated just a fraction too long, unsure whether to make a scene or not.

The man smiled at the waitress and ordered another two special coffees, one for himself, and one for his charming young friend. He held out his hand to Charlotte. 'Let me introduce myself. My name is Van. Liam's business contact. I am distressed to hear he is not coming. Allow me to make up for his absence. A brandy, perhaps? Or do you prefer advocaat?'

Charlotte gaped and didn't reply. Bea wondered why he'd homed in on Charlotte rather than on Maggie. Maggie was looking quite presentable in Bea's clothes and with her hair well brushed. Charlotte looked a mess, lumpy and ill at ease. Perhaps he didn't know that Maggie had also carried his stolen goods?

Charlotte fidgeted, murmuring, 'Nothing, thank you.'

The newcomer turned his light eyes upon Bea, assessing and then dismissing her as unimportant. 'And you are their chaperone, no? Trying to keep them out of trouble? I must apologize for our little misunderstanding earlier. My friend Herman is so . . . forceful. Well, this is a very pleasant meeting, is it not? Your first time in Bruges, Charlotte? I may call you Charlotte, may I not? Liam has spoken so much about you that I feel I know you already.'

Charlotte's eyes rounded, while Maggie leaned back in her seat, eyes narrowed. Maggie's body language indicated that she didn't like the man, while Charlotte's showed uncertainty.

The waitress said, 'Would monsieur like to order some food?' implying that she wasn't happy at this intrusion. Neither was Bea.

The man waved a hand with two gold rings on it at the waitress. 'Just the coffee.' The waitress looked at Bea for a lead and didn't get one, so went away.

Bea knew 'Mr Van' couldn't be a proper name. Maggie also looked sceptical. Charlotte started work on the tiramasu, a little doubtful about the newcomer, but reacting to the magic of Liam's name.

Bea said, 'How did you know where we were?'

He didn't look at her, but said dismissively, 'We went round the block and parked, waiting for you to come out. Naturally.'

Bea leaned back in her seat, not sure what to do. He thought her a nonentity. Perhaps it would be good if he went on thinking so.

'My dear Charlotte,' he said, lips parting in a grimace which he seemed to think was a smile. 'What a shame that you should have been stood up on your first night in this lovely city. May I take the place of your young man, and show you around? Perhaps a nightclub?'

Charlotte eyed him over a spoonful of chocolate dessert. 'I'm not really a nightclub person.'

'Ah, but I could show you' – he waved podgily-plump hands – 'a nightlife such as you have never dreamed of.'

Charlotte put down the empty dish and considered whether to take on the ice or the sorbet next. 'Liam was going to take me for a ride in a horse and carriage.'

Bea suppressed a giggle at the thought of this rather large man – who must, she thought, be in his late fifties – hauling himself up into a carriage and squashing Charlotte into a corner of the seat.

'Ah, well . . .' He waved his hands again, declining to take up the implied invitation. Wisely. Bea spotted more glints of gold at his wrist, a watch and a bracelet. Too much gold, Hamilton would have said.

'But we must do something to mark the occasion of your first visit to this beautiful city.'

Maggie was dipping into her desserts, a spoonful here and there. 'It is very kind of you, Mr . . . Mr Van . . .?' She made a question mark in her voice when she uttered the name he'd given. 'But we don't know you from Adam.'

'Naturally you are being careful. But who else would be meeting you at your friend Liam's request?'

Two more special coffees came, one for Bea and the other for Mr Van. Neither attempted to eat anything, though Bea sipped at her coffee.

The two girls considered Mr Van's proposal, and for once were in accord.

'It's very kind of you . . .' Maggie began.

At the same time Charlotte said, 'I don't think . . .' They both paused, looking at one another, and then returned their eyes to Mr Van.

Maggie said, 'It's our dreadful British upbringing, you see. We have to know someone well to entrust ourselves to them for a night out in a foreign country.'

'I quite understand.' Yet the temperature had dropped ten degrees. Mr Van was not pleased. 'You wish to make this a business arrangement only, yes? You have had your little trip paid for by our friend and you turn down my invitation, made with the most honest of intentions. Very well and good. So now you have to pay for your pleasure, no? We return to the hotel and you let me have my presents and no more will be said on either side.'

Charlotte gulped her coffee, while Maggie played with her spoon. Bea kept quiet. If the girls decided to hand the stolen goods over, she wasn't sure she could stop them doing so. And wouldn't it perhaps be best if they did?

'A coffee set. Supposedly.' Maggie gave him a tiny smile. 'I opened it to make sure nothing had got broken in transit.'

Charlotte giggling, choked on her coffee. 'Broken? Oh, Maggie!'

He ceased to play the part of genial uncle. 'You opened it?'

Charlotte nodded, still coughing. 'Nineteen beautiful boxes.'

'Nineteen?' He was sharp. 'There ought to be twenty.'

'Only nineteen,' said Charlotte. 'Honest! That's all there were. Maggie counted them several times.'

He switched his eyes to Maggie, who nodded. 'Nineteen.'

He narrowed his eyes at her. 'It was unwise of you to open the parcel. Did you open the second one, too?'

'We wanted to know what we were getting into.' Maggie was pale but defiant.

'Twelve in that one,' said Charlotte. 'Nineteen tiddly little boxes, and twelve pretty miniatures.'

He sipped his coffee, his eyes on Charlotte, who was giggling though with an undercurrent of tension, even of fear. A silly little girl poking King Cobra, half aware that she might get her come-uppance, but hoping for the best because she'd never really come up against evil before and wasn't at all sure that she believed in it.

Bea sat very still, watching and waiting.

He said, 'You are two very silly little girls, trying to play grown-up games with me, but now it is time for you to face real life. You will let me have my presents this evening, and that will be the end of it.'

'And if we don't?' said Charlotte, laughing but impressed despite herself.

His eyes were ice-cold. 'Of course you will do as I say. The alternative would be very, very bad for you. I have many connections in this city and in the police. Before you return to your hotel, I would have you arrested and with my property in your room, it would be – what you call it – an open and shut case. You would face a long sentence in jail. This I promise that I can do.'

Maggie was holding herself together with an effort. 'Wait a minute, if you inform on us, you'd lose your "property".'

'My connections with the police are good. Believe me, arrangements would be made to let me claim the lost items within days. So let us have no more of this nonsense, shall we? Waitress!' He signalled to her. 'The bill, if you please.'

Monday evening

As Liam's train drew into London, he made up his mind what to do. Rafael would be tied up at work tonight and early tomorrow, so it was safe to go back to the flat to pick up his things. And then he'd be out of there.

He wished things hadn't worked out this way. He'd had no intention of getting in this deep when Rafael first offered him a few hundred to run an errand for him. As for Charlotte, poor cow . . . he'd taken a risk in warning her and that was more than he'd really needed to do, wasn't it? She'd decided of her own free will to trade in her virginity for a free holiday, and it wasn't his fault if things had gone pear-shaped after that. He preferred blondes, anyway.

He stepped down from the train and joined the rush of people all anxious to leave the station. Once through Customs – he had nothing to declare – he went into the nearest toilet, stamped on Zander's mobile phone till it was in pieces, and dropped the bits into the nearest garbage point. Now nobody could connect him with stolen goods . . . or murder.

Thirteen

Monday evening

'Excuse me for a moment,' murmured Bea. 'I must pay a visit. Don't decide anything till I get back, right?'

Mr Van didn't take his eyes off the two girls while Bea edged herself out from her seat. Mr Van didn't think Bea was of any importance. Mr Van was happy in the belief that he'd cowed the girls into acquiescence. Bea was happy to let him think so.

She made her way to the back of the restaurant and down the stairs to the toilets. The seed of an idea had lodged itself in her head, and she needed time to think about it. Suppose . . .? But what if . . .? There would be a risk. Yes. Was it worth it? Mm, yes. It would be dangerous, of course, if she were found out. There would be danger on this side of the Channel and danger on the other. She wasn't sure which would be worse.

The simplest thing to do would be to contact the police, though not on this side of the Channel. She wasn't sure she believed Mr Van could manipulate the Belgian police in the way he described, but if he'd only one minor official in his pocket it would mean disaster.

She washed her hands and tucked her blouse into her waistband. She didn't try to pretty herself up because it was best that Mr Van continued to think her as of no importance. He thought she was just a chaperone. The term 'chaperone' was outmoded and she rather wondered how he'd come by it. His spoken English was good, but not perfect. Perhaps he'd never before come across an English businesswoman of a certain age, someone who'd been tutored by a wise man like Hamilton.

Here Bea did what she thought Hamilton would have done in such straits. She sent up an arrow prayer. *Please Lord, am I doing the right thing? These two girls' lives will be ruined if Mr Van has his way and . . . oh, you know all about it anyway, don't you?*

She thought about that for a moment and added, *At least, I hope you do know all about it. Sorry if I doubt you now and then, and you really are there and . . . oh, I'm just so muddled. What I'm saying is . . . help, please!*

Stop this, she told herself, and went back up the stairs to the restaurant. Pausing by the till, she gave the mâitre d' her card to pay the bill for herself and the two girls. The restaurant was long and narrow, with a bar down one side and tables on the other. From where she stood, she had a good view of Mr Van and the two girls, sitting sideways on to her. While she waited for her card to be processed she pulled out her mobile phone, and took a couple of pictures of Mr Van.

'Is everything all right?' asked the mâitre d', whose eyes were everywhere and who knew more about human nature than most people. 'The gentleman visitor. Is he satisfactory to you?'

Bea grimaced, stowing her phone away. 'He's no gentleman, we didn't invite him to join us and he is not welcome. But I can deal with him, I think. He's not Flemish, is he?'

'Dutch. If there is anything we can do . . .? We were so sorry to hear about your husband.'

'Thank you.' It crossed Bea's mind for a moment that she and the mâitre d' had known one another for so many years that a half embrace, or a kiss on both cheeks might be appropriate – and comforting. But, being British, she let the moment pass, and walked on to their table.

Mr Van was in the middle of an anecdote about a hunting expedition – really?

Maggie looked sullen, Charlotte feverish.

Bea slid into her seat and tried to act 'fluffy'. She thought of Velma and wondered how that clever airhead would have managed. 'Well, Mr Van . . . it's getting late and we've had a long day. I'd like to see the girls tucked up in bed pretty soon.'

'Of course, of course. As soon as I have my presents, I will leave you in peace to get your beauty sleep.'

Maggie shuddered and Charlotte asked if anyone had any

indigestion tablets. Bea found some in her handbag and handed them over.

'Now,' she said, in her new, bright tone of voice, 'there's just one tiny little thing that's been bothering me. I'm sure you mean well, Mr Van, but these girls are my responsibility and I don't want there to be any problem getting them back to London. Just imagine if they were stopped at Customs on their way back and accused of smuggling? Of course, they wouldn't have any stolen goods on them, but it could be very nasty, couldn't it? They might be held up and interrogated, and investigated and oh, I don't know what else.'

Mr Van almost laughed. 'You have my word this will not happen.'

'But can we trust you? I ask myself what would happen if these two girls' mothers found out that I'd let them run into such danger, I really don't know what they'd say, but I'm sure it would be . . . oh dear, am I going to cry?'

Bea found a handkerchief in her handbag, and applied it to her eyes. Maggie had never seen Bea act like this before and looked at her in some amazement, but Charlotte nodded.

Mr Van looked at his watch, bored with the conversation. 'The girls are in no danger from me, I do assure you of that. Now, shall we—'

'But how can I be sure of that?' twittered Bea. 'I can see that you are a very important man, with all sorts of connections and not to be trifled with in any way, so I've been trying hard to think how best to protect my girls *and* get them back safely home. I think I have come up with a solution!'

She beamed at them all. Maggie lowered her eyes to the table, but Charlotte was all attention.

Mr Van shrugged. 'So . . .?'

She spread her hands and smiled widely, expecting approval. 'You don't get the goods until the girls are safely back home.'

'What?' He hadn't expected this.

'But how . . .?' said Maggie.

'Simple.' Bea was delighted to explain. 'Tomorrow morning on our way out of town, I place the two boxes in my overnight bag and put them in the Left Luggage at the railway station. I post the key to you, we get safely back home, you get the key the next day, and everyone is happy. Isn't that a good plan?'

'Yes,' said Maggie.

'Oh, yes!' said Charlotte.

Mr Van scowled. 'It is a very bad plan. No, no. I cannot trust you. Besides, they have codes, not keys, at Left Luggage boxes nowadays.'

Bea maintained her sunny smile. 'Of course you can trust me. Oh, I'm so pleased that I thought of this. I couldn't think how to get the girls home safely, otherwise.'

His temper flared. 'Suppose I come to the hotel with you now, and we waste no more of my time!'

'You mustn't threaten me,' said Bea, keeping up her smiling face. 'Or I will ask the maître d' to call the police. I will say you have been making horrid suggestions to my girls about becoming sex slaves and working for you, and they will believe me. Girls, you'll back me up, won't you?'

Both girls nodded, eyes wide.

He gaped. 'But I have never been involved in—'

'Of course not,' said Bea, soothing his injured pride. 'Only in smuggling. I know. But you see, the hotel people were very upset at your man Herman's crashing in on their guests without permission, they know that the girls were supposed to be accompanied on this trip by boyfriends who failed to show up, and they have already jumped to the conclusion that you want the girls for prostitution. They took down the number of your car and told me that if we fail to return to the hotel tonight, they'll be on to the police. However, I don't think that will be necessary, will it?'

She was calling his bluff that he had an inside contact in the police force, but it seemed to be working, for calculation replaced indignation in his eyes.

Bea laid the restaurant bill on the table, with a pen. 'Write down your name and address on the back of my bill, and I'll fulfil my part of the bargain.'

He tapped on the table, eyes switching backwards and forwards. Bea held her breath. Charlotte gave a little squeak, napkin to mouth.

Eventually Mr Van decided to do as she asked. She watched while he wrote down the name of one of the town's most expensive hotels. Of course, he wouldn't give her his real name and address. He threw the pen down, grumbling, 'This is going to cost me extra, staying over for two nights. I am not best pleased.'

'Oh, don't be a cry-baby,' said Bea, pocketing the bill. 'Come, girls, I've settled the bill, so we can leave now. I'll get the maître d' to call a taxi for us, in case Herman's lurking outside.'

Back at the hotel, Bea thought she'd very much like to lie down and die, but was forced to revise her plan when Charlotte scuttled ahead to the girls' room and dashed in, leaving the door open behind her. Retching sounds came from the bathroom.

Maggie was disgusted. 'She was stuffing her face with junk food all through the car journey here. No wonder she's being sick.'

Charlotte appeared in the doorway, wiping her face with a flannel. Her skin glistened, and she was crying. 'Maggie, you are a nasty, horrid . . . I can't think of words bad enough to describe you. The doctors say I've got irritable bowel syndrome. Any stress will set it off, and I've had far too much stress today. Oh . . .!' She dashed back into the bathroom.

'Dear me,' said Bea, feeling limp and quite unequal to getting the pair of them to kiss and make up. 'Maggie, will you do something for me, dear? Pack all the stolen goods back into their containers and bring them to me in my room? I rather think a little lie-down is indicated.'

'You were very brave.' Maggie threw off her jacket and began to reassemble the goods. 'But may I say that I was a bit surprised at—'

'Hush, child,' said Bea, putting her finger to her lips. 'Trust me. Do as I say, and we'll all get home in one piece.'

Maggie shot a look at the half-open door to the bathroom, and nodded. 'Give me five minutes.'

Bea unlocked the door to her own room and shut it behind her. She didn't bother to switch on the lights, but went to the window and leaned on the sill, looking down past the brightly flaring petunias in the window boxes, down and down to the canal where some ducks were squabbling, giving a wide berth to a stately swan. It was a time of day that she loved. Distant bells chimed the half-hour. The sinking sun lit flares of colour across the towers and turrets of the city.

Had she done the right thing? Tangling with evil was not something a sixty-plus widow needed to be doing. If only Hamilton were still alive . . . she cut off that thought. Tried to think of nothing at all.

There was a knock on the door and Maggie entered with the

coffee set box and the tin which once contained shortbread. She hesitated, seeing that Bea didn't turn around to greet her. 'You must be tired, poor thing,' she said. She put the boxes on the big bed and left the room, taking such care to shut the door quietly that it banged into place. Bea was startled into a laugh. Trust Maggie to make a noise even when she didn't mean to.

Now, should she have a shower or indulge in a bath?

Ah. A knock at the door. Maggie had returned, half laughing and half dismayed. 'I'm sorry, Mrs Abbot, but Charlotte won't let me back into our room. I don't quite know what to do.'

'You upset her.'

Maggie shrugged. 'Chalk and cheese. Sharing with her was never going to be a permanent option. Can I doss down with you?'

'I'll speak to her.' Bea told herself that this difficult day would end sometime or other, and that tomorrow she'd look back on it and smile. She knocked on the door of the other room, said she was alone and worried about Charlotte, and might she come in?

Charlotte opened the door and let Bea in once she saw Maggie wasn't with her. Charlotte's face was the colour of uncooked pastry; she was definitely unwell.

Bea asked, 'Can I get you anything? Are you drinking plenty of water?'

'Nothing works when it's this bad. Just keep that cow Maggie away from me, right? All I want is a bit of peace and quiet and . . .' Charlotte dissolved into tears again. At this rate she'd be dehydrated from more causes than one.

'All right,' said Bea. 'I'll take Maggie's things next door. She can sleep with me tonight, and tomorrow we'll get you back home so that you can put all this behind you.' She went into the bathroom. 'Is this Maggie's toiletbag? Yes? And the suitcase she's using?'

'To make matters worse,' sobbed Charlotte, 'I can't even get through to Liam's phone now.'

'You poor thing,' said Bea, torn between wanting to slap the girl, and give her a comforting hug.

'Oh . . .!' Charlotte flung herself past Bea into the bathroom again.

Bea sighed, collected what she thought Maggie needed and returned to her own room. Maggie turned away from the window, where she'd been watching dusk settle over the city. Maggie had been crying, too, but had herself more or less under control.

'I longed to see this place, and it is beautiful, of course. But what with Zander letting me down and . . . everything . . . I'll be glad never to see it again.'

Bea switched on the lights and put a comforting arm around Maggie's shoulder. 'It's a beautiful city and one day you'll be glad to come back again, with another man, perhaps. I've been here many times with Hamilton and always loved it. Of course this time it's different, but I'll come back again, perhaps next spring, to buy some more clothes.' She thought with regret of the outfit she'd tried on that morning. If only Charlotte had made her appearance ten minutes later!

'It's different for you. You had Hamilton for company.'

'For thirty-five, nearly thirty-six years. Not long enough.' She straightened her shoulders. 'Go and have a good long shower or a bath, or whatever. We'll rescue the rest of your things in the morning.'

Maggie went into the bathroom and turned on the taps. Soon Bea heard her singing. Of course. Maggie needed noise to make sure she was alive. Maggie probably snored. Ouch! Well, it couldn't be helped. Hamilton had purred in his sleep, right up to his last few nights when he'd been silent, sedated with morphine to kill the pain. Well, best not to think about that.

Bea emptied the rest of her things from her overnight case – Hamilton's overnight case – and set to work.

Tuesday morning

The following morning everything went according to plan. Not Mr Van's plan, but Bea's. She'd spent some time wondering what she would do in Mr Van's place, and had come to the conclusion that he'd given in far too easily at the restaurant. Bea thought he'd set Herman to watch that she didn't leave the hotel during the night and when she did leave, she'd be followed and the case wrenched from her before she could get to the station.

So she took certain precautions.

She rose before Maggie, showered, dressed and popped her overnight things into the case Maggie was using. Her wrist ached, but not intolerably. After she'd roused Maggie, she knocked on Charlotte's door. The girl had slept badly, if at all. She looked dreadful, with greenish shadows under her eyes and reddened lids. The first thing she said was, 'I don't want any breakfast.' The second was, 'I don't think I'm up to driving all that way.'

'Shall I get the hotel people to call the doctor for you?'

'Don't be stupid. I'm not that ill. I'll be all right when I get back home.'

'I came by train but I could go back with you to help with the driving, if you like?'

'I suppose that would be best.'

Bea told herself that it was best to forget Charlotte's rudeness, and concentrate on how ill the child looked. 'I'll get the hotel to bring you up something to drink while Maggie and I go down to breakfast.'

'I don't want anything.'

Bea curbed her frustration. 'Very well. Now I've packed already. I'll take my overnight bag to the station after we've had breakfast, which will give you and Maggie time to finish up here. All right?'

'I suppose so.'

Bea went down to breakfast with Maggie, whose appetite was undimmed by their plight. Maggie relished every part of the Continental breakfast supplied, from the different types of ham and cheese to the selection of freshly baked rolls, the hard-boiled eggs, the cereals, the juices and the array of pâtés and jams provided. Bea could only manage one croissant and a cup of coffee.

Bea explained to Maggie that she'd take her bag to the station straight away, so would Maggie get Charlotte and all their luggage down to the foyer ready to leave in an hour's time. Maggie nodded and helped herself to a third plateful.

Paying the bill for the three of them, Bea explained to Erik that she was very nervous after that awful man had tried to get in to see the girls. Now one of the girls was really quite poorly and Bea had to get them back to London straight away, but she had various errands still to do.

For one thing, she'd been supposed to meet up with an old friend to return an overnight bag that she'd borrowed on her last visit, and she wanted to leave that in the left luggage place at the station and post the code to her. Could Erik lend her a piece of paper and a stout envelope for this, and did he know of a reliable taxi driver, who could help her get around?

Erik nodded. 'You need an extra big taxi driver, maybe?'

'Perhaps two?' Bea suggested. 'One to park his taxi and the other to go with me into the station to lodge the bag, and then help me post the letter? I'd pay whatever they ask.'

Erik reached for the phone.

By the time Bea had collected the bag from her room, a taxi was waiting for her outside the hotel with two large men inside. Both were wearing dark glasses and both were grinning. They weren't taking her fears seriously. After all, Bruges was a very safe place to live. On the other hand, she was offering them double their usual fares for squiring her around and her antics would provide them with a fine tale to tell their friends about in the bar that night.

They shook hands with Bea, introducing themselves as Jan and Dirk. Jan took the bag from Bea, commented on how heavy it was, and ushered her into the back seat. The radio was blasting out the news from a local station. As Jan got into the passenger seat, Bea thought she glimpsed a large dark car parked under the trees by the side of the canal. And yes, it moved off after her.

She tensed and then relaxed. Mr Van couldn't do anything to her with two such stalwart men to look after her.

'We protect you from the bad guys,' boasted Dirk, the larger of the two men and also the driver.

'I'm very grateful,' said Bea. And indeed she was. The large dark car followed them round the corner. There was a complex system of one-way streets on this side of Bruges and the car clung to their bumper all the way to the ring road, and turned with them on the way to the station.

Dirk stiffened, losing his smile. He muted the sound of the radio, but said nothing till they parked outside the station. The dark car pulled up behind them. As Bea made to get out, he held up his hand. 'One moment, please.'

He set the car in motion again, did a U-turn and regained the main road via the traffic lights. The dark car cut across several others to close up behind them. Dirk conferred with Jan in Flemish, as he drove the taxi neatly round to the far side of the station, where there was a large car park. He found a slot and eased the taxi into it. The large dark car cruised in behind them but could find no place to stop nearby.

Jan said, 'That car is following us, yes?'

Bea nodded. The driver's window had been wound down, and she'd had a good look at the two men inside; Herman and Mr Van. Her throat constricted.

'Dutch plates,' observed Dirk.

Bea said, 'Yesterday, the driver of that car tried to get into the hotel room occupied by two young girls, friends of mine. He tried to get me into the same car. Later his passenger forced himself on us at the restaurant and threatened us. The girls were very upset.'

Jan said, 'There was a programme on the television the other night about men taking girls for the sex trade. Your two girls are pretty, no? And you yourself might be appealing to a certain type of man.'

At the thought of a man finding her a sex object at her age, Bea was seized by a painful desire to scream with laughter. She fought it off, just. In a voice that wobbled, she said, 'Maggie is very attractive, but her friend is badly dressed and wears glasses.'

Dirk mused, 'My granny used to say you don't look at the mantelpiece while poking the fire.'

Jan thought this might be too coarse a saying for a lady passenger. 'Hrrm,' he said. 'Well, this is no joke.'

Bea reassured him. 'They won't try anything with you two around.'

Dirk took charge. 'We both come in with you. Let me carry the bag. Is too heavy for you.'

Bea was glad that they had both volunteered to accompany her because, as they walked along the busy central passage between the platforms, she caught sight of Herman dodging his way through the crowd, trying to catch up with them. Perhaps he'd left Mr Van to park the car?

The Left Luggage lockers were off the concourse in a room at the front of the station. Bea turned in the doorway, unzipping the bag and holding it up so that Herman could see the shortbread tin and the box which had once contained a coffee set. She saw his eyes focus on them as she did up the zip again.

She asked Jan and Dirk to stand behind her to prevent Herman from seeing exactly which locker she was going to use. She heaved the bag inside and slammed the door shut, testing the lock. So far, so good. She craned her neck around Jan to see if Herman was indeed watching her – which he was. She needed him to see that she was fulfilling her part of the bargain to the letter, so she asked Jan to move one pace to her left, so that Herman could watch her put the code for the locker into the pre-addressed envelope.

By now Herman was on his mobile, frowning, watching her every move. Perhaps he'd hoped to snatch the code from her as soon as she'd deposited the bag in the locker?

Jan and Dirk escorted her to a post box outside the station. Herman followed, still on his mobile. Bea dropped her letter into the box, checking that mail was collected at frequent intervals. Mr Van should have the letter tomorrow morning. As she walked back through the station to the taxi, the two men kept pace with her, one at either shoulder. She wondered if film stars with body-guards felt like this. She rather enjoyed the feeling. Herman trailed after them, still on his mobile, no doubt reporting to his boss.

Bea settled into the back of the taxi, but couldn't feel relief as yet. She was still wound up, on a high. She couldn't relax till she and the girls were all safely through Customs, and – oh dear – there was that long drive ahead.

Jan was enjoying this. 'Where to now, then? You want us to take you around the beauties of our wonderful city?'

Bea laughed. 'I wish I had the time. But yes, come to think of it . . . would you drop me off at Rubica's on the corner of Simon Stevinplein before returning me to the hotel? I need to pick up an outfit I tried on yesterday.' The diversion would give her an opportunity to check if Mr Van were still following her or not. If he'd been fooled, he'd now disappear. But if he had worked out what she'd done . . . she shuddered. She didn't like to think what he might do next.

Both men laughed. 'You are one wild dame!' said Jan, who obviously watched too many old films.

'I am that,' said Bea. 'Indulge me. I'm very happy to pay whatever you ask for the pleasure of your company.'

The two men conferred, delighted to sink themselves into the role of James Bond, rescuing a damsel in distress. What a wonderful change this made from the daily routine!

Jan decided he would go into the shop with Bea, while Dirk circled the block. Would it be possible for the lady to buy an outfit within ten minutes? They understood it usually took longer. Bea said that they could rely on her.

Jan ushered her into the shop, while Bea sought out Jeannine, explaining that she was in a great rush, had to get back to London unexpectedly early, but would love to take the outfit that she'd tried on yesterday with her, and here was her card.

When she had completed her transaction, Jan told her to wait inside the shop until he saw Dirk's car arrive and when it did, he rushed her across the pavement into it.

Jan had regained his smile. 'There is no more sign of that car. I would have seen them, if they had still been on our tail.'

Dirk wondered, 'Perhaps we should have called the police, no?'

'No,' said Bea, perhaps a little too quickly. She calmed down to say, in reasoned tones, 'Thanks to you, there's no harm done and calling the police would delay our departure and cost you both time off work. One of my girls is really quite poorly and I want to get her home as quickly as possible. Take me back to the hotel. I'm sure they won't follow me any longer.'

And indeed there was no large dark car on the way back to the hotel, or lurking under the trees beside the canal.

'You are two wonderful men,' said Bea. 'I'll remember you both in my prayers tonight . . .' Now why had she said that? It wasn't a thought that would normally occur to her. 'How much do I owe you?'

'Two taxi fares from the hotel to the station and back,' said Jan.

Bea paid him treble what he'd asked for, and thanked them both.

Tuesday early afternoon

Bea's wrist was aching like mad by the time they reached London again. She drew up outside the girls' flat and got herself out of the car, moving stiffened joints one by one. She didn't expect Charlotte to thank her for driving them home, and she wasn't disappointed.

Although Maggie had much the longer legs, Charlotte had insisted on sitting in the front seat, because she said she was always car sick if she sat in the back. Bea believed her. The girl had revived a little once they were back in England, but she hadn't exactly been a sparkling companion. Maggie had, predictably, hooked herself into her iPod and passed the journey by listening to some of her favourite tunes. The crackle of her music had nearly driven Bea to distraction. But there . . . Maggie had had something to complain about. Bea supposed.

Charlotte humped her case – the one she'd borrowed from Bea – out of the car and left it on the pavement, saying that she was too ill to carry it indoors, and that if Maggie would care to bring it up, she could pack her own things and get out of the flat. Maggie shrugged, but said she didn't mind if she did.

Bea enquired where she was to leave the hired car, and Charlotte came up with an address in North Kensington. They were all too tired to observe the usual pleasantries.

Maggie asked if it would be all right if Bea took Maggie's case on to her house, and Bea said she'd do that, particularly since – as she no longer had the use of Hamilton's overnight bag – she'd packed her own things at the bottom of Maggie's case early that morning.

Maggie disappeared into the flats, telling Bea that she'd be home soon. Bea tucked herself back into the car with a groan, for her wrist really did ache abominably and however often she'd adjusted it, the seat was all wrong for her. She got out her phone and alerted Oliver to expect her in an hour. She still had one more job to do before she could relax.

Tuesday early afternoon

Rafael could hardly believe it. He'd had a key to Liam's flat for ever because Charlotte had got locked out one day and so arranged for the people in the flat upstairs to keep a spare key, and vice versa. But when he'd kept his appointment with the scumbag, he found the bird had flown. Well, Rafael would catch up with him at work and wouldn't there half be a reckoning then!

Meanwhile, he'd been keeping an eye on the Weston house. From a neighbour, Rafael had learned that Philip's father was seriously ill in hospital, with his wife at his bedside. But, someone was still taking in the milk and newspapers.

Obviously, Philip was hiding out in the family home. Rafael couldn't think why it hadn't occurred to him before. He'd rung the bell but no one had answered, though he'd thought a curtain had moved at an upstairs window. Philip might not want to open the door to Rafael, but he'd have opened it for Liam, wouldn't he? Now Rafael would have to think of another way to get in.

*Van called from Bruges to say the old woman travelling with
the girls had pulled a fast one, shoving the goods in a locker at
the station, and posting the code to him. Van would have to stay
another night in an expensive hotel, till he could get the key and
retrieve the goods. He was not best pleased.*

Rafael found that amusing. As if Van couldn't afford it!

Now to phone Liam at work.

Fourteen

Tuesday afternoon

By the time Bea got back home, Oliver was shifting from
one foot to the other on the doorstep, on the lookout for
her.

'Mrs Abbot, Maggie's been on the phone, in something of a
state. Can you get back down to the flat straight away?'

Bea closed her eyes. She'd been dreaming of a cup of tea and
a rest in her own bedroom, with the blinds drawn against the
sun. Various bits of her were feeling unhappy, including her
temper. It wasn't Oliver's fault, but if he didn't help her out with
the luggage, she'd kill him or give him the sack or run him
through with a bread knife or something!

She curbed her rage with an effort. 'I need to get this hired
car back to the garage first.'

'Shall I drive it for you? Oh, and there's tons of messages,
lots been happening.' He swung Maggie's case out of the car,
and ran up the steps with it.

'I don't want to know,' said Bea, retrieving the bag from
Rubica. 'What's Maggie on about? Can't it wait?'

'She said it was urgent. Go on, let me drive the car. I can,
you know.'

'No, you can't,' said Bea, weary to the bone. 'Not till you've
passed your test, and we can't leave it here or it'll get clamped.
You take my stuff inside, I'll drive the car round to the garage

and take a taxi down to the flats. You can give me all the news later.'

'Are you all right, Mrs Abbot? You look sort of, I don't know, not quite as usual.'

'I don't feel it, either,' said Bea, inserting herself with an effort back into the driving seat. 'But at least the girls are safely back home, and that's the main thing.'

The girls were safely back home, and so were the goods. Tired as she was, she smiled, remembering Mr Goldstone's excitement when she handed the fabulous treasures over to him. He'd hummed with pleasure, touching each miniature, caressing each gold box even while he complained fretfully that there were still only nineteen in the consignment and not twenty. He said he knew exactly how to get the lot to the insurance people without any questions being asked, and volunteered that he'd split any reward money fifty-fifty.

Tired as she was, Bea had informed him that he must be in his second childhood if he thought she'd accept his offer. Ninety-ten, she said, with the larger amount to the agency. Her expenses on this trip had been enormous, and although Velma had said she'd pay, Bea couldn't really bill her because the trip hadn't produced anything to help them find or clear Philip. Bea felt really bad about that, because she could have spent the time searching for him, instead of rushing off to the Continent.

Mr Goldstone had haggled for a while, saying it would cost him something to set up a deal, no questions asked, with the insurance people. Finally he'd suggested a split of eighty-twenty, keeping her name out of all negotiations, to which she'd agreed.

He'd wanted all the information she could give him about Mr Van and Liam in order to track down the man who'd killed his friend. Bea got it down to a few sentences and, remembering the photograph she'd taken of Mr Van in the restaurant, punched buttons to send it to the old man's mobile. In return she asked him for a description of the twentieth box, in case she came across it anywhere.

About Philip and the missing picture . . . did Mr Goldstone have any news for her? No? Ah, well.

She spared a thought for Mr Van as she got back into the car. She didn't think he was going to coo with pleasure over the two litre bottles of mineral water which was all he'd find when he opened Hamilton's bag tomorrow. Which reminded her to put an overnight bag down on her expenses sheet.

Now Maggie had called for help again. No time for a cuppa, but she simply must change her shoes before she went out again, and grab a bottle of water from the fridge. Oliver followed her around, with a clipboard full of messages.

'Sorry about this,' said Bea, not listening to what he was saying. 'Can you hold the fort for another hour or two?'

Question marks were shooting out of his eyebrows, but to do him justice he reined in his tongue.

'Speak soon,' she said, and dashed out of the house again.

The porter wasn't in his little box in the foyer at the flats and she'd forgotten to pick up her keys to the flat, but when she announced her name into the speaker entry system, Maggie let her in and met her as she got out of the lift on the second floor.

'What's up?'

'You'll see.' Maggie was tense, looked worried.

The flat smelt of bleach, mingled with polish. Someone had been cleaning the place. Maggie threw doors open, one after the other. 'Zander. Liam.'

Their rooms were neat, tidy and bare. All traces of the previous occupants had disappeared. Even the beds had been stripped. It was as if the two men had never existed.

Maggie opened the door to the boys' bathroom. Spotlessly clean and shiny, there wasn't even a crumpled towel to be seen; in fact, there were no towels at all.

The kitchen. Every single shelf had been stripped of its contents except one. 'That's my food on the shelf, next to Charlotte's. Everything else has gone.'

Bea gaped. 'What about Philip's room?'

Maggie opened the door. The room looked the same as when Bea had last seen it, down to the black plastic bags that Bea had filled on her first foray into the flat. 'What remains of his belongings are still here, but his food's gone from the kitchen. I suppose clearing out both bedrooms is Liam's farewell trick. Charlotte disagrees, of course. She thinks Liam's been kidnapped so she's sitting by the phone, waiting for someone to ring and demand a ransom.'

'Come off it!'

'Agreed. He knows we've tumbled to his smuggling operation

and has scarpered in case we set the police on him. He's covered his tracks by getting in a cleaning firm to expunge all traces of his occupancy, fingerprints and so on.'

'That makes sense, but why clear out Zander's room as well?'

'I haven't a clue.' Maggie was close to tears. 'Guess which cleaning firm he used?'

Bea put a hand to her head. 'He knew that you worked for a domestic agency, so he asked *our firm* to arrange it?'

'The bill is on the kitchen table. It was made out to Liam Forbes, but he's crossed his name out and put mine on instead. Oliver must have accepted the job because he knew that I was living here.' Maggie picked the bill off the table and handed it to Bea, who put on her reading glasses to note that Oliver had sent the Green Girls team to do the job. Four women aged forty to sixty, all experienced cleaners. Oliver had chosen well.

Bea supported herself against the nearest wall. She'd just had a horrid thought. 'Surely there's only one reason why Liam cleared out Zander's room? He knows Zander's not coming back. Was Zander also involved in the smuggling, I wonder?'

'I can't believe that. I expect Zander came back unexpectedly to claim his things, and Liam saw him and . . . no, that doesn't make sense. I suppose we could try to contact Zander in the Midlands to see if that's what's happened.' Maggie declined to look into the abyss.

Bea was getting a bad feeling about this. 'How do we know that he's in the Midlands?'

'Well, Charlotte said . . . and then Liam borrowed Zander's phone and . . . why should Liam lie?' Maggie was getting confused.

'I don't know. What I do know is that yesterday morning when I came here to clean, Zander's shaving things were still here in the boys' bathroom and his belongings were all over his room, though someone had attempted to pack them up for him. There was even a laptop which hadn't been in the room when I cleaned it earlier. At the time I wondered why Zander hadn't taken it with him, and now . . . everything's gone, shaving things, clothes, laptop and all. Maggie, do you know which firm Zander works for? Yes? Could you get the number and ring them? We need to make sure he really did go to the Midlands.'

Maggie gulped but did as she was told, while Bea went to check on all the wastepaper baskets in the flat. Trust the Green

Girls to have cleaned them out. Each empty basket now had a plastic bag neatly inserted into it.

Bea called out, 'Maggie, what do you do with your rubbish?'

The door at the end of the corridor opened and Charlotte appeared, looking even more dishevelled than before. Her T-shirt and jeans were the ones she'd travelled in and both looked the worse for wear since she'd been stuffing her mouth with chocolate on her return and got some on her clothes. She had a bottle of Coca-Cola in her hand and looked wild. 'You! What are you doing here? Did I ask you to come? If you don't know where Liam is, you might as well get lost. We've got some proper cleaners now, much better than you.'

'True,' said Bea. 'Four people can always work more quickly than one.'

'You are beneath my contempt,' said Charlotte grandly, and glugged down some of her drink.

Maggie was still on her phone, wide-eyed with distress. She put her hand over the receiver to speak to Bea. 'His office doesn't know what's happened to him. He wasn't asked to transfer anywhere and he hasn't been seen since last Friday. They're worried that he might have been taken ill. They've tried ringing his home number and his mobile, but no one replies. That would be because there was no one here and,' she swallowed hard, 'because Liam has Zander's mobile.'

'Tell them to report him missing,' said Bea. 'We have to bring the police in on this.'

'No police!' Charlotte spluttered and hiccupped but got the words out somehow. 'Don't you dare! I won't have it! Not while Liam's been kidnapped!'

Bea took Charlotte's arm and guided her back into her bedroom. Over her shoulder she said to Maggie, 'Tell them to call the police and then get on to Oliver, ask him to trace the Green Girls and find out what they did with the stuff they took away from here. Say I'll give them a bonus if they let me see it all.'

She sat Charlotte down on her bed. 'Now listen to me, Charlotte. Three men have disappeared from this flat over the last week, and the police have to know about it. It's not just Liam, but Zander and Philip as well. I think Philip went voluntarily and is hiding out from his creditors somewhere. With any luck we'll be able to track him down and produce him alive and well.

'But the others . . .! We know Liam was involved in trying to smuggle goods out of the country and he's done a runner since we found out about it. I don't know what's happened to Zander, but I'm beginning to wonder if he learned something about the smuggling operation from Liam and has been, well, dealt with. Everything we know about Zander's supposed transfer to the Midlands came from Liam, didn't it? Yet Zander's office say he wasn't given a transfer, he didn't turn up to work yesterday or today, he didn't take any of his belongings away with him when he was supposed to have left, and Liam's using Zander's phone. I think Liam knows what's happened to Zander, and that's another reason why he's disappeared. This is serious, Charlotte. The police have to be informed.'

'Not in cases of kidnapping.' She hiccupped. 'Hick!'

'Charlotte, try to think clearly. Liam's behaviour is criminal. He's out of it. But Zander seems to have been a straightforward sort of person. Don't you think you ought to find out what's happened to him? Suppose he came across the same men who were threatening you last night in the restaurant?'

'Hick! That's ridiculous! Anyway, they can't do anything to us. We let them have the stolen goods, and they let us go. End of story.'

Well, it wasn't the end of the story, as Bea very well knew. Possibly Maggie had guessed as well. That big suitcase had been as heavy this morning as it had been on the journey out.

Charlotte tossed her head. 'Anyway, they're in Belgium, and we're in London.'

'We crossed the Channel. So could they.'

'You're trying to frighten me and it won't work!'

Bea was silent, waiting for the girl to acknowledge the truth of the case that had been put to her. Charlotte began to retch. All that Coca-Cola and chocolate on an empty stomach! Bea held back a sigh, guided Charlotte into the girls' bathroom and left her to it.

Maggie came to the door. 'Is she being sick again? Oh, honestly!'

'Did you get on to Oliver?'

'He says Florrie Green is calling in at the office later to collect her money and she'll speak to you then about clearing the flat.'

'Good. Now can you go downstairs and have a word with the porter – what's his name? Randolph, yes – ask him what happens to the rubbish cleared out of the flats. If you can find the bag which the Green Girls used when they tidied up this place, see if he'll let you have it.'

'He'll think I'm mad.'

'Tell him you've lost your bus pass, think it might have been dropped in the kitchen and that it could have been thrown away by mistake. Ask him if he saw anyone but Liam from the flat today, or if Liam had any visitors while he was here. Randolph may not have been in the hall all the time, but it's worth a try.'

Maggie was holding herself together with an effort. 'Do I tell him Zander's missing?'

'Let the police do that. I want to get clear of this place before they arrive. I don't want to have to answer questions about smuggling and I don't want to draw their attention to Philip if we can help it.'

She knew very well that once the police started to ask questions about Zander's disappearance, the other vanishing acts would have to come out. It was a dilemma. On the one hand she couldn't keep quiet about Zander, and on the other she must try to keep Philip out of it.

Maggie disappeared, and Charlotte came out of the bathroom, still hiccupping, hair plastered to her head and T-shirt sodden. The girl ignored Bea to go to a cupboard and pull out a fresh T-shirt and jeans.

Bea said, 'I know you don't want Maggie to stick around any longer, so if you'll show me where her things are, I'll pack them up for her.'

Charlotte looked horrified. 'You're not going to leave me here by myself in this empty flat? This place is spooked! I'd die!'

Bea wanted to tell the girl to get lost, but couldn't. She sighed, telling herself she was terminally soft-centred. 'Very well, then. You may come back with us and stay in my spare room for a couple of nights. Just till you can get the locks changed and new tenants in.'

Charlotte hiccupped again. 'I'm not changing the locks. Liam might come back.'

So might Philip, come to think of it. 'Oh well, we'll think of something.'

Charlotte clapped both hands to her cheeks. 'I've just realized the rent's due next week. I'm responsible for collecting it from the others, and they aren't here to give me their share!'

'We'll see what we can sort out later. Now let's pack, shall we?'

Perhaps Velma would be understanding about the rent, since she owned the flat. Perhaps Philip would turn up, with a wad of money in his pocket, having made a killing in the club. Perhaps pigs might fly.

Maggie came out of the lift with a bulging rubbish bag which she'd rescued from the bowels of the earth. 'This is the only one I could find. Randolph didn't see anyone but Liam and the cleaners coming and going before Charlotte and I came back from our trip. And no, he hasn't seen Zander since Sunday. Liam told Randolph yesterday morning that Zander had landed a job in the Midlands, and Randolph said to wish him well. End of story.'

So, on with the next.

Bea's first priority when she got home was a cup of tea. She told Maggie to help Charlotte settle in and sank on to a stool in the kitchen, waiting for the kettle to boil. Oliver followed her in with his clipboard full of messages but was wise enough not to speak to her until she'd downed her first cup, poured a second and reached for the biscuit tin.

Oliver was tentative. 'Can you bear to listen to what's been happening here?'

She shook her head. She was developing a headache. Nervous tension.

He said, 'Did the Green Girls mess up at the flat? Mrs Green wasn't best pleased when I gave her your message.'

Bea shook her head. 'They did just fine. Any news from the hospital?'

'Mrs Weston phoned. She wanted you to go round by her house to collect the post and pay her cleaner. I didn't say you'd gone after a lead on Philip because I wasn't sure you'd want her to know about the smuggling. She gave me the code for the alarm and said she'd ring her Polish cleaner and tell her someone was coming and that they were to be asked for the alarm codes before she let them in, to make sure it was the right person. I said you were tied up but I'd find someone to go for her. I got your old book-keeper to go, gave her some cash to pay the woman, and get a receipt. She took the letters on to the hospital. Mrs Weston was waiting outside for them. She asked after you, and I said you'd ring as soon as you were back.'

Bea rubbed her eyes and yawned. 'You've done well, Oliver. Just keep everyone off my back for a while, will you?'

The bell rang downstairs in the agency rooms and Bea groaned. Oliver said, 'That'll be Mrs Green. Shall I put her off?'

Bea shook her head, got to her feet, clutched her mug of tea and tottered down the stairs to let Florrie in.

'Sorry to bring you in, Florrie. Oh, you've brought Yvonne and Maria as well? Go through to the room at the back, will you?'

'You look rough, Mrs Abbot,' observed Florrie, humping a couple of black bags in with her. Yvonne and Maria were also humping black bags. Three large ladies, they installed themselves on the big chair and the settee in Bea's office.

Florrie, aged sixty but dyed to look forty and almost succeeding, had a florid complexion and muscles of iron. The other two had identical blonde poodle haircuts and looked as stringy as long-distance runners. A formidable crew.

Florrie was the spokeswoman. 'Tillie couldn't make it. Had to pick up her grandson from school. You've caught us between jobs but we can't stop long because we start cleaning the school at the back here in an hour. So what set the alarm bells off, eh?'

Bea eyed the sacks. 'Is that all the stuff you took from the flat this morning?'

'All but what Tillie's taken home already, a duvet and some pillows, almost new by the look of them.'

Bea sank into her chair. 'Sorry, sorry. I know you have a right to keep anything you find when you clear a flat, unless instructed otherwise. This time, well, the man who let you into the flats . . . it was a man, wasn't it . . .?'

'Youngish, rat-faced, on the landline most of the time we were there. His name was Liam, if you can go by the name he gave when he answered the phone. Told us his name was Forbes and he'd pay cash, then found he hadn't got any cash and said Maggie something would pay as she was living there at the moment and worked for you. That was after we'd cleaned, of course. So what's pressed the alarm bell?'

'Do you know who Liam was on the phone to?'

Florrie shrugged. 'Wasn't listening. Some girl or other. Kiss kiss, mucky talk about crotchless panties.' She turned to the others. 'Anyone else hear anything?'

Yvonne nodded. 'Times of trains. Boat trains. Ireland, at a guess.'

Maria contradicted her. 'Flights out of Heathrow, I heard. Airport, anyway. Gatwick, maybe Stansted? We usually fly from Stansted when we go on holiday.'

'Ireland?' asked Bea, sipping tea. 'Oh, sorry, ladies. Would you like a cuppa?'

'Just had one,' said Florrie. 'Thanks all the same. What's this all about, then? He cleaned out the kitty and did a runner?'

'Something like that. One of Liam's flatmates thought he was going to propose to her on a city-break in Bruges, but he didn't turn up and now he's missing. She wants me to find him if I can.' Which was all true, sort of.

'Ireland,' said Yvonne. 'He was asking some friend about a job "back home". Southern Ireland, by his accent. I know the type. She's well rid of him, if you ask me.'

'Only thing,' said Florrie, 'was he going with a boyfriend? He didn't look homo, and I should know with my youngest being that way.'

Bea followed this with difficulty. 'You thought Liam might have been going off with one of his male flatmates, because he wanted his and another man's room stripped out?' The three women nodded. They'd obviously talked about this already.

Florrie said, 'Makes sense. He said to clean his room and the one next to it, but to leave the third man's and the girls' room alone. He showed us what we could clear out of the fridge and the kitchen, take the lot except for what was on one shelf. He said that belonged to the girls and to leave it alone. So what are we supposed to have done wrong, eh?'

Bea tried to make sense of this. 'One of his flatmates – a man called Zander, who kept his room neat and tidy – went off some time last weekend, leaving all his belongings behind. They were still there first thing yesterday morning, but they're not there now. There was a lot of stuff.' She looked at the three bags the women had brought in with them. 'Did you find a telly, a load of books, a laptop, a briefcase and a really good leather jacket?'

Yvonne shook her head. 'There wasn't that much left in the room you're talking about. Some bedding. Tillie took that.'

Florrie confirmed it. 'The cupboard was bare. Hardly any rubbish, either.'

Bea was flummoxed. 'Then what happened to all his stuff?'

Maria was indignant. 'You think we tell lies?'

'No, no. I believe you, but it doesn't make sense. Anyway,

let's look at what you did take. If there's anything I need for this girl Liam bamboozled, I'll buy it off you. Otherwise, ladies, it's all yours.'

They spread out the contents of the three bags on the floor one by one. There was some bedding, old clothes, shoes that needed repair, paperback books. There were towels, some clean, some used, a useless mobile phone, some CDs without their cases.

'All from Liam's room,' said Florrie. 'There was some magazines – the top shelf sort, you know? – but you wouldn't be wanting them, would you?'

Bea agreed she wouldn't. 'You didn't touch the third man's room – Philip's?'

'Liam said not to bother, so we didn't.'

'You say Liam was on the phone a lot. Did he write anything on a pad by the phone? People often do when they're getting times of trains.'

Florrie said, 'There was a wodge of paper in the wastepaper bin. It went out with the rubbish.'

'What about the tins and foodstuffs you took from the kitchen?'

Florrie sighed. 'That sack was heavy. I left it in my little car outside, which reminds me that I'd best get it moved, or it'll get clamped. Do you need the tins?'

Bea shook her head. 'No, I don't think I do. Thanks, Florrie. And you, Yvonne and Maria. Tell Tillie thanks from me, too. Now I'll get your money and you can be off to your next job, right?'

Rafael was fit to be tied. Liam's office said he'd been called home to Ireland unexpectedly, a death in the family. No address. Rafael had lost his second-in-command just when he needed him most!

He told himself to calm down. He'd had set-backs before and overcome them. It had been a set-back when his usual courier got himself written off, but now he'd got the girls and they'd be even better. They'd delivered the gold boxes and miniatures so he could wipe that off his list.

Only, without Liam to keep the girls happy, they might start talking. Rafael checked with the hotel which Liam had said the girls were using, only to be told that they'd left that morning. So far, so good. He'd catch up with them later.

Now for the Weston house. Rafael had taken another turn

*round there in his lunch break and noted that the milk and papers
had been taken in again. Philip was certainly there, and where
Philip was, the Millais was bound to be.*

*Philip had talked a lot about how rich his new stepmother
was, and how she always wore several expensive diamond rings.
They would do very nicely, plus the Millais, of course. Would
the diamonds be kept in a safe? Well, Philip would know.*

Yes, he would pay Philip a visit tonight.

Fifteen

Tuesday early evening

Maggie galumphed down the stairs to Bea's office in the
basement. The girl had changed into a T-shirt and jeans
but they were a good fit and the colours suited her. Maggie was
learning what she could wear and what she couldn't. The problem
was that most of what suited her had been 'borrowed' from Bea's
wardrobe. Bea recognized one of her favourite T-shirts, but was
too weary to object. Her headache was increasing.

Maggie was full of nervous energy. 'Charlotte wanted to use
your bathroom but I told her "no". She's complaining that she's
used to a bath and there's only a shower cubicle in her en suite,
and I still said "no". She said she'd be sick on the stairs if she
had to climb to the top floor to use my bath, and I said that if
she was sick, she could clean it up herself. So she feels much
better now.'

Bea hadn't thought she could laugh again, but she did.

'Charlotte's got a new bee in her bonnet. She's decided that
Liam hasn't contacted her because he's been beaten up by his
so-called "friend" for warning her about the smuggling. She's
ringing round all the hospitals to see if Liam's been admitted to
one of them.'

'You can tell her Liam's been enquiring about trains and flights
to Dublin.'

'I don't think she wants to be confused with facts.'

'Poor girl,' said Bea. 'Hasn't she ever had a man pay attention to her before? No, don't answer that. Of course she hasn't.'

'I was like that, once,' said Maggie, reddening. 'All awkward corners and grateful for the slightest attention. You were very good to put up with me.'

'A pleasure,' said Bea, almost meaning it. 'And before I forget, I'm really pleased to have you back.'

Maggie fidgeted with her belt. 'Mrs Abbot, what about Zander?'

Bea took the bridge of her nose between two fingers. 'I know. It's worrying. I checked with the cleaners and they didn't take his belongings. When you went out with him on Sunday to feed the ducks—'

'Kew Gardens. It was fun.'

'He didn't say anything to you then about going to Bruges the next day?'

'No, it was Liam who told us about that. Liam said he and Zander were going to plan it all later that evening but they were ever so late getting back. I think I was asleep before they came in. Charlotte, too.'

And nobody had seen him since. Bea tried to think it through. Liam told Charlotte that Zander had been called away, something to do with work, but his toilet things were still at the flat on Monday morning and his belongings didn't get packed up till later that day . . . by someone who was far from neat, which didn't sound like Zander.

'I'm wondering,' said Bea, 'if Zander got caught up in the smuggling ring, too. Liam wasn't the boss of the smuggling ring, was he? Liam was taking orders, seemed afraid of whoever it was. Liam's boss is the mastermind behind these art thefts. We know he's already killed twice, so it makes sense that Liam's scared of him.

'Suppose Zander told Mr Mastermind that he wanted out and got himself killed as a result. Mastermind then told Liam to make up a story to account for Zander's absence and either he or Liam removed Zander's belongings to make it seem that he'd disappeared of his own volition.'

Maggie opened and shut her mouth in horror. 'That's . . . awful. I'm sure you're wrong, but . . . oh, no! You think he's dead? But . . . but if we went to the police, it would all come out that we'd been smuggling stolen goods out of the country, wouldn't it?' She ran her fingers up through her hair and held on to her head. 'Mrs Abbot, I haven't thanked you yet for getting us back in one piece. Believe me, I'll be grateful till the day I die. But if we tell the police what we suspect . . . can you think of another way?'

'I glanced through a newspaper yesterday at the station and there was nothing about a body having been found. Suppose you start ringing round the hospitals yourself. Ask if a man answering Zander's description has been brought in. Say he's a flatmate of yours, hasn't been seen since Sunday afternoon.'

Maggie said, 'I'll try.' And collided with Oliver on her way out.

Bea got to her feet. 'Sorry, Oliver. I've no time for agency business. I have to find rubber gloves and go through some rubbish.'

He put on a 'wounded but willing to follow you till death' expression as he followed her up the stairs. 'Let me help.'

'Is this what I pay you a fantastic salary for?'

Icily polite, he said, 'If you think this is more important than attending to business, then so be it. Tell me what we're looking for.'

She found a pair of rubber gloves, spread newspapers out on the work surface in the kitchen, and emptied out the black bin bag Maggie had extracted from the basement of the flats. 'We're looking for anything which might give us a lead as to where Zander, Philip or Liam might have gone. A telephone number for Mastermind would be helpful, too.'

'Who's Mastermind?'

'I'll tell you all about it as we search through the debris. We want till receipts. Scraps of paper with names and addresses on. You know how people doodle when they're talking on the phone? Initials, telephone numbers. Liam was apparently taking down times of trains, possibly to Ireland. Bank statements might be helpful. Doctor's prescription forms. Letters or notes from friends or relatives. Photos. This is the sum total of what was taken from the wastepaper baskets in the flat today, plus . . . yuck . . . fast-food containers, opened packets of food, and this must be stuff from the fridge. You'll need rubber gloves, too. Put everything even faintly possible on to one side and we'll go through it in detail.'

'You remember asking me to get some numbers off Philip's phone? Well, I did that and have a list here. Will that help?'

'I'm sure it will. We'll look at them later.'

Maggie padded into the kitchen, showing too much white around her eyes. 'Central Middlesex. They've got a man answering to Zander's description who was knifed, beaten up and left to die in a car park near a Tube station somewhere on the District line. He was found by a commuter early yesterday morning, probably been there all night. Robbery, they thought, because he's no ID, no money or other forms of identification on him. Unconscious when brought in, but showing signs of coming round now.'

Bea and Oliver suspended operations to listen. Maggie said, aiming for jaunty, 'Of course, it might not be him. What would he be doing out there, eh?'

Bea guessed, 'Meeting Mr Mastermind? Remember Liam said he was going to have a meeting with Zander late Sunday night? You'd better go out there, see if you recognize him. Order a minicab, one of those the agency always uses, put it on our tab. Get the driver to wait for you, no matter how long. Don't get caught in dark alleys.'

Maggie turned even paler than before. Clearly she hadn't realized – as Bea had – that the three of them might become targets once Bea's trick was exposed.

'Trust me.'

Maggie reached for her phone.

Oliver looked affronted. 'Could anyone bear to let me know what's going on?'

The front doorbell pealed. Maggie yelled, 'I'll get it,' and disappeared. They heard her open the front door and greet someone by name. Piers.

'Bother,' said Bea. 'I forgot to ring him back.'

Piers strolled into the kitchen. 'Any chance of a cuppa, Bea, since you stood me up last night? Or something stronger?' He took in the mess, and grinned. 'Let me guess. You're creating the latest entry for the Turner Prize, or you've lost a cheque that ought to have been paid into the agency account.'

Bea wasn't sure whether to hit him or kiss him. 'Sorry about last night. Things got a trifle difficult. Have you any news about Philip and the missing picture?'

Oliver interrupted, holding up a fan of tickets. 'Eurostar tickets. You want them?'

'Definitely. Piers, I suggest you stand well back. You don't want to get those good clothes dirty.'

'*You're* not wearing an apron, I notice.' With the tips of his fingers Piers withdrew a sheet of lined paper from a crushed pack of cereal. 'Suppose I arm myself with a knife and fork? Or perhaps a spoon and fork? There's some broken glass here that's posing a nice threat to my earning capacity. Are we looking for anything in particular?'

Bea sighed. 'All right. Let me tell it from the beginning, if I can work out where the beginning was. Philip Weston – Velma's stepson – disappeared with an important picture. I don't know whether his disappearance was connected with what happened next or not, but this is what I've worked out so far . . .'

As she talked, the bells of St Mary's Church proclaimed the hour, and with one part of her mind Bea recalled the chimes of Bruges. She wondered what Mr Van would do when he discovered he'd been fooled. She didn't think he'd write the episode off to experience. He'd be on the phone to his partner over here, the man who had killed twice already, who'd be on her trail straight away. She'd gained a day with her subterfuge, but was up against time. She must find some clues to the vanishing men and tell Mr Goldstone, who could tell the police, before Mr Van informed Mastermind that she'd walked off with the prize.

Her headache increased.

Oliver made a disgusted sound, scraping what looked like soft cheese from a piece of paper with pen marks on it. 'I think this says "Boat" followed by some figures. Times the boat-train leaves? The paper's torn across just under it.'

Bea tried not to gag as she investigated something murky. 'I wouldn't mind a gas mask. Try to find the other half.' She lifted out some scraps of paper. A photograph, torn in pieces? Lots of junk mail. The stubs of a chequebook. Lloyds Bank. No amounts, payee names or dates had been filled in. Nothing infuriated Bea more than people not filling in cheque stubs. Which one of the three had banked with Lloyds? Who would know? Charlotte?

Where was Charlotte, anyway? The house was very quiet. Too quiet. When Maggie was in the house it resounded with music but Maggie was on her way to be reunited with her boyfriend. Maybe.

'I think that's the lot,' said Piers, prodding a mess of what looked like chutney. Or maybe it was jam. 'Now, who's good at jigsaws?'

Bea shovelled the debris back into the rubbish bag, and they laid out their finds on the kitchen table.

Piers said, 'I suppose I'd better take the photographs.' He set to work.

Bea shuffled Euro tickets. 'He didn't spend long in Brussels, did he? No sooner had he arrived than he caught the next train back.'

Oliver bent over scraps of paper, trying to fit them together. 'At least two different handwritings. One uses black ink, the other bright blue . . . and here's something in pencil.'

'Pretty girl, this,' said Piers, professional instincts to the fore as he pieced a girl's torso together. 'Too much cleavage in front and too little up top, but some men would like her. There's a name on the back. I think it's "Pat", or maybe "Dot". Or . . . hang about, there's another bit here.'

Bea took off her rubber gloves to rub her forehead. 'No bank statements, no credit-card statements, no communications from mobile phone companies. Nothing with a name or address on it. I don't think there's anything here from Philip's room, but I can't for the life of me remember whether I emptied his wastepaper basket or not when I did his room. I think probably not because I was interrupted before I finished, and it's usually the last thing I do.' She was dying for another cuppa, and turned away to fill the kettle and search for some aspirin.

'Not "Dot",' said Piers. '"Patsy". Would you believe! I didn't think anyone labelled their daughters with names that had another connotation nowadays.'

'Patsy,' said a voice from the doorway, 'is Liam's sister. So what are you doing with her photo, may I ask?'

Piers said, 'Some sister! Who are you?'

Bea couldn't find the aspirin, but switched the kettle on and reached for the biscuit tin. When had she eaten last? 'This is Charlotte. Everything in this case revolves around her. She's staying with me till . . .' Bea turned round to introduce Charlotte properly.

What Bea saw then switched her from fatigue to fury. 'WHAT ON EARTH ARE YOU WEARING?' Rage tumbled through her mind and sent her reeling. This girl! This . . . no word was too bad for her, this misbegotten . . .! She screamed out her frustration and dislike. How dare this criminally-inclined, ugly little . . .! Bea was going to kill her, chop her into tiny pieces and feed her remains to the fishes!

Normal service, everyday habits of restraint and politeness were forgotten. Words such as 'cow' and 'ungrateful toad' leaped out of her mouth. She heard them and with one part of her mind she was shocked at herself. With the other, meaner part, she cheered herself on.

How dare Charlotte assume she could take Bea's clothes to wear, and not only clothes out of her wardrobe, but the very clothes she'd bought that morning from Rubica, that she'd never worn herself! Worse, she was too dumpy to wear them gracefully, the skirt was too long and the brand-new jacket had been stretched out of shape over her bulges!

Charlotte crumpled into tears. Bea rejoiced. Let the girl cry! It was the only thing Charlotte knew how to do well! As soon as there was the slightest thing wrong, the girl wept!

Bea slammed both her hands down on the table, and the girl jumped. So did both men, who looked shattered. They were not accustomed to seeing the cool Mrs Abbot giving way to rage.

Bea began to shake. She leaned on the table, thinking, My head's going to burst! I'm going to faint. I'm not going to faint. No. She rapped out an order to the men. 'Get that girl out of my sight. And get those clothes off her. Now!'

The two men jumped again. Both had their mouths open. Charlotte wailed, blundering to the door. They heard her footsteps going down the hall, and then the front door opened and closed.

Bea felt limp. She was *glad* the girl had gone. She remembered then that Charlotte had nowhere to go. She'd be wandering the streets, perfect prey for any man who tried to pick her up. Bea dropped on to the nearest stool and cleared her throat. 'One of you had better go after her. We can't let her rush under a bus and kill herself. She's perfectly capable of it. Needs a full-time carer.'

The kettle screamed and shut itself off. Silence.

Oliver murmured to Piers, 'Shall I go?'

'Uhuh. I'll look after Bea.'

Bea ground her teeth. 'If anyone dares touch me, I'll . . . I'll bite!'

'Wouldn't dream of it,' said Piers. He motioned to Oliver to get going, and walked right round Bea to get some mugs down from the cupboard. 'Tea or coffee? When did you last eat?'

Bea turned her head away, refusing to answer.

'Tea, then,' said Piers, making a pot. 'And you were going to get a couple of biscuits down you, right? Here. Take a chocolate one and shove it in your mouth. Good for you. When you've eaten three or four, I suggest you go and have a little nap after which you can doll yourself up in something pretty and I'll take you out for a meal. Something cheap and filling. Italian do you?'

Bea crammed a biscuit into her mouth and sent him a poisoned dart of a glance.

He didn't seem to notice, putting a mug, milk and sugar on the table in front of her. 'Been overdoing it, have we? Just like old times. I'd come back after spending all our money plus having a raving good time in bed with another woman, and find you prostrate on the sofa after you'd been out cleaning all day to earn a few miserable pennies while at the same trying to keep Max happy. I remember there was always a nourishing stew on the stove for your ungrateful husband.' His memory was accurate.

He poured her out a mug of tea, added milk and sugar and put it in front of her. She took another biscuit, ignoring him.

'Drink!' It was an order.

She shrugged, but did as she was told. 'Good girl. Now up we go to bed. Would you like me to carry you?'

'Tcha! As if!' In fact, she wobbled on her way to the kitchen door, but managed to remain upright. Reaching the stairs, she decided that this was no time to start mountaineering. She wasn't going to let Piers carry her, either. She turned in to the living room and made it to the big settee. Her eyes closed on her. She thought she might have heard the front door slam, and maybe she heard Piers say 'Shush!' to someone out of sight. But that was it for the time being.

She woke slowly. There was a burble of sound in the distance, the radio or the television, turned low. Voices, men's. A door slammed and someone exclaimed, 'Shush!' She tried to sink back into sleep, and remembered . . .

She shot upright, throwing off something that had been laid over her to keep her warm. Piers had put the spare-room duvet over her, and eased off her shoes.

She remembered. And groaned. Had she really used the word

'cow' to Charlotte? And various other terms which she preferred not to bring to the forefront of her mind? How could she! Oh. Dear.

It was one thing to sling words at someone who could take it, but that poor little scrap Charlotte needed support, not annihilation, even if she was the most irritating child in existence. Maggie had been bad enough in the past, but Charlotte was the pits!

What was the time? How long had she slept? She caught her breath. She'd wasted time, and time was in short supply. She only had till tomorrow morning to sort this affair out. The moment Mr Van realized he'd been fooled, he'd swing into action, and there were too many people dead or seriously injured in this affair already.

Her headache was still there, but not as bad as before. She shuffled into her shoes, yawned, took a good look at herself in the mirror and reached for a comb and lipstick. She really needed a long relaxing shower and clean clothes, but first she must find out what information the men might have discovered in the rubbish. And apologize to Charlotte. She supposed.

The two men were in the kitchen, bending over a mess of paperwork.

'Where's Charlotte? Did you manage to retrieve her?'

'She was teetering on the brink of crossing the High Street against a red light, so I hauled her back and handed her a box of tissues. She talked solidly for half an hour about how nothing was her fault and Liam was a princely treasure and now she's washing her hair,' said Oliver, sliding papers into files. 'She says Maggie is always borrowing your clothes, so she didn't see why she shouldn't do the same.'

Bea bit back a sharp rejoinder. 'Any word from Maggie?'

'None.'

Bea sank on to a stool. 'Sorry for losing it. Sorry for leaving you to it. Somewhat tired. Been a long day. But we've only got twelve hours left before Mr Van discovers what's happened and alerts Mastermind. What have we got?'

Piers indicated various piles. 'This lot is all junk mail. I think we can throw it. Next is unidentifiable paperwork, cheque stubs included; I suggest we keep all that on one side in case we get a brainwave. We did ask Charlotte to help us, by the way, but she says we're biased against poor Liam and she won't listen to a word against him. Which put the kybosh on that idea.'

Oliver pointed to a spread of paper and photographs. 'That's all the stuff that we think came from Liam's room and the notes he'd written on the pad by the phone. We matched his handwriting and bright blue ink with signatures in the paperbacks he'd discarded, and some doodles on his porn magazines. Neither of the other two men use black ink or seem to have been addicted to porn so it's safe to say these are Liam's.'

Piers took up the tale. 'There are two photographs of a girl in the almost altogether. This one is signed by someone called Patsy. She's definitely not Liam's sister, as there's a torn up card here from Patsy featuring a heart and some roses on the front, with a message to her "dearest, darlingest, lovingest L". She thanks him for some "delights" which she says she's keeping in pristine condition against his return.'

Bea nodded. 'Crotchless panties were mentioned by Liam when he phoned someone this morning.' She rubbed tired eyes. 'Charlotte thinks she's his sister.'

'She would, wouldn't she?' Oliver had obviously taken Charlotte's measure.

'The other photo is of the same girl gone blonde, in an even more revealing pose.'

Oliver resumed, 'The doodlings from the phone pad – you can see it's been torn off a pad – are in pencil but match Liam's handwriting. The figures are for times of trains and flights to Dublin. We checked, but the airline won't confirm that Liam was on any of the possible flights, and we've no way of knowing if he charged his credit card.'

'Any recognizable phone numbers?'

Oliver indicated another pieced-together scrap of paper. 'He had to get one number through Directory Enquiries, which he wrote down and then altered it by one digit after he'd double-checked it. Piers phoned the number. It belongs to a travel agency in Dublin.'

Bea said, 'That makes sense. One of the Green Girls said she'd overheard him applying to an "old friend" for a job on the phone. He also spent time chatting up a girl.'

Oliver wasn't entirely convinced. 'If he was going off to start a new life, with a new job and a new girl, why didn't he take the photos of the girl with him? He was pretty careful not to leave any other paperwork behind.'

Piers said, 'I wonder how many pairs of crotchless panties

he was distributing? Maybe he had several girls in tow and this one was going to be discarded in the same way he discarded Charlotte.'

There was a stir in the doorway and there stood Charlotte, hair springing out in a wild bush. She was wearing a T-shirt and jeans of her own, and looked as creased as Bea felt. 'He has not discarded me! How dare you say that! And as for you' – she turned on Bea – 'you owe me an apology, I think.'

'Do I?' said Bea, telling herself that it would do no good to get aerated all over again. 'Then that makes two of us, doesn't it? I will apologize for calling you a . . . whatever I did call you . . . if you will apologize for abusing my hospitality.'

'Humph!' Charlotte seated herself at the table, unasked. 'Where's Maggie? And what's for supper? I'm starving.'

'Maggie's out, trying to locate Zander. And supper is what you make of it.'

'Well, I think it's a pretty poor do.' Charlotte's eyes were drawn to the papers on the table. She pointed. 'Hold on a minute. What are you doing with Philip's chequebook? You've no right!' She pulled a face. 'Come to think of it, I believe the bank's closed his account. It's all very well the boys going off like this, but they're leaving me in a horrible situation. I'm really worried about making the rent next week. Liam will send me his share, of course. If I remind him. Sometimes I have to remind him. Did you say he's gone to Ireland to see his sister?'

How long had she been listening at the door? Bea said, 'There's a card here from Patsy. She doesn't sound like his sister.'

Charlotte glanced at it, but didn't read it. 'Well, she is. I expect he's staying with his family. Have you got his home phone number there? Somewhere just south of Dublin.'

Bea said, 'We thought *you* might have it. No? Is there anything else here that you can identify as being Philip's – or Zander's?'

Charlotte gave a deep, put-upon sigh, and separated out some till receipts. 'I suppose these till receipts are Philip's. They're from the convenience store up the road. Philip likes his drink.' There were a few instant meals on the receipts but the bulk of the items came in bottle or can form.

Charlotte pushed some other receipts across the table. 'Zander used to get his food – mostly fruit and vegetables – from market stalls near where he worked in Soho, so no till receipts. He was pretty nearly a vegetarian, but he did get some stuff in from Covent

Garden specialist shops now and then, and these two will be for his cheese and pasta, stuff like that.'

She separated a third lot. 'I shop in the M and S store in the High Street. I've got an account there which I pay monthly. I always keep my current receipts until I know my account's been cleared. These are old receipts from last month. We each buy our own food.'

'And Liam?'

Colour rose in Charlotte's face. 'He was a bit absent-minded about shopping for himself, so I usually shared what I had with him. He paid me back by getting in pizzas or other takeaways a couple of times a week.'

Oh, yeah! thought Bea. Then she remembered the mess of foil plates that had been in the flat when she first went in to clean it, and had to admit that maybe Liam hadn't been all on the take.

'What's all this?' Charlotte had homed in on the porn. Her eyes found the bright blue doodles, and some of the colour left her face. She laid the magazine down.

'Well, I suppose men have to have their little ways, don't they?'

'Some men do,' said Piers. 'It's rather hard on their women-folk, isn't it?'

Charlotte made an effort. 'Oh, that sort of thing doesn't bother me.'

The front door slammed and Maggie walked into the kitchen. She looked pale and tired. 'It's him,' she said. 'But not him. A policeman's waiting at his bedside for him to remember what happened.'

Early Tuesday evening

Rafael left the gallery early, giving the excuse that he had a headache. And indeed he had. Tension, of course. He always felt tense before a job. Afterwards, he was higher than a kite without the need to resort to drugs. He didn't do drugs.

He took the bus back to Kensington High Street and walked down through back streets to the Boltons, noting residents returning from work and play. Rich kids, wealthy parents, 4 x 4s. Shopping bags from Harrods and Harvey Nichols. Day nannies, foreign. Live-in au pairs, likewise. Money, money, money.

When he reached the house, he thought he heard water running from a down pipe somewhere. There was an unobtrusive door set to one side of the main building; it looked like an entry to staff quarters. Bingo! That's where Philip was hiding out! Under the protection of his father, but not under his feet.

Rafael decided to wait till it was dark and ring the bells at both the front and side doors, pretending to be Liam. One way or another, he'd be in there tonight.

He rubbed his temples. The headache wasn't going away. Curse Liam! Everything was so much more difficult without him. The girls ought to be back from Bruges by now. Perhaps it would be as well to check on them, make sure they didn't talk to anyone about what had happened. He'd pop in to see them on his way home.

Sixteen

Tuesday evening

Maggie made for the nearest stool. Unusually, she looked frail. 'Is there a cuppa on the go? Quiet in here, isn't it?' She switched the television on automatically as she sat down, but didn't notice when Piers reached behind her to switch it off again.

Bea switched the kettle on again. 'Take it slowly.'

Charlotte was spoiling for a fight. 'Where have you been? I've been at my wits' end, wondering what had happened to you, and that woman you say is your boss was so rude to me, you wouldn't believe!'

'I'm exhausted, Charlotte,' said Maggie, pressing fingers to eyelids. 'So would you please shut up for once? Other people have their troubles, too, you know.'

'Well!' Charlotte stormed out of the room, and could be heard banging her way up the stairs.

Bea hoped Charlotte had gone to pack, but didn't count on it. She passed Maggie a mug of tea. 'It is Zander, is it?'

'I think so, but he didn't know me. He's had a kicking.' She shuddered. 'His head's shaved and bandaged. He's concussed from here to eternity. He was stabbed in the back but thankfully that's not done too much damage. There was a policeman there, waiting for him to come round. The policeman wanted to know my name and address but I said I wouldn't give it until I knew if it were my boyfriend or not.

'Zander opened his eyes a couple of times, but didn't recognize me. At least, I don't think he did. The policeman leaned over him to ask what was his name, and did he remember what had happened to him. He thought a bit. You could see it hurt him to think. He said, "I don't know. Am I in hospital? What's happened? I can't remember." Only he couldn't speak clearly because his poor face had been banged about.

'I was going to say, "Your name is Zander," and give the address of the flat, but I didn't. I wasn't at all sure that it was Zander, you see. Or rather, I was sure, but if he'd been beaten up by Liam and was afraid to say who he was, then I wasn't going to give him away. So I said he wasn't my flatmate and came away. It's Zander, all right, but he doesn't want to admit it. And I'm not going to cry!'

'Brave girl,' said Bea, and the two men harrumphed agreement. 'Well, I suppose he's safe for the moment. Like us, he's playing for time.'

Charlotte banged back into the room. She was wearing the jacket in which she'd travelled that morning, and she dragged her suitcase behind her. 'I'm not staying here. You can argue all you like but I know when I'm not wanted. I'm not staying at the flat all by myself, either, so Maggie had better come back with me.'

'You must be joking,' said Maggie, hunching her shoulders and taking both hands to her mug of tea.

Bea looked at her watch. How many hours till Mr Van discovered that he'd been fooled? Answer; not enough.

She said, 'Charlotte, cards on the table. For your own safety, you'd better stay here. I'd never forgive myself if you went back to the flat and ended up in hospital.'

'Why should I? I'm in no danger.'

'As soon as Mr Van discovers he's getting two litre bottles of water instead of gold boxes and miniatures, he's going to—'

'What? Why should he? You handed the presents over, didn't you?'

Bea told herself not to lose her temper. Through her teeth, she said, 'Of course I didn't hand them over. I substituted something that weighed approximately the same as—'

Charlotte said, 'I don't believe this! You cannot be serious! Why, when he finds out, he'll—'

'Be rather cross,' said Bea. 'Yes. He'll come after us with a hatchet, if I read him aright.'

'But that's . . . you've got to ring the police!' Charlotte thought about that, and recanted. 'But that would get Liam into trouble, wouldn't it? We must warn him.'

'Liam,' said Maggie, 'can go to—'

Bea intervened. 'That's not helpful, Maggie. Charlotte, Liam's back in Ireland, we think. With a girlfriend, who is not, repeat not, called Patsy. He's applied for a job in a travel agency there. If you can think of any way to contact him, then please do. We need to talk to him, urgently. Somewhere out there Liam's boss is waiting to hear that the stolen goods have reached Mr Van safely. Some time tomorrow morning he's going to hear that they haven't, and he's going to come looking for Liam. When he doesn't find Liam, he's going to come looking for you two girls, and he won't be bringing you bunches of flowers. Think, Charlotte! Who is it who got you into this smuggling lark? It must be someone who knows you as well as Liam.'

Charlotte put on a sulky face. 'I don't know anyone like that.'

Maggie stared at Charlotte, unbelieving. 'Think, Charlotte. This man's capable of murder.'

Bea went one further. 'You think, too, Maggie. There's a limited time scale here. You only moved into the flat last Friday. Who did you meet who fits the bill? Remember, this is someone who knows you, or knows about you through Liam and Charlotte. Think hard. Who did you meet at the flat?'

Maggie put her hands to her head. 'Not Philip; he'd already disappeared. Zander; it can't be him, can it? No, no. He's no mastermind, and anyway, he's been in hospital since Sunday night.'

Charlotte gaped. 'Zander in hospital? Why?'

'He got knifed and beaten up.'

Charlotte grinned. 'There you are then. He's the mastermind and it was he who persuaded Liam to take us over to Belgium. He's the one!'

Maggie snapped a look at Bea, shaking her head slightly. 'It's not Zander; he's too scared to admit who he is. It's not Liam; he's so scared, he's done a runner. The only other people I met at the flat were upstairs at the party.'

Charlotte was scornful. 'Not a party. Just a friendly get-together, which we have most Friday nights. Sometimes it's up in their flat, sometimes it's in ours. Sometimes next door. It's the same people, all the time. Well, mostly. They come and go. Brian and Fudge from upstairs got married in May and moved out and someone else moved into Brian's room, but they're keeping Fudge's room on for a bit because they've got the builders in at their new place and so they're storing a lot of their stuff at the flat for a while. A girl called Lou something moved into Brian's room. Works in a bank. Tall girl.'

'I remember her,' said Maggie. 'Six foot two plus high heels. Black. All over a tubby little fellow with thinning hair—'

'That's Alfred. He's something important in the City, gets big bonuses. He's moving out soon, buying a flat in St Katherine's Dock. Then there's the gay couple who share the biggest bedroom, the one that's like mine, but it wouldn't be them. Nor Ralph. He works in an art gallery somewhere, never has anything to say for himself but always brings a girl, never the same girl twice, don't know where he gets them from or what they see in him. And Sprouts. Well, his name's not really that, of course; it's a nickname because he says he likes Brussel sprouts. Now he's weird, if you like. Sort of dark and glowering, eats crisps all the time, drinks Perrier water, no fun at all, if you ask me. Though sometimes we get stuck with one another watching a DVD late at night, if you know what I mean. It can't be any of them . . . except perhaps Sprouts, I suppose. Yes, it could be him.'

'That's six people,' said Bea, who'd been counting on her fingers. 'I thought the flats only held five?'

'Well, a couple of them are from another flat across the landing. Sprouts and the banker. Either of them could be it, I suppose.'

Bea was trying to keep up. 'Are you telling me that anyone in the building has an open invitation to your Friday nights?'

'Sort of. I suppose. People bring friends. People move on and come back to visit us. Brian and Fudge came back last Friday . . . no, maybe it was the Friday before. Do you remember them, Maggie?'

'I didn't talk to anyone much except Zander,' said Maggie. 'Wish I had.'

Oliver was trying to slot names into box shapes on his pad. 'How do you divide up the rent, and how do you get new flatmates?'

Charlotte explained, 'One of us takes on the lease and collects the rent, which we divide equally between the five of us, even though some rooms are nicer than others. I hold the lease for our flat. If a room falls vacant we usually know someone who's looking for a place, or we advertise in the *Telegraph*. Occasionally the estate agency contacts us to say they've got someone enquiring for a room but usually, between all the people we know, we can fill the vacancy.'

The front doorbell rang. A solid, urgent peal. Everyone jumped. Piers said, 'I'm nearest,' and went to open the door.

In stalked Velma.

At least, it was a walking, trembling semblance of Bea's old friend. Her lipstick – usually so carefully applied – was a scarlet slash that went crookedly over one cheek. She was wearing a designer black-and-white summer dress . . . and bedroom slippers.

She didn't take her eyes off Bea. In a high, unnatural-sounding voice, she said, 'I don't think I parked the car too well. Would someone see to it, please?'

Bea said, 'My dear, what is it?'

Velma opened her mouth wide and screamed. Eyes closed, hands clenched, she screeched so loudly that birds in the garden below took off in fright.

Bea whispered, 'My God. Sandy's dead!'

Velma flung herself on Bea, still screaming, punching her, hands raised to scratch.

Piers grabbed Velma from behind and hauled her off, kicking, still screaming.

Bea tried to grab Velma's flailing hands, and managed to capture and hold one of them, while Oliver caught the other.

Velma went limp, head going down, arms relaxing, knees buckling.

Piers said, 'I've got her. I'll carry her through to the sitting room. Get her a brandy, someone.'

'We don't have any,' murmured Bea, her mind racing. Velma was in shock. What an awful thing! Piers laid Velma out on the

settee and pulled the spare-room duvet over her. Velma's eyes
were closed. She still trembled, but there was no more fight in
her.

Bea pulled up a stool and sat beside Velma, taking one of her
hands in hers, stroking it, feeling her friend's grief flow into her.

Charlotte said, loudly, 'So that's where the duvet off my bed
went to!'

'Hush,' said Maggie. 'Mrs Abbot, what can I do to help?'

Velma opened her eyes, staringly bright, whites showing. She
focused on Bea. 'I trusted you to find Philip, and you failed me.'

'We did our best,' said Bea.

'Not good enough,' said Velma. She shook off the duvet and
threw Bea's hand aside. 'I was going mad at the hospital, sitting
at his bedside, talking to him, telling him he was getting better
all the time when I could see that he was marking time, waiting
for Philip. And then I realized, silly me, that of course he loved
Philip far more than he loved me, and I hadn't let myself believe
it before, but finally I did and I went off home for a break to
change my clothes and have a shower and they rang me . . . they
rang me. A massive heart attack, they said. So sorry, they said.'

She pulled herself into a sitting position, head hanging, fingers
twitching.

'Yes,' said Bea, pulling one of Velma's hands back into her
own and chafing it. 'You felt guilty at leaving him even for such
a short time and . . .'

'Did you?' Velma asked, tucking in her chin, lifting her head
to look sideways at Bea.

Bea nodded. There had been one day when she'd left
Hamilton's bedside and walked and walked, she didn't know or
care where, so long as it was away from the hospital. When she
got back, worn out, later that evening, they told her he'd asked
for her, before slipping into the coma from which he never woke.
Yes, she knew that guilt.

Velma pulled away from Bea, and clapped both hands over
her eyes. She rocked to and fro, keening. 'He died as soon as
my back was turned. He loves me, he loves me not. He loves
Philip, he loves me not.'

'He loved you a lot,' said Bea. 'I saw it in his face when we
met. Of course he loved his son, too. But he loved you with all
his heart.'

'Stupid, stupid!' Velma struck at her breasts, her eyes wide, unfocused. 'He loved me not. And now I've got to start all over again.' She got to her feet. 'Did I come in the car? Where's my handbag? Has someone got my car keys? I must go home and see to things. I don't know exactly what it is I have to see to, but there must be something.'

'I'll drive you,' said Piers.

She flinched. 'Do you think I'm not capable? I know that I'm not quite myself at the moment, but I am perfectly capable of driving myself home.'

Oliver said, 'I'm learning to drive. Can I sit in the car with you, watch how you do it?'

Velma smiled at him, and the smile almost came naturally. 'What a nice boy you are. Of course you may. Oh, and Bea,' she turned back to her old friend, 'that's it, for Philip. He can go to the devil now, for all I care. Tell the police he's missing and has taken a Millais with him. Let them sort it out. I'm not spending another penny on him.'

She made a three-point turn, eyeing up the door, focusing on it. She took a deep breath and walked in a dead straight line through it and out into the hall. Oliver scuttled ahead of her, opening and shutting the front door for her.

Bea let herself down on to the settee which Velma had just vacated. She, also, stared into space. Sandy dead! So everything they'd done to find Philip had been in vain. They could have gone straight to the police the moment the girls had been involved! They could have given Mr Van away to the cops in Belgium.

Poor Velma. Heart-stricken.

All was dust and ashes.

Bea was sure that Sandy had loved Velma more than he'd loved Philip, but maybe he'd worried about his son more than he'd worried about Velma. Because, let's face it, Velma was a pretty strong personality when you looked under the fluffy blonde exterior. Velma had been knocked off balance by guilt at having left her husband's side for an hour, and by grief, but she would survive.

Philip might not.

Bea didn't give a toss about Philip. Selfish, weak, needy . . . he hadn't only wrecked his own life, but his father's and Velma's as well.

Someone was shouting. Bea blinked, and brought herself back to the task on hand. Maggie was trying to soothe Charlotte, who was crying. Of course, she would cry. Piers was standing with his back to the room, looking out on to the garden. The sky beyond Piers' figure was a dull blue, the leaves of the big sycamore tree losing their colour as the sun dropped lower and lower in the sky.

Charlotte sobbed, 'I don't understand anything! Who was that woman, and why is she going on about Philip?'

Maggie controlled her irritation pretty well. 'That was Mrs Weston, who is your landlady, by the way. If you speak nicely to her – no, not at this minute! Can't you tell she's upset? – she might be understanding about the rent. Philip was her stepson. She asked us to find him because . . . oh, why do I bother! Mrs Abbot, would you like me to rustle up something to eat? It seems ages since breakfast.'

Bea started, trying to deal with thoughts which were rushing round her head screaming *Urgent!* And *Action!* 'Yes, Maggie. That would be good. Or get takeaways for once.'

Charlotte revived at the thought of food. 'I wouldn't mind a Chinese, but not sweet and sour pork.'

Maggie said, 'Come and help me choose,' and deftly removed Charlotte from the room.

Piers was fiddling with his shirt cuff, an annoying habit he'd had as long as she'd known him. 'Bea, if I've followed this correctly, as of tomorrow morning you're going to be number one target for Mastermind and his cohorts?'

Bea was already punching numbers on her mobile. 'You're telling me. Mr Goldstone, can you talk? I'm a little concerned about what's going to happen tomorrow when . . . oh, I see.' She held up her hand to stop Piers interrupting as she listened to what the art gallery had to say. Which was quite a lot. Eventually she nodded. 'Right. I follow your thinking. Have you a name for your contact in the Fraud Squad or whatever it calls itself? The Art and . . .? No, I haven't got that right, have I? What's his name again?' She seized the phone pad and made some notes. 'Well, thank you. Have you heard anything more about the Millais, or the frame? No? Oh well. It was a long shot, I suppose . . . yes, I will keep in touch. Promise.'

She switched her phone off. 'Piers, my friend Mr Goldstone has already given the boxes and the miniatures to someone in the insurance company, someone who welcomes the return of stolen goods without asking any questions. As far as he's concerned, he's done his bit and all he has to do now is wait for the reward to plop through his letterbox. He's not contacted the police about the thefts because he thought I'd do it, and he wasn't sure how much to say since he knows I wanted to keep quiet about Philip, which of course I did. Then. He's not worried about Mastermind, because Mastermind doesn't know he exists.'

'Mastermind knows far too much about all of you, to my way of thinking. First he'll try Charlotte; at least, that's what I'd do. Can we trust her to keep her mouth shut?' Piers answered his own question. 'No, we can't. We might persuade her not to answer any calls to her mobile, but some time or other she's going to have to go back to work and to the flat. If asked, she'll tell the world what she knows, and I can't see any way to stop her.

'However, a moment's thought will make it clear to Mastermind that it's you and not Charlotte who knows where the goods are. You used your own name in your dealings with him, yes? Well, even if Charlotte doesn't give him chapter and verse, there aren't that many Abbots in the phone book. So, within days – or more likely hours – he's going to know how to get hold of you. Yes, it's definitely time to call in the police.'

'It's late. I hope someone's still there who can deal with it.' She punched numbers and asked for the man whose name Mr Goldstone had given her. She was passed on to someone else, began to explain . . . only to be passed on to a third person. She had barely got her name and address recorded the third time when she put the phone down with a grimace.

'They took a message but want me to ring back tomorrow morning. Office hours. I suppose I'd better alert the local nick and ask for protection.' She looked doubtful. Piers did, too. She braced herself, reaching for the phone directory as her landline rang.

Piers muttered, 'I'll get that.' He picked up the receiver, listened . . . and said he'd ring back in a minute.

Bea, punching numbers, raised her eyebrows to ask who it was who'd called.

'Oliver. Worried about Velma, who's coming unbuttoned. I said you'd ring him as soon as you could.'

Bea hesitated, but decided to contact the police first. The following quarter-hour was one of the most frustrating of her life. She gave her name and address twice to different people,

said she had some information about a robbery which had led
to the murder of Lady Farne, repeated her name and address to
a third person, was asked to hold – which she did. Then asked
if she wished to leave a message.

By the time she got round to doing so, Piers was answering
the phone again, frowning, fiddling with a pen he'd picked up.
She tried to hear what he was saying, at the same time as she
talked to the police.

She spoke slowly into the phone. 'Yes, that's right. We realized
that there was a link between Lady Farne's murder and her godson
who lived locally. Then . . .' She was interrupted by someone at
the other end. She listened, biting the remains of lipstick off her
mouth, not liking what she heard. 'No, I quite understand. It is
rather complicated. The problem is that I think the man who
masterminded the theft and presumably committed the murder is
going to find out some time tomorrow morning that he's been
fooled, and as he's killed at least once already . . . yes, yes. Of
course I really need to talk to whoever is dealing with Lady Farne's
death. You say he'll be in tomorrow morning and will contact me
then? Yes, I'll be here.'

She put the phone down with a gesture of defeat. 'How much
do I tell them? Do we leave Zander's name out of it? Is it really
Zander in hospital? If we blow his cover, won't that put him
into danger again? I mean, he must be safe while he's in hospital
and Mastermind thinks he's dead. What do we say about Philip
and Liam? They've disappeared into the undergrowth like rabbits
diving into their burrows. Possibly different burrows, but possibly
the same one. Has Philip fled to Ireland, I ask myself? And
what's going on with you, Piers?'

Piers cupped the receiver of the landline in both hands. 'Oliver
again. You'd better speak to him.'

'Mrs Abbot, is that you?' Oliver, trying to control excitement.
'I don't know what to do. She's throwing all her husband's things
out of the window into the garden at the back and as fast as I
can pick them up, she's throwing more . . .' A crash at the other
end. 'That was a television set, would you believe?'

Bea groaned. What more trouble could this day hold? 'You
want me to come round?'

'Yes, but . . . the thing is, she wants to give me his car, and
it's a Peugeot that she gave him for his last birthday, and I keep
saying I can't take it, and she says that she wants to give it to

me because I'm a nice boy, nicer than Philip, and if I won't accept it, she says she'll take it down to the Embankment and drive it into the Thames! I don't know that that's possible – to drive it into the river, I mean – but I do believe she'll crash it or something. What do I do?'

Bea tried to think. Had Velma the right to dispose of her husband's belongings? Perhaps Sandy had made a will, and if so, then maybe everything – or a lot of things – might now belong to Philip. If he could be found. 'Oliver, can't you reason with her? No, silly of me. Of course you can't reason with a woman whose temporarily off her rocker. If it were just Philip's things she wants to destroy . . .?'

'At the moment it's her husband's stuff. Clothes, shoes, DVDs, you name it, and it's raining down into the garden. I've had to take refuge in the kitchen doorway.'

Bea tried to think clearly. 'Suppose you retrieve as much as you can, and stow it in the Peugeot. Then we can remove the car with its contents and garage it somewhere till she's calmed down. Yes, that would be best. But you mustn't try to drive it.' She held on to the phone but looked up at Piers. 'Piers, did you get the gist of that? Do you think you could rescue the car for us? Oliver's not passed his test yet and we don't want him getting picked up for driving and taking away – or worse.'

Piers nodded. 'I'll get round there straight away.' He disappeared.

Maggie arrived in the doorway. 'Ta-da! Supper is served!'

Bea held up her hand to silence Maggie while she returned to the mobile.

'Oliver, Piers is on his way. He'll take the car and put it somewhere safe. Don't try to stop Velma throwing things out because she'll only turn on you. Make her a cup of sugary tea, see if you can get her to drink it and to eat some biscuits. Carbohydrates help with the shock. She'll wear herself out soon. I'll come down to help you when I've got things sorted at this end, right?' She put the phone down with a tired sigh.

Maggie went into her mother-hen mode. 'Oh, you poor thing. You must be worn out. You must eat something or you'll be no good to man or beast.'

'True,' said Bea, trying to smile. 'Eat first, and then I'll go and see what I can do to help Velma. You can look after Charlotte, can't you?'

Charlotte came into the room, munching a huge slice of pizza. Pizza? thought Bea. Weren't we having a Chinese?

Charlotte pounced on the duvet which had covered Bea while she napped. 'At last! Honestly! How could you!'

Bea had had enough. 'Charlotte, has it never occurred to you that you'd get on better in this world if you thanked people for helping you, instead of criticizing them every time you open your mouth?'

Charlotte bridled, stuffing another mouthful of pizza in. She spluttered through it, causing flakes of pizza to fall on to the ivory carpet together with a string of melted cheese. 'You have to take me as you find me.' She cleared her mouth partially and continued, 'I'm no hypocrite, pretending to be charitable to a poor girl who hasn't got anyone to stand up for her, and then making her life a misery!'

'You are a very rude and ungrateful little girl,' said Bea, who'd had more than enough of Charlotte. 'And while you're a guest under my roof, you abide by my rules. You will say please and thank you when appropriate, and you will refrain from borrowing my clothes. Is that clear?'

Charlotte opened her mouth and wailed. Tears spurted.

'Now look what you've done,' said Maggie, but she was half laughing as she steered Charlotte out of the room. 'Come along, Charlotte. Mrs Abbot's quite right, you know. You really should mind your Ps and Qs more. What I think is that we're all so tired now, we're not exactly at our best, right?' Her voice faded away as she led Charlotte into the kitchen.

Bea began to laugh and caught herself crying.

This would never do. Oliver needed her, and so did Velma. Poor Velma! Bea found a tissue, mopped up, blew her nose, and told herself she'd be much better for getting some food inside her. She followed the girls out to the kitchen.

Later Tuesday evening

Rafael stood in Charlotte's room at the flat and felt his headache intensify.

There was evidence that the girls had returned from Bruges and repacked to leave in a hurry, leaving clothes half in and half out of the wardrobe, on the bed and spilling from a chest of drawers. Or was this how they'd left it when they went off yesterday?

Rafael hated it when things didn't go according to plan.

Calm down, he told himself. The girls left the hotel in Bruges this morning. Perhaps the car has broken down, or they've had an accident on the way.

He rang the garage. Had the hire car been returned yet? It had? All was well, then.

Or not. For if they'd got back safely, where were they now? A thought: he went into the girls' bathroom. There was no sign of their toilet bags. Wherever they were, they intended to stay away tonight. This was more than slightly worrying. Suppose they'd talked to someone at the hotel who'd advised them to go to the police or . . .

Ridiculous. They couldn't risk that, or they'd be had up for smuggling.

There was one way to find out. He had no opinion of Charlotte's discretion, and had warned Liam never to let her suspect that he, Rafael, might be involved in anything illegal. He didn't want her to think anything was wrong now, either.

Suppose he pretended Liam had been on the phone to him, said he was leaving the country? Suppose he, Rafael, made himself available as a shoulder to cry on, she'd be so grateful that she'd tell him anything he wished to know, wouldn't she?

He pulled out his little book and found her mobile phone number.

Seventeen

Tuesday mid-evening

Bea got as far as the kitchen door only to see Charlotte sobbing noisily at the table, while Maggie patted her on the back. Bea hesitated, and Maggie looked up.

'Oh, Mrs Abbot, you do look tired. How about I bring you something on a tray in the other room, and you can eat there in peace and quiet?' Maggie being tactful? Or did Bea really look as much of a wreck as she felt?

In late years she and Hamilton had usually eaten in the kitchen even when they had guests, but there was a perfectly good dining table in the living room. It would be a treat to sit down there and be served food, even if it were only pizza. In fact, it was Chinese, because Maggie had ordered both. As she set the dishes in front of Bea, Maggie explained that there was more than enough over for Oliver and Piers when they returned. 'And now I'll get back to Charlotte, poor thing.'

Bea had an uneasy feeling that she ought not to be sitting down to eat while so much was happening but she had hardly eaten anything all day, and knew she'd cope better when she'd got some food inside her. She pulled a library book towards her and found her place. Something soothing by Ann Tyler; enough pathos to help you identify with her characters, and enough humour and hope to reassure the reader that life was worth living.

She still felt jaded after she'd eaten but could get on with life again. The landline rang as she took her tray out to the kitchen. There was no sign of Charlotte, but Maggie had taken the call. 'Mr Piers says he's loaded up his car and the Peugeot with the stuff that Mrs Weston's thrown out, and he'd like to know where you want it. Is he to bring the car here?'

'I suppose it had better be garaged somewhere. What about the place that your hire car came from? Can you give Piers the address? I could meet him there and give him a lift back to Velma's.'

Maggie relayed this, and nodded. 'Yes, I'll tell her.' She nodded some more as Piers talked. When she came off the phone she said, 'Piers says OK, he'll meet you at the hire car place. He says Oliver's in with Mrs Weston, who's stopped throwing stuff around and is working through mountains of paperwork, stuffing it into plastic bin bags. The men are not sure what important papers she might be getting rid of, so Oliver's offered to take them away and shred them for her. She's agreed.'

'Oliver's worth his weight,' said Bea, looking round for her handbag. 'I'd better get going, then. Where's Charlotte? Washing her hair again?'

Maggie half laughed, shaking her head. 'I'm sorry for her, you know? Well, most of the time I'm sorry for her. The rest of the time I could kill her. I explained that Mrs Weston needed you with her now her husband's died, but Charlotte's so self-centred she can't take anyone else's troubles on board. She's had a phone call from a friend, someone who works in the library with her, who's offered to take her out for a drink, so she got changed and went to meet him. I didn't give her a key – I didn't think you'd want her to have one – but I said I'd be around to let her in when she returned. She shouldn't be that late.'

'Fine,' said Bea. 'I'm thinking Mrs Weston might like me to stay with her for a while, but if she does I'll have to drop back to pick up for some overnight things. Can you manage here? Yes, of course you can. Maggie, I really am delighted to have you back.'

Maggie twisted her body, embarrassed. 'Well, I'm pleased to be back, too. That Zander thing, it was horrid, you know? I did fancy him, of course I did, but when I saw him in hospital, I went off him. Isn't that awful?'

'My dear.' Bea put her arm round Maggie's shoulders. 'It happens. How many times do we fancy a man when we meet him at a party and the next time we see him, kerplunk! We realize he's not exactly the Prince Charming we'd thought him.'

'That's it. It was such a wonderful party and I haven't had many of those, not like that with everyone welcoming me, and Zander was so handsome. I suppose I got a bit above myself, as my mother would say. Now I've come down to earth with a bump. Only, I keep worrying what he's going to do, with all his belongings gone and . . . do you think Charlotte will allow him back?'

Bea rubbed her forehead. Was her headache coming back full strength? 'Let's deal with that when he's ready to leave hospital.' She collected her handbag and located her car keys. Where had she said she'd go first? Ah, the garage. Piers might even be there by now.

Piers was. Fortunately the garage people had space for the Peugeot, at a price. Bea paid, grimly wondering how much out of pocket she was going to be in this affair. Without Velma to bankroll them, her expenses were going to have to come out of any reward the insurance people might come up with. *If* Mr Goldstone was as good as his word.

Piers got into the passenger seat of her car, and she drove off.

He was yawning. 'Rescuing damsels in distress makes one feel quite good about oneself. Trying to rescue a damsel who doesn't want to be rescued is something else. I've an appointment at eight that I'd rather like to keep, but I must get home and change first.'

'Has your car been loaded up with some of Sandy's stuff as well?'

He slid down in the seat, closing his eyes. 'Don't remind me. I told young hopeful that I refused to accept anything I couldn't sell in a charity shop. He was trying to load some skis and a bag of cricket impedimenta into the boot at the time. He gave me a slit-eyed look and said he was doing his best, but he did take the hint and removed the sporting gear. I fear he's formed a low opinion of my capacity for brotherly love.'

'Thank you, Piers. You've been wonderful.'

'I wish you could say that as if you meant it.'

'I do mean it. Maggie's saved some Chinese for supper for you, if you want it.'

'Dinner date. Tell her I'll drop by for some of her own cooking some other time. She's a good kid, if noisy.'

'It seems to me that anyone under thirty-five makes too much noise.'

'Us oldies,' said Piers, yawning again, but unfolding himself as they drew up behind his car outside the Weston house. 'I'll just collect my keys from Oliver and be off. You know where to find me.'

At that moment Oliver came out of the house, carrying two large black bin bags. Two more were in the porch. On seeing Bea, he brought them down to stow in the boot of her car. 'That's all the paperwork for the time being. I've stowed a lot of stuff in a garden shed. She caught me at it said she'd set light to it later on, but I told her it would be difficult to get a fire in the back garden under control because the houses are so close together you couldn't get the fire engines anywhere near it.'

Piers, chuckling, got into his car and drove off.

Bea put her arm through Oliver's. 'Thank you, Oliver. You've been so clever. Maggie's keeping some supper for you.'

'I'll go back if there's nothing else I can do, but if you want me to stay, I will. Mrs Weston's like a hamster on speed. Surely her battery will run down soon.'

'Did you get her to eat or drink?'

He shook his head. 'Made a pot of tea, found the biscuits. She wouldn't look at them.'

They walked up the path to the door, and Oliver let them in. 'I've been using the spare set of keys that was in the little cupboard, the one with the alarm pad in it. You'd better have them now.

I've deactivated the alarm for the time being, because we've been in and out all the time. Something occurred to me . . . can you spare a minute before I go?'

'I'll just check on her and get back to you.'

Bea could hear someone talking on the phone as she went down the hall. Velma was in the study, a large room with a bay window which was both library and study. She was sitting in a circle of light thrown by a desk lamp, at an old-fashioned desk. On seeing Bea, she clapped her hand over the mouthpiece of the phone long enough to say, 'Cancelling his credit cards.'

Bea nodded, and left her to it. She found Oliver in the kitchen, switching on more lights. Oliver was looking thoughtful. 'It may be important or it may not. I've been thinking about the amount of stuff that was removed from Charlotte's flat. Look how much time and effort it's taken to cart away Sandy's stuff from here. Two car loads full, plus all the sports gear that I've put in the shed. Now I suppose Zander and Liam didn't have as much as Mr Weston, but . . . how did it all get spirited away from the flat?'

Bea tried to concentrate, and failed. She shrugged.

'Look,' said Oliver, seizing a 'To Do' slate off the wall, and taking it to the table. 'Let's make it simple. Did Philip have a car to take away his stuff in? No. Philip was skint, didn't own a car. Did Liam or Zander have cars? No, apparently not. Liam hired the car which took the girls over to Belgium. Lots of people who live in Kensington manage without cars because public transport is good, cars are expensive to run and there's nowhere to park.

'Now we know Zander's been in hospital since early Monday. He didn't clear his own room; presumably Liam was doing it on Sunday night and Monday morning, which made him late for getting on to the train. Liam's room was also emptied by the time the Green Girls went in to clean on Tuesday morning. So . . . where did Liam put everything? You saw the two rooms before they were cleared, didn't you? How much was there to get rid of?'

She thought back. 'People who live in rented flats usually accumulate more than they bring in at the start. Liam had a couple of big suitcases in his wardrobe, and that's all. I imagine his belongings might well have gone into the two cases, possibly with a couple of big plastic bin bags as well. That's taking into account that he discarded a lot of things which were picked up later by the Green Girls. I don't know if he'd have managed his telly as well. It wasn't very big, a portable, newish, and it's gone.' She thought about it. 'Yes, it would have been quite a lot to cart away, but if he'd dumped the telly somewhere, he could have got it all into one taxi.'

'What about Zander?'

'He had much more in his room. For luggage all he had was a suitcase and a sports bag. When I saw his room early on Monday, someone had started to pack up his clothes but hadn't by any means got it all in. In addition, there was a flat-screen TV, a sound system, laptop, a camera and a stack of books. Also a briefcase. You'd need three or maybe four large cardboard boxes to pack all that in. Maybe more.'

'That's what I thought. Now this evening I've been going up and down the stairs and to and from the garden like a demented yoyo. How many trips would Liam have had to make to get rid of everything? Possibly two trips for himself – if we discount the telly. For Zander . . . seven, eight? Probably more. Each time he'd have to haul the stuff out of the flat to the lift, take it down to the ground floor, and then haul it out again into the lobby. And then what did he do with it? Put it into a couple of taxis and take it . . . where?

Bea tried to think. 'A self-storage place?'

'It would have taken him hours. First he had to pack, and then take all those trips up and down in the lift, take two taxis, arrange to store the stuff and pay for it . . . and then get to St Pancras to catch the train. Did he have time to do all that before he got on to a Eurostar train in the early afternoon?'

'No, he didn't. That flat-screen TV, for instance. It's far too big to cart around easily. We must ask Randolph if he saw Liam carting stuff away in a taxi or two.'

Oliver was eager to explain. 'There's another possibility. Look, we know that there is accommodation for five people living in Charlotte's flat, and five people in the flat above. Charlotte even told us that somebody from the flats might be linked to the crimes we're investigating, which is something we need to tell the police about tomorrow.'

'Or the flat next door.'

'True. But I'm looking particularly at the top flat, because when we add up how many people are living there, we find a vacancy. Remember Charlotte said that two tenants in the flat above got married and moved out, but are still paying rent for one of their rooms because they left a lot of their stuff in store until they can get the builders out of their new place. Right? So there should be one room vacant in the flat directly above Charlotte. It has a lot of the married couple's stuff in it, but perhaps there was also room for Zander's plus, perhaps, Liam's telly.'

Bea picked on a flaw. 'How would Liam get hold of a key to the flat above?'

'Mastermind lives in the flat above, that's how.'

Bea was dubious. 'We'll suggest that to the police tomorrow. Can you make your own way back? Or shall I call a taxi for you? On the house, naturally.'

'I'll pick up a taxi on the way.' He left, closing the front door softly behind him. Bea poured away the pot of tea he'd made earlier, and made another. There was milk in the fridge, and not much else. She carried a mug of tea in to Velma, set it down at her elbow, and waited for her to finish her phone call.

Velma pushed the tea aside. 'I'm not an invalid.'

'No, indeed,' said Bea. 'Have you found his will yet?'

Velma pointed to an envelope on her desk. 'Mutually helpful. He to me, and I to him. All to one another.'

'Which proves he really loved you, Velma.'

'And pigs might fly.'

'Nothing for the prodigal son?'

'His Rolex. It's one he bought for himself years ago. It's at the hospital still – if no one's pinched it. I couldn't give a toss. Anyway, it's not likely that Philip's going to come out of the woodwork now to claim it. I think he must be dead, too.'

Could Philip also be dead? It was an alarming thought, but there was a lot to be said for the reasoning behind it. If so, the Millais would probably never be recovered, and Philip would go down in history as the man who killed his godmother.

Bea didn't like the hard voice her friend was using. How to divert her? Could it be done by turning her mind to different tasks? Taking them at different speeds? If only Velma would break down and cry.

Bea said, 'I expect you could do with a break from the paperwork. Shall I help you change the bed? You won't want to sleep in the same sheets that Sandy used.'

'Good idea.' Velma went over to the mirror, exclaimed at the sight of her dishevelled hair, and reached for her handbag to find a comb. She sang to herself, '*I'm going to wash that man right out of my hair.*' She smiled at her image in the mirror. 'Am I on a roll, or am I on a roll?' She was strung up so tightly she almost twanged. '*I'm going to wash that man right out of my hair . . .*'

She led the way up the stairs.

Rafael sipped his wine, trying to absorb what Charlotte had told him. He'd treated her to a dish of lasagne and a couple of glasses of wine at a local bistro, and his reward had been bad news.

His voice cracked with the effort of keeping it steady. '*What an adventure! You say you only got back safely because this woman – what's her name, Abbot? – substituted bottles of water for the stolen goods and brought them back with her to London?*'

Rage built up inside him. How dare this woman interfere with his plans! An ice-cold thought dropped into his mind; Van was going to be furious!

Charlotte drank more wine, giggling. '*I think I'm just a little bit tipsy. It's like it all happened to someone else. Last night we were in Bruges at this weird restaurant where they cook dear little bunny rabbits to eat, though I didn't have any, of course. Then I was poorly in the night and when we got back Mrs Abbot insisted I stay at her place, though I really didn't want to much, because she's such a cow!*'

He poured more wine into her glass. '*Anything else?*'

'*That's it, I think. Oh, Maggie found Zander in hospital some-where, except that it may not be him after all. Hit and run? Badly hurt, anyway. Not fully with it*' – *she tapped her temple* – '*you know?*'

Zander was still alive? Another blow. Rafael wanted to hit someone but forced himself to sound concerned. '*I thought he'd moved away. You're sure?*'

'*Mm. It's upset me ever so much. First Philip disappears, then Liam and now Zander. However am I going to pay the rent next week?*'

Rafael decided that Zander could wait. He was in hospital, might never come out. Perhaps Rafael would pay him a visit to make sure he never did. Meantime, he tipped the last of the wine into Charlotte's glass. '*This Mrs Abbot; does she live at the address where I picked you up? What's she like?*'

Charlotte was beginning to slur her words. '*She's a blonde of* sorts. It's probably dyed. She's really old and quite horrible, not at all sympathetic. Not like you.' She reached out to caress his hand. 'I thought you didn't like me. But you do really, don't you?'

'Of course I do. What has this woman done with the things she brought back? Put them in a safe?'

'How should I know?' She rolled her eyes at him. 'Shall we go on somewhere quiet?'

He consulted his watch, running through various scenarios in his mind. 'What time do you have to get back?'

'Any time. Maggie said she'd wait up for me.'

Rage boiled up inside him, and all the time the silly fool was grinning at him, pawing him . . . he wanted to strike her hand away, but . . . no, not yet. 'Why don't you ring Maggie, tell her you might be late? That you're still out with your friend from the library. You did tell her that I worked in the library, didn't you? You didn't give her my name or anything? Good. It's our little secret, isn't it? Who else beside Maggie lives at Mrs Abbot's?'

'There's Oliver, but he's out this evening, I think. Student. Looks like a schoolboy still.' Charlotte got out her phone and squinted at it, mouthing the numbers as she pressed the buttons.

Rafael got out some cash, deciding against using his credit card to pay the bill. Much better not to leave any traces of himself at the restaurant.

'Is that you, Maggie? I'm out with my friend still.' She giggled, rolling eyes at Rafael. 'Yes, it's the one from the library. You didn't expect me back early, did you? . . . oh, that's all right then. I might . . . if I'm lucky . . . I might just stay out very, very late, if you know what I mean.' She laughed, too long, too loudly, and cut off her call.

She was so coy, it made him grind his teeth. But he was used to hiding his feelings. He smiled and patted her hand.

She said, 'Maggie's all alone, poor thing. Got no one to take her out. But I suppose Oliver will be back soon. Mrs Abbot's staying over at her friend's house. I hope she's going to be understanding about the rent.'

'How's that?'

'Mrs Weston. She's our landlady, you know? Philip's stepmother.'

His nostrils flared. So Mrs Abbot had a connection to Philip at the Weston house? Was visiting it tonight? Well, well! Perhaps luck was running his way again. He could kill two birds with *one stone; no, three. He was sure Philip had taken refuge there, and Philip needed to be taught a lesson and yield up the Millais. Then there were his stepmother's diamonds to consider and now . . . the interfering Mrs Abbot was there as well. He wanted words with Mrs Abbot. More than words. He wanted what she'd taken of his.*

Three against one? He hesitated for a moment, but decided the odds were still in his favour, if he showed them his knife. He'd been carrying a knife since he was in his teens, in case anyone thought his small stature made him an easy target.

He was annoyed with himself about Zander. He must have aimed a trifle too low. But women – easy. He only had to press his knife into a woman's breast and they let him have whatever he wanted. Philip? Well, Philip was no threat to man or beast.

First, he must get rid of this tiresome girl with her clack-clacking tongue. He couldn't let her run around, telling her story to all and sundry, could he? As she got up from the table she clutched his arm, pretending to be even more drunk than she really was. She repulsed him.

She swayed and giggled even more when they got outside into the open air. 'Where shall we go now?'

'Your flat. With the boys gone, it'll be quiet. No interruptions.'

She clung to his arm, tottering along beside him. When he'd killed before, it had been in the way of business. This was the first time he'd really enjoy it.

Eighteen

Tuesday late evening

B ea heard the front doorbell as she was taking a bundle of bedlinen down the stairs, so she called back up to Velma, 'I'll get it.' It would be some charity caller, or a neighbour who'd taken in a parcel, perhaps.

Maybe it was Oliver, returning for some reason. She remembered that he'd cut the alarm off. She must remember to turn it back on. There was no reason to anticipate trouble until tomorrow, when Mr Van would discover how he'd been tricked.

She switched on the lights in the hall and, still carrying the bedlinen, opened the door.

A nice-looking young man stood there. Smiling, diffident. Smaller than her and not at all threatening. 'Is Philip in? I'm a friend of his.'

'Are you? Oh. Well, I'm sorry, but he's not.'

He pushed at the door, not aggressively, but moving it inwards. 'I'm so sorry, Mrs Weston. I know Philip's been a naughty boy, but I really am a friend of his and need to speak to him, urgently. I owe him some money.'

'I'm afraid I'm not . . .' Bea glanced back up the stairs. 'And Philip's not here. Nobody's seen him for ages.'

'Oh, but . . .' He frowned, puzzled. 'He rang me, told me he'd taken refuge here. Somewhere at the back of the house? In the staff quarters? He asked me to bring him some money round. Which I have.' He smiled, the open, blue-eyed, honest smile that had taken in many an older and wiser person.

He pushed at the door and Bea gave way, confused. Might Philip really be hiding out somewhere in the house? No! It wasn't possible. And yet, it was a big house with a top floor which was never used and a flatlet at the side for a live-in help.

Bea dumped her armful of bedclothes. 'Look, as far as I know, he's not here but if you'd like to hang on a minute, I'll check.'

She started back up the stairs, only to find he was close on her heels. Tail-gating, you'd call it if you were in a car. She didn't like it, and repeated, 'Please stay in the hall, and I'll get back to you.'

His eyes were on her hands. A wedding ring, but no diamonds. This was annoying. He'd understood that Philip's stepmother always wore a couple of good diamond rings. He stayed where he was, halfway up the stairs, till she'd reached the landing. And then set off after her.

Velma came out of the master bedroom, flapping open a laundered pillowcase. 'Who was that, Bea?' Her diamond rings flashed in the light from the chandelier hanging over the stairs.

'A friend of Philip's. Says Philip's rung him to say he's hiding out in the staff quarters here. Is that possible?'

Rafael kept his smile, trying to work out which woman was Mrs Abbot, and which was Mrs Weston. He said, 'I was round here the other day and heard water running at the back of the house, so he must be here. Also the milk and papers had been taken in. He rang and said he was short of money. I said I'd bring some round for him. I don't like to think of him being in need.'

Velma hesitated, but threw the pillowcase back into the bedroom and reached for a small bunch of keys hanging behind what looked like a Lowry doodle on the wall nearby. 'You heard the cleaner, I suppose. And we've been back and forth, taking milk and papers in. But . . .' A shrug. 'I'll check the flat to make sure, if you like.'

She unlocked an inconspicuous door at the end of the corridor and went in, Bea and Rafael following on her heels. Again Rafael got too close to Bea and again she experienced a sense of discomfort.

All three piled into a sizeable living room. No Philip.

'No one here,' said Velma, switching on lights. She crossed the living room to open doors and switch on lights in a bedroom, bathroom and small kitchen.

Bea touched the top of the television set. No dust.

Rafael pushed past her to check on the rooms Velma had looked into. What a rude young man!

Velma jingled her keys. 'We haven't had any live-in help for some time. The cleaner comes in every now and again, otherwise . . .' She shrugged. She began to turn off the lights in the empty rooms.

Rafael was poised on his toes. Suddenly he didn't look quite so harmless. 'So where is he?'

Velma gestured him to precede her out of the flat. 'How should I know? As far as I'm concerned, he's dead.' Again her diamonds flashed in the light.

'What about the top floor?'

Velma stared at him, exasperated. 'What about it? Junk rooms. My first husband's train set. Philip's not been here for a couple of months, and if he did come back now, I'd slam the door in his face.'

Rafael moved rapidly down the corridor in the main part of the house, throwing bedroom doors open as he went. 'Which is his room?'

'Don't be ridiculous!' said Velma. 'And now, if you don't mind, I'd like you to leave.'

Bea followed behind him, closing the doors he'd flung open, thinking that she didn't like this intrusion much, wondering where she'd left her mobile phone in the event that she had to call for help to get their visitor out.

His demeanour had changed; he was no longer projecting the image of a nice, wholesome young man, but becoming harder, tougher by the second.

As they reached the master bedroom, he caught hold of Bea's arm and propelled her in. 'What?' She tried to pull herself free. He was a lot stronger than he looked, and kept her tightly clasped to his side.

Velma had left all the lights burning in this room. The lower half of the tall sash windows gaped open on to the night, overlooking the garden. Some way off a neighbour was having a party; lights, booze, karaoke. What fun.

It was no fun inside.

Bea yelped, pricked by something sharp.

Rafael said, 'Let's stop playing games, shall we, Mrs Abbot? You are Mrs Abbot, aren't you? This is a knife that I'm holding, close to your breast. It's something of a disappointment that Philip's not here, Mrs Weston, but I'll catch up with him later. Meanwhile, dear Mrs Abbot, I think you have something that belongs to me.'

'Ouch!' Bea tried not to wince as the knife bit into her.

Velma stared. Her eyes were unfocused.

'That's right,' said Rafael. 'You keep your distance, Mrs Weston, or I'll be forced to do something extremely nasty to your friend here. Oh, and in the meantime, you can take off those rings and throw them to me. As for you, Mrs Abbot,' he smiled, bringing his head close to hers, whispering into her ear, 'no one interferes in my business and lives. Understand?'

'I haven't got them,' said Bea, through stiff lips. 'I gave them to Mr Goldstone, the fine arts dealer, and he has already passed them on to the insurance people.'

'You're lying! Bitch!' His fury increased.

She jerked as his knife bit further into her breast. She tried to free her arms but he was holding her so closely that they might have been one person. Tears shot from her eyes. He didn't believe her! 'It's the truth!'

Velma was breathing hard. 'I have never in my life . . .! How dare you! Let go my friend or I'll . . .!'

'You'll what?' He laughed.

She lunged forward, long-nailed fingers reaching for his face, her mouth squared, screeching.

He let Bea go to defend himself.

Bea hooked her leg around one of his, catching him off balance. His knife flew wide.

Nothing could stop Velma. Shrieking, she brushed aside his arm as if it was a matchstick. Still shrieking, she drew her fingernails down his cheeks.

Bea caught at one of his flailing arms, but could not hold him.

Velma got him by his hair and shook him as a terrier shakes a rat.

He screamed, a thin, grating sound.

Blood trickled down his cheeks.

He stumbled towards the bed, but Velma did not let go. She swung him away from her. Yelling, his legs wobbling, disorientated, he teetered sideways and stumbled headlong out through the open window.

Bea heard the soft thump as he hit the garden below.

She closed her eyes, sobbing, hands holding her side where blood seeped through her fingers.

She remembered that the front door might still be on the latch, the alarm not set. She gasped out, 'Front door. I'll get it.'

She tottered to the landing, looked at the flight of stairs and wondered if she could make it safely down to the hall. Forced herself to do so. Wondered if she were leaving a trail of blood. Couldn't be bothered to look.

Leaned against the front door, put the chain on, shot the dead bolt.

Wondered if the man were dead. Hoped he was.

There was no sound from upstairs. She must phone the police. If they'd killed the man . . . oh, dear.

Her side hurt. Her top was sodden with blood. She picked up one of the pillowcases that she'd brought downstairs earlier and wadded it, holding it against her breast.

'Velma, I'm going to ring the police.'

No reply. Bea picked up the phone and hesitated. Why hadn't Velma replied? Had the knifeman managed to wound her as well

. . . perhaps even stabbed her fatally? No, surely the knife had flown wide?

Bea put the receiver down and, panting, climbed the stairs, trying not to think of what she might find.

Velma was half lying, half sitting on an upholstered chair near the open window. Her eyes were open, but unseeing. Bea touched her hand. No response. Velma was warm, she was breathing. Lightly, but she was breathing. Bea couldn't see any blood.

The open window nearby bothered her. Suppose the man hadn't been killed, but was even now climbing up to the first floor again?

She forced herself to look out, fearful of what she might see. A lifeless body, or a man climbing up towards her?

The lights from the bedroom threw oblongs of brightness across the garden below. She squinched her eyes up, trying to see what lay below. Nothing. No body. No climber. He'd gone.

How? He must have broken bones in his fall, surely? There was a herbaceous border immediately below her and she could now see that for half its width the plants had been crushed and broken. He'd broken the plants, but not himself in his fall.

He was nowhere to be seen. And Velma was unconscious.

Bea pulled down both sash windows and locked them. She drew the curtains against the dark night outside. She reached for the bedside phone and summoned an ambulance.

Midnight Tuesday, to early Wednesday morning

'Looks as if she's had a slight stroke,' said the paramedics, brightly. 'We'll take her in straightaway. And what have you been doing to yourself, then?'

'I'm all right,' said Bea, fighting off waves of dizziness.

'What's been happening here, then?' asked the paramedic. 'Was it a domestic?'

'Burglar,' said Bea. 'Had a knife. Gone, now.'

'Did you call the police?'

'Can't remember. Tried to, I think.'

'We have to report it, you know.'

'Fine,' said Bea. She insisted on finding her handbag and Velma's, setting the alarm, locking up the house, and walking to the ambulance behind Velma on her gurney. She sat in the ambulance, holding the pillowcase to her breast while watching

Velma for the slightest sign of recovery. Her mind zigzagged between the memory of the knife biting into her, and the terrible rigidity, the waxen look on Velma's face . . . or was that the light in the ambulance? What time was it? She tried to turn her wrist to read her watch and released more blood from her wound.

She must ring Maggie. But not yet. All in good time.

Velma stirred, nestling into the blanket around her. Opened her eyes. The relief!

As they arrived at the hospital, Velma tried to sit up. The paramedic told her to lie still, they were nearly there.

'What happened?' said Velma.

Bea let herself relax, and saw the world go black around the edges. As she fainted, she heard the paramedic yell for help.

Accident and Emergency Department. A fire bell was ringing somewhere inside the hospital, notching people's nerves up even further than they were already. A multiple car crash had brought nine people in, bloodied, groaning, unconscious, dying. Nurses and doctors moved around, no panic, but get a move on, will you . . .

Bea was stitched up, told that her friend was doing fine and she could see her in a minute, but they were both being kept in overnight, just in case.

'I must ring home. They'll be so worried.'

'I'll do that,' said the nurse. 'The number to contact is in your handbag, is it? Right? Now the best thing you can do is stop worrying. You've lost some blood but the scar won't show where it is just under the breast. I don't suppose you'll be wanting to wear a bra for a few days, but your friend's coming on nicely.'

'Did she have a stroke?'

The nurse didn't reply and despite the noise and the bustle around her, Bea drifted off to sleep. She half woke when they moved her bed, but went off again.

Early the following morning she sat up, wincing at the pull of the stitches under her breast. She was in a small ward. Across the room from her was Velma, out of bed and struggling into the clothes she'd worn the previous day. They smiled at one another.

'Bathroom's thataway,' said Velma, pointing to the right. Her speech wasn't slurred, her face looked normal, and she was using both hands.

'You're a fraud,' said Bea, heaving herself off the bed with an effort. 'You had me so worried, I passed out.'

'Ditto, ditto,' said Velma, grinning. 'The nurse said they'll want to keep us in for tests. How's about we stage a mass walkout?'

'*Chicken Run*. Definitely.' Bea pulled her bloodied clothing out of the bedside locker. 'Only, do I dare let my public see me dressed like this?'

'And me!' Velma ran her fingers through her hair, which had been so expertly cut that it fell back into shape straight away. 'You might have thought to bring my make-up bag when you called for an ambulance.'

A nurse bustled in. She was alarmingly large and spoke to them both as if they were children. 'What's all this, eh? Back to bed, both of you. The doctors will be round after breakfast, and they'll be the ones to decide if you're going home today or not.'

Velma sank into the chair beside her bed, while Bea did exactly as she was told. After the nurse had done her obs – or observations – Bea said, 'Velma, what do we say to the police? I told the paramedics it was a burglar. But what we saw in the flatlet . . .'

No reply. Velma lay back in her chair and closed her eyes.

Bea lay back, too. It would sort itself out in the end. She supposed she ought to be giving thanks to God for saving her . . . but in a few hours' time, Mr Van was going to discover that he'd been tricked and if she'd read him aright, he'd be straight on the phone to that nasty young man with the knife. And then . . . what had happened to their assailant . . .? God knew, of course. She had to trust he'd keep on looking after her. Trust and . . . there was something that went with the word 'trust' but for the moment she couldn't remember what it was.

She drifted off into a doze.

Later that morning Maggie organized some clean clothes for Bea, delivered via a passing nurse. Although Maggie hadn't been allowed up on to the ward, she phoned Bea with various titbits of news. Charlotte had stayed out all night with her new boyfriend. The police had rung to make an appointment to see Bea, had been told she was in hospital and said they'd connect with her there. Piers had rung to ask how Velma was doing, and Oliver had gone off to see a friend about something, Maggie wasn't sure what.

Both Velma and Bea had been told they could go home if they reported to their GPs, took some medication, and didn't get into any more hassles with burglars . . . and oh yes, the police would be contacting them at home.

Velma looked limp, but declared she'd be fine when she could get at her full array of make-up again. Only, 'Bea, I really don't understand what's going on, and I'm not sure that I want to know but one thing's for sure, I can't face going back to that big house by myself. Would you . . . could you . . .?'

'I'll tell you everything, once we're out of here. I was thinking, myself, that you wouldn't want to be alone for a bit. You can have my guest room. Charlotte was in it, but she was out all night and anyway, she drives me nuts, so if she does turn up, she can either go back to her flat or bunk down on a mattress on the floor in Maggie's room. I don't owe her anything.'

'I owe you a new outfit of clothes. Harvey Nichols for lunch?'

'I'll hold you to that, but not today, I think.' She ordered a taxi. 'Let's pick up some clean clothes for you and get you settled at my place.'

Velma said, 'I must look a hag. Do you think I should have some Botox treatment?'

Bea scrutinized her friend's pretty face. Yes, there were a few lines around her eyes and mouth, but even now Velma looked young for her age. Anyway, she got by on charm and pizzaz. 'Botox tends to give one a stiff face, doesn't it?'

As they turned into the Boltons, Velma broached a matter which had been on both their minds. 'You noticed someone had been in the flat, didn't you?'

Bea nodded. 'Men never think to turn equipment off at the mains, or take out the garbage.'

'He'd used the telly, the microwave, the shower in the bathroom – and left the seat up on the toilet.'

'Not recently, though. The telly was cold. He wasn't in the flat yesterday, I think. He knew how to get in?'

'He had his own key to the main house, knew the password for the alarm. But I'm thinking Sandy let him in as soon as my back was turned, and that's why he kept saying he was sorry.

If he were here now, I'd give him a piece of my mind, but . . .'
She sighed. There was no more fight in her.

As Bea paid off the taxi, Velma stared up at the cream cake
façade of her house. 'What a carry on. Poor little me, and that
big house. Shall I give it to charity and become a nurse?'

Bea couldn't help laughing, which made her hold on to her
ribs. 'Ouch, that hurt. Why not go on a cruise and find some
ancient but exceedingly rich man who wants a pretty woman to
care for him in his declining years?'

'Never again,' said Velma and let them into the house. Alarm
off. Milk, papers and letters taken in. The pile of bedlinen was
still on the chair at the bottom of the stairs, where Bea had left
it. 'I owe you a pillowcase. Remind me.'

'I owe you more than that. I wasn't exactly in my right mind
yesterday, was I? And that nice lad of yours – what was his
name? No, don't tell me. I can't pack any more information into
my head at the moment. Shall we look into the affair of the
flatlet first?'

They climbed the stairs, rather more slowly than they'd done
the day before, took the keys from behind the picture, and let
themselves into the flat. The stand-by lights were still on. The
blinds were still in the same position over the windows. Bea
took the bathroom first. 'The soap bar is hard. No one's used it
for some time, but someone has used the shower since the cleaner
was last in, and left scum round the washbasin. Men never bother
to clean up after they've shaved and showered.'

Velma called back from the kitchen. 'There are two pizza
boxes in the garbage, some banana skins, an empty bottle of
booze, an empty carton of milk and half a loaf of bread. The
bread's stale, showing mould.'

'Which means,' said Bea, switching off stand-by lights, 'that
he was here for a couple of days some time ago. Maybe four
days, maybe five. Perhaps he came here as soon as he left
Charlotte's flat.'

Velma hugged herself, shivering, cracking up. 'Sandy must
have let him in when I went off to see the dentist, but warned
him to keep out of sight. No wonder Sandy ran out of cash; he
was subsidizing that rat! It's creepy, to think he was so close
and *all the time Sandy knew!*'

Bea sank on to the double bed, and looked around. 'What
about your cleaner?'

'She's Polish, hardly any English. She's got keys, comes in twice a week for a couple of hours at a time, Tuesdays and Thursdays. Ditto the gardener. If Philip stayed in the flat while they were around, he was safe. He could have stayed here for days and nobody would have noticed. What I don't understand is why he left.'

Bea remembered the day she'd first come to the house to collect things for Velma. There'd been a puff of air, an almost soundless closing of a door upstairs. 'I think he must have overheard me talking to the police when they wanted to search the place. I sent them away, but after they'd gone I thought I heard a door close upstairs. I didn't think anything of it then, but if Philip was there and realized the danger, it would have been enough to send him on the run again.'

Bea got to her feet, moving with care. 'Velma, could you help me tip up the mattress? It's on the soft side and I think I can feel something hard underneath. Philip kept some correspondence under his bed in the flat. I hardly dare hope, but . . .'

Velma helped her tip up the mattress and they stared at a sheeted package underneath. Velma whipped off the covering and met the bold eyes of a teenaged girl in a dark dress against a blue sky.

'Bingo!' said Bea.

'Millais. Genuine. Those eyes go right through you.'

'Do we leave it here?'

'It's as good a place to hide it as anywhere, I suppose.' She let the mattress drop. 'One more thing before we go.' Bea had noticed a telephone with an answerphone on it in the living room. A red light winked.

She depressed the play button, and heard a young girl's voice. 'Philip, are you there still? I gave you the wrong number. It's two-oh-eight, not two-eighteen. I told her you'd be there before closing time and it's late on Thursdays and Fridays. Divine, right?'

It was the only message.

'Doesn't make sense.' Velma sagged against the wall.

Bea said, 'Come on, put a few things into a bag and I'll take you home.'

Velma locked the door of the flat. 'Your car or mine?'

Bea held on to her ribs. 'A taxi. If either of us tried to take a car on the roads at the moment, we'd be arrested for dangerous driving.'

'In that case,' said Velma, 'I'll bring a bottle of champagne.'
'You're on medication!'

'Champagne's better for me than medication.' She turned pathetic. 'I've lost my bubble, Bea.'

'But not your squeak,' said Bea, at which they both laughed inanely.

'Better than crying,' said Velma, who was doing just that.

Bea wondered how soon the knife man would strike again . . . and how long it would be before Mr Van arrived on her doorstep.

Rafael had gone back to the flat in Kensington because he couldn't think, for the moment, what else to do. Two gardens he'd had to cross, two walls he'd had to climb before he almost fell into the lap of an elderly man who'd been having a surreptitious cigarette before turning in for the night. Rafael had explained that he'd had a fight with someone at the party nearby, that a woman had scratched him, that he needed to get away. Could the gentleman kindly let him out into the street through his house?

Kind gentleman had done more than that, offering to clean him up, and brush him down. He'd even offered to call the police. Naturally Rafael had refused to have the police involved; it had been a quarrel over a woman, he said. So he'd limped out of the front door of the man's house and with a couple of rests on the way, had managed to get home.

Those two bitches were going to call the police, weren't they? Fortunately they didn't know who he was, or where he lived. There was nothing to connect him with the Weston house except for Philip – who was still missing – and Charlotte, who was out of their reach. All the Maggie bird knew was that Charlotte was going out with someone from the library, and Rafael had never worked in a library. But if Charlotte had talked to Maggie about Ralph, alias Rafael, if Zander recovered full consciousness and named him . . . he couldn't risk it. He'd better pack up and move on.

Could he, dare he keep his job at the gallery? It had provided him with information about collectors, it had been useful to him in so many ways, he was reluctant to let it go, but if they once connected harmless-seeming Ralph with the burglaries then he was looking at a long stay in prison. He'd best move on. He could get another job, not in the West End perhaps, but in any city which boasted an antiques shop or two.

His cheeks burned where that woman had struck him with her talons. Before he left London, he'd get even with her. As soon as he'd replaced his knife, his precious knife.

What would he tell Van? By midday Van would realize he'd been tricked.

Rafael shrugged. What could Van do about it? Rafael took a padded envelope out of his breast pocket, and unwrapped a gold box. Its gleam drew the eye. Total simplicity, costing not less than everything. It was the only thing he'd ever kept from his little jaunts. Its beauty had seduced him as no woman had ever done.

He phoned the gallery to say he'd gone down with flu and wouldn't be in for a while. Now to find another place to stay for a couple of nights, and to buy another knife . . .

Nineteen

Wednesday morning

B ea paid off the taxi at her door, and helped Velma up the steps with her overnight bag and make-up box. Velma sagged against the doorframe as Bea sought for her front-door key.

Maggie heard the key in the lock, and rushed out to meet them. 'Are you all right? Oliver's still missing but he did phone to say he was with an old friend, doing some kind of experiment, if you please. The phone's been ringing off the hook with your son trying to reach you, and Mr Piers and, oh, lots of people. But I don't suppose you want to be bothered with all that. You poor dears, you do look awful. You ought to have let me fetch you from the hospital, and now the police have arrived, but I'm not sure you're up to answering questions, either of you. Are you?'

Velma said, 'I don't think I am, but I suppose I'd better try.'

Bea held back a sigh. Her ribs hurt and she ached all over. 'Neither of us is up to it, but ditto. Maggie, could you make up the spare room bed for Mrs Weston? She needs looking after for a while. Perhaps we can persuade Charlotte to—'

'Oh, she never came back. I waited up till two and rang her mobile, but she didn't answer so I suppose she's with her new boyfriend. I'm really rather cross with her, and if she does come back I'll tell her to go to a B and B or something, right? Would you like some coffee, or some soothing camomile tea?'

'Camomile tea,' said Bea.

'Strong black coffee,' said Velma.

'Camomile tea,' said Bea, firmly. 'Mrs Weston needs to be careful for a while.'

Velma handed Maggie her bottle of champagne. 'Too careful means having no fun at all.'

'Have it just before lunch,' said Maggie, being diplomatic for once. The telephone rang in the agency rooms below and she disappeared, saying she'd deal with it.

Bea and Velma went into the living room. A tall grey man in a grey suit rose from where he'd been contemplating Bea's game of patience by the window. He pulled his ID from his pocket.

'Detective Inspector Greene, three "e"s.'

A WPC with a sniffly nose materialized behind him, producing her own ID. She mumbled her name so much that Bea failed to catch it.

Bea waved everyone to seats, and sank into one herself. 'What kind of policeman are you, Detective Inspector? Stolen arts department, common assault, or murder?'

'Or all three?' Velma subsided on to the settee, graceful even in her fatigue. She closed her eyes. 'Pretend I'm not here. Wake me when the champagne comes up.'

The DI had a thin smile and heavy lines under his eyes. 'You rang the station last night. Something about smuggling art treasures. Suppose you tell me all about it.'

'I suppose,' said Bea, 'I ought to begin with Lady Farne's murder. Do you know anything about that?'

Velma opened her eyes. 'Now this I do want to hear.'

'The Farne case. Yes,' said the grey man. 'We were asked to look out for the boxes that were stolen.'

'Not only the boxes,' said Bea. 'A picture also went missing, which is where we came in . . .' She tried to tell him the events of the past week in order, and he let her talk, only interrupting a couple of times when she'd not been absolutely clear as to the sequence of events. The WPC took notes, sniffing occasionally.

'The missing Millais is genuine,' said Bea. 'I've got a reproduction of it somewhere. I also took photos on my mobile phone of the boxes, the miniatures and of the man who was supposed to collect them from the girls.'

'Nineteen boxes, you say? There should be twenty.'

'So I'm told. But there were only nineteen in that consignment.'

At this point Maggie brought in a tray with a cafétiere of coffee on it, and a pot of camomile tea. 'No champagne?' asked Velma, but accepted tea without further demur.

Bea asked Maggie to remain. 'We believe one of the missing young men – Charlotte's boyfriend, Liam Forbes – has gone back to Ireland. I expect you can check that. Another one, name of Zander, may have ended up in Central Middlesex Hospital.'

Maggie said, 'There's a man there who's been knifed and beaten up and looks like Zander, but he didn't seem to recognize me. I didn't like to argue because he looked so poorly, and anyway, there was a policeman at his bedside.'

Bea looked at the clock on the mantelpiece, but it had stopped. It was an old clock with a pre-battery movement. She must have forgotten to wind it. Her watch reported that the day was still young. How soon would Mr Van be arriving?

She forced herself to continue. 'The man who knifed me last night knew all about the smuggling. I assume he's the mastermind behind the murders of Lady Farne and of Mr Goldstone's friend Leo. He certainly had no compunction about sticking his knife into me. I'm hoping the police will locate him before he finds me again.'

Bea checked her watch again. 'Now, about this time of day the man called Van should be accessing the bag I left at Bruges station and then all hell will be let loose. He will not be pleased, and I won't feel safe till he knows I've passed the stuff on to the insurance company.'

The DI considered what she'd said. 'Let's get back to the young man whom Mrs Weston threw out of the window. You say there was no sign of him when you looked out, but you failed to search the garden to see if he were badly hurt.'

Bea said, 'I was in no fit state to search for him. Mrs Weston had had a stroke. I called an ambulance and we got out.'

'Do you have a name for this man, or a picture of him on your phone?'

Maggie looked thoughtful. 'Mrs Abbot, you told Charlotte and me that the man behind the murders must somehow or other be connected with our flat. You say he was small? Not as tall as me?'

Bea said, 'Mid-brown hair, conservatively cut. Slight build, soft voice, nondescript. If he wore an anorak and jeans you wouldn't look at him twice, but I would say his suit was a good one. He was much stronger than he looked, and when he got going, he projected an aura of, well, violence.'

'I marked his cheeks,' said Velma, with satisfaction. She spread her beautifully-cared-for hands out. 'I haven't had time to do my nails since. Do you think I've got his DNA under my fingernails?'

Maggie muttered a name, and repeated it. 'I think you're talking about Ralph something. From the flat above ours. Works in an art gallery in . . . Bond Street? I didn't have a chance to talk to him, but Zander said Ralph always had a pretty girl in tow, and he did that night. She was a model, I think. She looked like it, anyway. They left the party early. I can't think of anyone else who matches your description.'

Velma was still holding up her hands. 'Do we scrape under my fingernails and put the bits in a sealed envelope or something?'

The DI stood up. 'I'll get someone round to do it for you, Mrs Weston. In the meantime I'd like a look in your house to see if we can find the knife you say this man used on you, and also to check that he's not still lying injured in your garden.'

'The walls round our gardens are all high, and if he were injured he probably couldn't get out. Serve him right!' said Velma. She tried to get up, and fell back in her seat. 'But if you don't mind, I'll give you my keys and you can explore as much as you like on your own. I need a restorative nap.'

Bea said, 'You stay here and rest, Velma. Inspector, I'll come with you, if you like. I know how to turn off the alarm.'

'We'll need detailed statements from all three of you. And from the other girl . . . Charlotte, is it?'

'Tell the truth,' said Maggie, 'I'm a bit worried about Charlotte. I know her manners are appalling and she's so self-centred she's practically a nut-case, but I did think she'd surface some time this morning before she went off to work. I've tried her mobile and she isn't answering. I rang the library, too, but they say they haven't seen her. If she's gone off with another boyfriend without saying a word . . . well . . . she might, mightn't she?'

Bea got to her feet and checked her appearance in the mirror over the fireplace. She realigned her fringe, and sought for lipstick in her handbag, saying, 'Charlotte is a very silly little girl, with a tongue loose at both ends, but . . . Oh, I do hope I'm not right, but I'm just wondering how Ralph knew my name and that I'd tricked Mr Van out of the art treasures. Because he did know. Could Charlotte have told him? Could he have been her date last night? Only, Ralph doesn't work in the library, does he?'

Maggie pressed buttons on her phone. 'Is that the library? Yes? Has Charlotte turned up for work yet? She hasn't? . . . You've been ringing her but she doesn't answer? She went out last night with someone called Ralph, who works at the library . . . there isn't anyone at the library called Ralph? Sorry to have troubled you.' She shut off the phone. She'd lost all her usual colour. 'So where is she?'

The DI got to his feet. 'Do you want to report her missing? It sounds like a night on the tiles went on too long.'

Bea wasn't sure. 'I'd agree, if I hadn't been on the receiving end of Ralph's knife. Suppose we leave it for a couple of hours and contact you if she doesn't turn up? Meanwhile, I'll come with you to Mrs Weston's place.' She looked out of the window to see if she should pick up a jacket. 'Bother, it's raining.'

Maggie wailed, 'It would! I left my umbrella and raincoat at the flat. Can you drop me off there on your way?'

Bea dithered. 'Someone needs to stay with Mrs Weston.'

'I'll be all right,' said Velma, closing her eyes and nestling further into the settee.

The DI said, 'If we go round by the flats first, I can have a word with the concierge, see if he confirms any part of your story.'

Bea would have liked to splat him, but realized it would take too much of her waning energy to do so. 'We can't leave Mrs Weston alone. Maggie, I'll just check that I've still got the keys to the flat. If I have, you can stay to look after Mrs Weston and I'll fetch your umbrella and raincoat while the DI is busy talking to Randolph downstairs.'

'I'll keep on ringing Charlotte,' said Maggie, seeing them out. 'She's probably stayed overnight somewhere and overslept.'

Bea checked her watch again. How long had they got before the sky fell on them?

Back at the flats, Bea left the DI talking to Randolph in the foyer, while she and the WPC went up in the lift. 'I'll come with you,' said the WPC. 'I might spot something you've missed.'

'I doubt it,' said Bea, but didn't object when the WPC opened doors for her. As Bea fitted Maggie's key into the door of the flat, they heard a phone trilling inside.

The flat was silent. Open doors let on to empty rooms. The phone stopped.

'The girls' room is at the end,' said Bea, telling herself there was nothing to fear in an empty flat.

The phone started again as they walked down the corridor. The door to the girls' room was ajar. The phone kept on ringing. Bea saw Charlotte's shoes first. One was on the floor at the foot of the bed. The black skirt and off-the-shoulder peasant blouse came next. The white blouse was stained with congealed blood. Ralph's knife had found its target perfectly this time. At her side lay her handbag, containing her mobile phone, still trilling. A bluebottle skittered around the room.

The WPC lunged past Bea to test for signs of life. There weren't any. 'You recognize her?'

Bea nodded. 'Charlotte. An irritating child, but she didn't deserve this.'

The WPC got out her own phone.

Bea was almost weeping with fatigue by the time she reached home again. The search for a body in Velma's garden had proved fruitless, but they could see where Ralph had broken branches on a small tree, scrambling over the wall, and a house-to-house call later turned up the kindly gentleman who had helped Rafael to get away. His bloodied knife was found under Velma's bed, and later DNA tied that blood not only to Bea but also to Zander, to Lady Farne and to Rafael's first victim, the fine arts dealer from whom he'd stolen the twelve miniatures.

Bea went to bed and tried to sleep. As did Velma.

How long did they have before a knife snaked its way into their hearts? A uniformed policeman had taken up a position in the hall, but how long would he be able to stand guard over them? One day? Two? And then what would happen . . .?

Late that afternoon, Bea was called down from where she'd been resting on her bed, to hear that she had a visitor. Oliver had returned from his mysterious errand and let him in, his credentials apparently satisfying the policeman on guard duty. Oliver didn't recognize the visitor, but Bea did.

As she entered the living room, he turned from the card table, a patience card in his hand. 'Mrs Abbot. Red queen on black king. I hope you don't mind?' He placed the card in a new position.

She ordered her breathing to calm down. 'Mr Van. I've been expecting you. Do take a seat.'

He did so, producing a business card. 'The name and address of my firm in Amsterdam. I am, what you call, a recovery agent, working for insurance companies. A short time ago I was asked to look out for a thief, a man who had stolen twenty valuable boxes and twelve miniatures.'

Bea was indignant. 'I thought you were a receiver of stolen goods, and now you say work for an insurance company? Or are you freelance? The way you treated us all . . . and in particular the way you treated the girls . . .!'

'A misunderstanding. I believed that you and the two girls were all part of the gang. I ought to have told you the truth, and there would have been no need for hiding bottles of water in the Left Luggage.'

'Charlotte's tongue wagged once too often. Ralph killed her last night.'

He frowned. 'And the stolen goods?'

'Were passed to a British insurance company yesterday. An art dealer acted as go-between, and he will share the reward with me. I'm afraid you've had a wasted journey.'

He scratched his jowl. 'How many boxes did you find?'

'Nineteen. I presume Ralph kept one for himself.'

'Your police are looking for him now?'

'Yes, but he's left his flat and no one seems to know where he's gone.' She shivered. 'To tell you the truth, he terrifies me.' She rose to her feet, indicating the interview was over. 'I hope you find him before he kills again.'

He stood, too. 'What makes you think I can find him before the police do?'

'You have his mobile phone number, and he has the twentieth box.'

He gave her a little bow. 'My deepest respects to you, madame. Perhaps one day we will work together on a different case.'

'I doubt it,' said Bea. 'I like to be on the side of the angels, and I'm not sure where you stand on that issue, Mr Van.'

When he'd gone Bea took a look at her neglected game of patience. More than one card had been moved in her absence. She swept the cards away. She had no time for play while Ralph was still at large.

Wednesday evening

The minutes, and then the hours ticked by. There was no news from the police.

Piers dropped in to find out what had been happening, and Velma tottered down the stairs to demand a glass of champers for medicinal purposes. Piers behaved beautifully towards her, and she revived somewhat, attempting a return to her pretty, coaxing ways. It wasn't a very good attempt and before long she left the room, tears welling from her eyes.

Piers said, 'Interesting what grief can do to a pretty woman. Sometimes it makes them paintable. I wouldn't mind having a stab at her now.' Bea remembered he'd once said he wanted to paint her, but had failed to follow up on his promise. But then, she'd never been a pretty woman, had she? The mirror over the fireplace reflected a hollow-eyed, tired face. Velma still looked adorable; Bea didn't.

Was she jealous? Perhaps, a little. Not that it was any good wasting emotion on jealousy where Piers was concerned.

Maggie insisted that they should all have a good, home-cooked meal that evening. She said it would do them good to eat at the dining-room table, with candles and napkins and wine glasses even for those who were drinking mineral water. They had to agree – as they seated themselves at table – that Maggie had the right idea.

'After all,' said Velma, 'we have much to celebrate. We are all alive and kicking, if feebly.'

Bea thought, Thank God. I ought to be on my bended knees, thanking Him for delivering us from evil, and instead I'm sitting down to celebrate with friends. I'm an ungrateful woman, only

too quick to ask for help and tardy at giving thanks. And oh! I
forgot to pray for the two kind taxi drivers who helped me out
in Bruges. I told them I'd remember them in my prayers and I
completely forgot! So, please remember them, dear Lord. And
of course I know it's not over yet, so please, dear God, keep on
watching over us.

'Thank God,' said Piers, unexpectedly echoing her thought.

'Yes, indeed,' said Velma. 'Who'd have thought it? And as for
you, young man,' looking at Oliver, 'I keep forgetting your name,
but I don't forget you, I promise.'

'That's all right,' said Oliver, who had brought a sheaf of
papers with him to the table. 'It's been kind of fun, really.'

'Put those papers away,' said Bea. 'Tonight we must eat, drink
and be merry. No work till tomorrow.' *Oh, dear . . . the tax return!*

Oliver pulled a face, but did as he was told. Maggie's roast
chicken, flavoured with garlic and herbs, was a dish to be
savoured. Maggie removed the lids from various vegetable dishes,
to reveal roast potatoes, her own special stuffing, tiny carrots,
and calabrese. 'Apple pie and cream to follow.'

'I'll put on weight,' mourned Velma, ladling food on to her
plate.

'Who cares!' said Bea. 'I'm sure I've lost weight this last
week, so I'll merely be replacing what I've lost.'

They tried to be merry, and succeeded pretty well. Piers
proposed a toast. 'Here's to a quiet conscience, and peace to
those no longer with us.'

Velma's hand trembled as she put down her glass. 'I owe
everyone an apology for what I said and did yesterday. I wasn't
myself. Of course Sandy loved me, and I loved him. And of
course Philip must have his things – if we can find him.'

'Speaking of which,' said Oliver, producing his wodge of paper
once more, 'I think I know where he is.'

Velma fixed her large eyes on Oliver. 'You are a clever boy,
as well as a good one.'

Oliver wriggled. 'Well, Mrs Abbot gave me Philip's phone which
was quite dead. I charged it up and listened to the messages on
it, but they weren't much help. There were a couple from a man
who never gave his name – though I think it was Ralph – telling
Philip to meet him at the usual place. Then a couple more, angry
when Philip didn't turn up. I got a list of names from the phone's
memory bank and started ringing around. It took a while because

I didn't even know what areas some of the codes were for, so I took the phone and the list to a friend of mine whose father can make computers do whatever he wants.'

'A hacker?' said Piers, eyebrows slanting.

Oliver coloured up. 'What we did wasn't illegal. At least, I don't think so. We sorted out what codes were London, and those which were Scotland . . .'

'Scotland!' Bea closed her eyes. 'He went up to his mother's? I'd forgotten all about her.'

'No, he's not there. We asked. He's working in a hairdresser's in South London, in Peckham, sweeping floors and taking towels to the launderette.'

Sensation!

Velma said, 'My jaw has dropped so far I'm almost speechless. What's he doing there? Oh. A girl?'

Oliver nodded. 'There were several girls' names listed. All except one said that they hadn't seen him for weeks and didn't care if they never saw him again. But there were three numbers listed for one particular girl; Rachel. A mobile, which was permanently switched off. A landline for a solicitor's office in Peckham. I asked for Rachel there, but they don't let their employees take personal calls at work.

'I got through to the third number eventually. It's a pay phone in a house share. A man with a strong accent, probably Jamaican, answered the phone. He said four people share the house and he thinks there's someone dossing down in Rachel's room. Name of Johnno.'

'Johnno?' repeated Velma, in tones of disbelief.

'I know,' said Oliver. 'The name "Johnno" didn't sound like Philip to me, so I asked if he were a big strong black bloke, and my informant neighed with laughter and said he was a little white scrap of a lad. Which sounded hopeful. My informant also said that if I wanted Johnno urgently, he'd be working in the High Street at Divine's.'

Bea half closed her eyes. 'Divine's. Of course.'

'So I got on the internet and discovered that Divine's is a specialist hairdressers . . .'

'Number two-oh-eight,' said Bea, remembering the message left on the answerphone at the Westons' house.

'You knew?' Oliver was annoyed.

'Not really, no. Tell me more.'

'Well, I rang them and spoke to the manageress. She said one of her stylists had asked her for a job for this young lad and he was getting on quite well considering he was a cack-handed white boy. I understand that Divine's has a predominantly black clientele. This particular stylist is called Chrissie. She couldn't come to the phone then because she was busy, but she agreed to ring me back after hours, which she did. Chrissie lives in the same house as Rachel. Rachel had asked Chrissie to find a job for this young layabout, and she'd obliged. Chrissie's a strong Christian. She believes in giving a helping hand to people when they need it.'

'A hairdresser's?' Velma muttered, now smiling and now frowning. She began to laugh, but stopped herself. 'Earning his crust for the first time in his life? In some ways, I wish we could leave him in peace, but he doesn't know his father's dead. He doesn't know about Zander, or Charlotte. He has to be told. Afterwards . . . what am I to do with him? He's not due anything under his father's will, but I suppose I could give him something. His father's car, for a start. I can't think he'll want to make a career in hairdressing.'

Bea wasn't so sure about that. 'He's probably better off there, than losing money at the tables.'

Piers said, 'If Lady Farne willed him the Millais he could sell it, clear his debts and buy himself an annuity. If he's got any sense at all – which I rather doubt – he will beg Rachel and Chrissie to go on looking after him.'

Velma drained her glass. 'Give me the phone number where he's living. I'd better talk to him before he realizes someone's rumbled his hideout, and he runs off again. I'm not letting him back into my house though. He's got to stand on his own two feet sometime.' She got to her feet, holding on to the table, and then let go of it, straightening her back. 'There's the funeral arrangements to make, people to advise, solicitors . . . oh fiddle! And an empty flat down the road to re-let. Maggie, do you fancy taking on a new lease for it?'

'Me? No!' Maggie toned down her refusal. 'I mean, crime scene and all that. Besides, Mrs Abbot really needs someone here to look after her.'

'I do indeed,' said Bea. 'Thank you, Maggie.'

Velma arched her back, testing out her muscles. 'Maybe I should have the builders in, have it gutted, replumbed with a shower room to each bedroom. Then bring in the decorators, replace the furniture and put it back in the hands of the estate agents, who can let it for double the present rent. I'm not sure I can face the work involved.'

'Maggie's good at organizing make-overs,' said Bea. 'She's arranging for it to be done downstairs in the agency rooms.'

'I'll pay well,' said Velma. 'Which reminds me that I owe you rather a lot of money, Bea Abbot. I also need someone to help me sort out Sandy's affairs, all those papers that I threw out yesterday . . . the future looks bleak.'

Bea went to her friend, and gave her a hug. 'The future looks good. You'll survive and thrive. We'll help.'

'And I'll paint your portrait this autumn,' said Piers. 'I'm supposed to have a full calendar, but we'll find time somehow, won't we?'

Velma shook her finger at him. 'Oh, you flatterer! I know your sort. I don't want a replacement for Sandy, you know. He was . . . something special.' Her eyes starred with tears, but she held herself together.

Twenty

The weekend and after

Life trickled back into some semblance of normality, though Ralph was nowhere to be found, and Bea started having nightmares. Velma continued to occupy the spare bedroom, but began the slow process of stitching her life back together again. She spent part of every day back at her own house, making funeral arrangements, advising friends and relatives what had happened.

Philip left Rachel and the hairdressing salon to find himself a room in another Kensington flat, paying for it with promises. Velma had the locks changed on her house in The Boltons, but gave him his father's Peugeot and as many of Sandy's belongings as he wished to take.

The police allowed Maggie to take the remainder of her belongings from the flat before it was put in the hands of builders and
decorators. In the flat above, they discovered Ralph's room,
empty, while the adjacent bedroom contained Zander's belongings as well as those of its previous occupant.

On Saturday morning Ralph's body was found on Hampstead
Heath, partially hidden in some undergrowth. He'd been shot
once through the back of the neck. The money in his wallet was
intact, but there was no gold box to be found. The police put
the killing down to a gangland execution.

That afternoon Bea received a massive bouquet of flowers.
There was no message with it, but Bea guessed it came from
Mr Van. Maggie rushed to the phone and left a message at the
hospital for Zander, reporting that Ralph was dead.

On Monday morning Maggie received a phone call from
Zander, asking if she'd come and collect him from the hospital
as he was about to be discharged, had no clothes and nowhere
to go.

'What do I do, Mrs Abbot? He's heard that Ralph's dead, so
thinks it safe to resume his old identity. But he can't go back to
the flat because it's going to be pulled apart by the builders.
Anyway, his stuff's no longer there. We can't put him up here
because Mrs Weston's in the guest room. And anyway, I feel sort
of odd about him. I mean, I did like him at first, but then . . . is
he for real, I ask myself?'

Bea sighed. Why was it everyone seemed to think she could
come up with the answers to every problem? 'If I read him aright
he'll soon make his own arrangements, but in the meantime could
he move into Ralph's room in the flat above Charlotte's?
Remembering that all his stuff is in the room next door?'

Maggie laughed, clapped her hands, and said she'd see to it.
That was one good thing about Maggie; she might not be brilliant
on a computer, but give her something practical to do, and she
was right on it.

Oliver came in with a bundle of papers, wearing a Monday
morning sort of face. Bea interpreted this as; he wasn't sure she
wanted to work, but felt she ought to do so, and was going to
push her until she did.

'I've been a poor sort of creature lately, haven't I?' Bea focused
her mind on agency problems, and remembered the missing tax
form and the solicitor's letter of complaint. Ouch. She wasn't

sure she could face telling him about either, but she'd dug herself into such a deep hole that she couldn't get out without help. Oh dear.

'Before we start, Oliver, we must discuss your ambition to go to university. What can I do to help?'

'I've decided against it. I've talked it over with my friend's father, and thought about it a lot, but it isn't what I want to do in life. Going to university would be like entering a virtual world where nothing matters except computers. Seeing people get hurt and being able to help . . . well, that's different. It's real. I felt I made a difference. I did, didn't I?'

'Yes, Oliver. You did. You helped Velma when she was half out of her mind with grief. You found Philip for her. You kept juggling the balls at the agency while I was too distracted to help. But I have to ask you if you are quite sure, because you could do anything, be anything, if you wanted it enough.'

'I'm sure.' He lowered his eyes, half-smiling, picking out a form from the bundle. 'I hope you don't mind but I took one or two things out of the wastepaper basket, the day all this started. Maggie would have thrown them away, if I hadn't rescued them.' His voice leaked virtue; here was a man sorely tried by a feckless woman, but being a nice, kind person, he was going to make allowances for her.

'This tax bill, for instance. Every time I tried to ask you about it we were interrupted, so I e-mailed Mr Max about it. He e-mailed back to say he'd put more than enough aside to cover it in a separate account in the Halifax, and had left all the forms for getting it out, already signed, in the safe. I've got them here, so if you'll just countersign I can organize payment.'

Bea was stunned. *Dear Lord, you really are looking after me, aren't you! Talk about miracles! Thank you a thousand times.*

Her next thought was, How dare Oliver be so patronizing! She wanted to hit him, he looked so smug.

Another nasty thought; did she really want to keep him now, now she'd lost his respect? No, she didn't. So, she must give him his notice, *now!* She wasn't being unfair? No, of course not. She had every right to sack him if she wished.

At least . . . what would Hamilton have done? He'd have admitted that he'd behaved badly, and thank Oliver for rescuing him. Well, she wasn't that generous, was she? She couldn't possibly apologize. Too humiliating! She couldn't do it. *Dear*

Lord, what do I do now? For a heartbeat, she wasn't sure . . . and then she braced herself.

'Oliver, you are brilliant, and I'm ashamed of myself. Whatever would I do without you?' Once the words were out, she meant them.

He gave her a forgiving, sunny smile. 'Well, I suppose everyone's entitled to a mad moment now and then, and there's lots of things I can't deal with. This solicitor's letter, for instance. There's nothing in the complaints file on anyone called Smythe. Is that the right spelling, do you think?'

This started a new chain of thought for Bea but before she could say so, the phone rang. It was Max, her extremely busy and important son.

'Mother, I've just heard from a friend of the Westons . . . I can't believe it, not even of you! I'm ringing from the Maldives, so I'll have to keep this short, but . . . you haven't really got involved in a murder case, have you? I mean, I can't afford to be dragged into—'

'The agency doesn't *do* murder, dear,' she said in a creamy voice. 'This was a simple case of looking for a picture that had got mislaid. Was there anything else, because I'm rather busy at the moment? We've got a letter in from a solicitor about a woman named Smythe. You wouldn't happen to know anything about it, would you?'

'No, I don't! Really, Mother! I'll ring you when we get back.' Max turned into Mr Hufflepuff and put the phone down.

'Where were we, Oliver?'

Oliver was smiling. 'We don't *do* murder, Mrs Abbot. Or so you said.'

'Certainly not. Now I do seem to remember something about a woman calling herself Ms Smith, some years ago. Maybe five years. Do you think it could be the same one? As I recall, this was a particularly difficult client, who . . .'